Wysard

Wysard

Carolyn Kephart

by
Carolyn Kephart

Sterling House

Pittsburgh, PA

ISBN 1-56315-144-8

Paperback Fiction
© Copyright 1999 Carolyn Kephart
All rights reserved
First Printing—1999
Library of Congress #98-88552

Request for information should be addressed to:

SterlingHouse Publisher, Inc.
The Sterling Building
440 Friday Road
Pittsburgh, PA 15209
www.SterlingHousePublisher.com

Cover design: Michelle Vennare - SterlingHouse Publisher, Inc.
Typesetting: Drawing Board Studios

Printed in Canada

Chapter One

<CO>arkul the Best and Highest rose in sharptoothed towers eternally enmeshed in mist, a bristling walled island of black and green and gray that surged up from the flat sweep of the Aqqar Plain as if the continual damps had spawned it overnight. In the skin-smooth, horizon-vast steppe this citadel was the sole interruption. It had dominated the plain for a thousand years, and Ryel had lived within its walls for nearly half of his birth-life. By the reckoning of Markul he was twelve years old, a mere child; by the reckoning of the World he was twice that and two years more.

He stood on the western wall, scanning the gray-brown mist-obscured monotony of the land. One might never discern the sun was setting, but for the faintest hint of radiance on a horizon only guessed at. Far beyond the endless overcast lay the Inner Steppes, Ryel's homeland, and countless times he had stood at this place on the wall, remembering the World-years of his boyhood. But now though his eyes were again fixed on the uncertain dusk, Ryel's contemplation roamed not to vast lands and swift horses. His thoughts made his eyes burn, and his breath come painfully.

Edris had been dead almost a month now. In the reckoning of Markul he had died young, on the threshold of his thirtieth year. Even the World would have deemed him dead too soon at fifty-eight. His body had been carried in great state to the jade tower at the joining of the western and southern wall, where among the most illustrious of the City's lord adepts Edris lay as an equal.

Ryel drew his cloak about him against the cold—Edris' great mantle of dark scarlet. *You are great in death as you were in life, my teacher,* he thought, his sorrow heavy within him. *But I cut that life short. With my pride I killed you, dearer to me than father. All because overreaching ambition would not let me rest, driving me to seek knowledge beyond reason or my own desert. And now —*

A stifling oppression drove the thought from his mind and the breath out of his body, even as an alien voice arose from some chartless place within him, murmuring at the base of his brain, making him sweat. But though it answered his meditations, it was not the voice of Edris.

Fool, it sneered. *Fool, to mourn that lumbering botcher, and squander your sweet young life and limit your Art among these graybeard dotards. To have wasted your self's substance in this desolate place, when the World and all its pleasures has waited for you. To have never had a woman—*

Ryel put his hands to his temples as he labored to breathe. He stared about him, wildly, uselessly. "Who are you?"

An insinuating snicker in reply. *You'll learn. But no enemy, young blood. Far from it.*

The air lightened, and Ryel could draw breath again. Sharp wind struck him full in the face, pushing back the hood of his cloak, chilling the sweat that had sprung upon his cheeks, prickling the nape of his shaven head, thrusting icy fingers into the rents of his robes. Those few who also stood on the wall had turned toward him in astonishment when he cried out to the air, and now they whispered among themselves. Hushed though their voices were, Ryel heard them.

"No, Lord Ter," he said, resigned and weary, to the one who stared most fearfully at him. "I haven't gone mad ... yet."

Lord Ter paled yet more, and ran a trembling hand through his ragged white beard. "I never thought you might, my Lord Ryel. Lord Wirgal and Lady Haldwina and I were merely remarking our pleasure at seeing you in health, and unmarked by your late ordeal."

"Unmarked. Yes. In every place but one." And Ryel turned to face them, meeting their eyes with his. They recoiled, huddling back against the stones of the wall.

"Yes," Ryel continued. Every word he spoke came lead-heavy. "Mine were eyes you used to praise once, Lady Haldwina—a color that people who have seen the World call sea-blue." He gave a bitter smile. "You haven't praised them lately."

"You looked upon forbidden things," the lady replied, veiling her face with a fold of her headdress. "For that you lost your eyes."

"Not lost," Ryel said. His voice felt too tight for his throat, and each syllable came forced. "I still see. But it seems that all of you have gone blind. I assure you that I have not changed in any way since—"

"Worse than blind you look," Lord Wirgal snarled. "All black. No white or color in those accursed eyes of yours—only continued black. The eyes of an Overreacher."

Ryel smiled. It felt strange on his face, and probably looked so. "Is it not the aim of our Art to learn all that may be learned?"

"Our Art is in the service of life, and the aim of our Art is Mastery, not death-dealings," Lady Haldwina said, her glance still averted. "You attempted the cruel Art of Elecambron, and in forsaking the true path have been justly punished."

"The adepts of Elecambron are our brothers," Ryel replied. "The First of this City all attempted the Crossing, notably Lord Garnos who learned the secret of immortality thereby."

"And died of it," old Wirgal hissed. "I will not speak of Lord Aubrel, who returned from the Outer World raving mad according to the Books, and committed the foulest crimes before his miserable end. And what did *you* gain from the folly that deformed you? Nothing, by your own past admission—nothing save the death of Lord Edris, rest be to his lost soul."

The others shrank back in terror lest Ryel avenge Wirgal's hard words with some malign spell. But the wysard only abruptly turned and without reply moved to another part of the wall, flinching at the burning pain in his eyes, that no tears would now ever cool.

Forcing his thoughts away from intruding voices and rancorous adepts, Ryel again drew his hood over his head and faced away from the night-blurred plain to survey the city of Markul with what was left of the light. Before he had come to Markul, Ryel had never seen buildings of stone, and what had amazed him at fourteen enthralled him still. He grew calm again, and breathed deeply of the herb-scented mist.

"Of all the Cities you are fairest," he murmured. "Most high, and best."

There were four strongholds of the Art, one at each quadrant of the compass: Markul to the east, Tesba south, Ormala west and Elecambron far, far to the north. Brilliant and gaudy Tesba was built of many-colored glass, drab dirty Ormala of wood and brick and plaster. Great Elecambron towered coldly pale as the icebound island it stood on in the eternal snows of the White Reaches. But even haughty Elecambron deferred to Markul with a respect that was entire, if unloving.

The Builders of Markul—Garnos of Almancar, Nilandor of Kursk, Aubrel of Hryeland, Riana of the Zinaph Isles, Khiar of Cosra, Sibylla of Margessen—had founded the first and greatest City of the Art. Shunned and persecuted by the World of men, they had sought refuge in the barren ruleless regions of the Aqqar Plain that drove a thin wedge between the realms of Turmaron and Shrivran and the wide empire of Destimar. Joining mind to mind as other men join hands, the Builders had created massive reality from mere imagination, their visions of peace and strong-walled security translated into the fortress of Markul.

Ryel embraced a porphyry column with one arm, and his robe's wide sleeve slipped down to his bicep. In that moment the air closed in around him, and the voice again intruded into his thoughts, its soft insinuation laced with a connoisseur's approval.

Most impressive, it breathed. *Especially amid these creeping hags and half-men. We're far from the paltry tents and stinking herds of the Inner Steppes, yes. But there are greater cities than this, young blood. Fair cities with women in them fairer still. And there's more. Far more.*

Ryel had at first stiffened in anger at this new intrusion, but temptation warred with anger and won. The wysard pushed his sleeve down to his wrist and turned from the city to the voice, slowly. "Show me more, then."

The voice laughed. And then it seemed that the nebulous gloom beyond the wall filled with white-flecked blue, a living burning blue such as Ryel had never known. The wind of the plain no longer howled and moaned, but calmed to a steady breathing, each breath deep and deliberate as a sleeper's. Ryel clutched at the parapet, lean-

ing out. And it seemed then that the mists parted to reveal dia-
mond-clear daylight, and the sun fell full on the infinite azure that
now rippled and tossed in great waves, surrounding the city and
dashing against the walls.

Ryel winced at the brilliant light, his eyes burnt and smarting
with salt. But only for a moment before darkness again closed
around him in drizzling mist, and a harsh wind tried to claw away
his cloak.

"Again," Ryel whispered, imploring the air. "Show me again."

No voice's reply, no sea's resurgence. Chilled and weary, Ryel
pulled his hood forward against the damp, then slowly descended
the wall. As he made his way through the several levels of the town
to his dwelling, he passed here and there small knots of mages in
discussion, witches trading lore on lamp-lit doorsteps. As he passed,
they all greeted him with mumbled formalities, low bows and down-
cast eyes, and all fell silent for some time after he had gone. Reaching his house after many courses of stone steps, Ryel entered and
shut the door tightly.

Here was peace, and warmth, and silence. The clutter and
paraphenalia usual with a wysard's apartments were absent here, for
Ryel's learning had long surpassed the necessity for outward Art-
trappings. In the east room was a wide bed curtained with thick silk,
pillowed in softest down laced with fragrant herbs to induce slum-
ber, needful for Ryel who often spent entire nights and days rapt in
his study of the Art, until exhausted he fell on his bed sleepless from
the fevered racing of his thoughts. Here he was lured into a spice-
scented oblivion, deep and dreamless.

He lay down and waited for that deliverance which had never
failed—until now. Sleep he could not, and he dreamed with his eyes
open.

In the winter of Ryel's thirteenth World-year, Edris came to
Risma. As the snow fell in the night had Edris come, and as quietly.

"The only problem with a yat is that there's no door to knock
on."

At the sound of that voice, so deep and ironic, Ryel started
about. A stranger stood framed in the yat's inner portal, without a

trace of snow upon his great scarlet mantle, although yet another blizzard howled outside. The mantle's hood shrouded his face save for a white gleam of teeth, a keen glint of eye.

Ryel's father leapt to his feet at the sight of him, his hand on the knife at his side. "Who are you? How did you get past my dogs?"

A laugh, warmly resonant, in reply. The stranger threw off his cloak and now spoke in the dialect of the Inner Steppes, although his first words had been in Almancarian. "Well met in this rough weather, twin-sib."

Yorganar took a step backward. "By every god."

The newcomer was clad not in Steppes gear but in long robes of somber colors. Like Yorganar he was hulking tall, and extremely similar to Yorganar in looks, save that his hair was cropped close and his face shaven smooth, contrary to Steppes custom. But Ryel then noted that the greatest difference was in the stranger's eyes, which were wonderfully subtle and acute.

"By every god," Yorganar said again. His voice trembled for the first time in Ryel's memory. "Edris."

The stranger nodded, unperturbed. "You live well in this weather, brother. I had forgotten how warm are the yats of the Triple Star when the wind blows wild." He gazed around him, noting everything with cool approval. "You've done well. Rich in goods you always were—richer still now, in a fair wife and a strong young son."

"I do not know you," Ryel's father at last replied, rough and harsh.

Edris smiled, then shrugged. "Then give me welcome as your people do for the least of wanderers. That much is mine by right."

Ryel's mother rose and came to them. She looked up into Edris' face as Ryel had never seen her look into Yorganar's, and it troubled him.

"Enter and rest, my husband's brother," she whispered.

Yorganar glared at her, but she withstood his displeasure un-flinchingly, and spoke ever in her soft way, but now with an edge of defiance. "Whatever else our guest may be, husband, he is your clos-est kin, and was at one time your dearest. Let him enter."

Yorganar said nothing, but after a long moment he moved aside, and let his brother pass.

Following Steppes custom, Ryel's mother poured out wine in a goblet of gold, and offered it to Edris. He took the wine, and his hand for an instant closed over hers. Slight and brief as the contact was, Ryel noted it and was angered. Mira saw his anger, and her smile faded.

"I'll leave you now," she said, and would have stood up to depart. But Edris' deep voice stayed her.

"Wait. I have not yet drunk your health, Mira. Nor would I have you withdraw as a Rismai yat-wife feels she must, but keep the gentle custom of your native city, and remain to grace a stranger's welcome. Yet in truth we were not always strangers to one another, you and I."

Ryel had never in his life heard any man other than his father call his mother by her name. It was unfit, as it was unfit for a married woman to remain in the presence of an newcomer after the first greetings were done, or speak to her brother-in-law, or oppose her husband in anything. But his mother was not of the Steppes, and had kept the ways of her city. What shocked Ryel even more was that his father had not ordered her to withdraw, nor rebuked her for her presumption. He felt confused and uneasy at so much law-breaking.

Edris saw Ryel's emotions, and threw an ironic glance at Yorganar. "You've trained your boy well in the ways of the Steppes, brother. I came almost too late, it would seem." Turning from Ryel and Yorganar, he again addressed Mira. "What else has become of the brat, sister? Has he grown up unlettered and ignorant, like every other horse-breeding lout of this tribe?"

"I made sure he did not," Mira replied proudly. "Ryel reads and writes fluent Almancarian, both the common and the palace dialect."

Edris' dark brows lifted. "Ha. Impressive. The latter is damnably difficult."

"Ryel learned it easily," Mira said. "He also has come near to mastering two of the Northern languages."

"Good," Edris said, clearly pleased. "What of mathematics? Astronomy? Music?"

"I have caused the best masters to instruct him—"

"—fetched from afar at great cost, and for no good," Yorganar growled. "What need has a horseman of the Steppes for such fool-ery?"

Edris studied his brother with far more pity than contempt, then leaned across the fire to Ryel who sat opposite. When he next spoke it was in Hryelesh, one of the Northern tongues Ryel had learned, one that neither his mother nor his father understood, one that en-wrapped him with his uncle in a bond half feared, half desired.

"Come over here, lad."

Half against his will Ryel went from his mother's side and knelt before Edris, who looked long on him, so long that Ryel almost be-came afraid. Edris' next words made him uneasier still.

"Are you still maiden, boy?"

Ryel lowered his head, and his long black hair fell around his suddenly flushed face.

Edris persisted. "What do you not understand—the language, or the question?"

Ryel felt his face burn and sweat. "I understand both," he mut-tered.

"Then answer. How much of your innocence have you lost?"

Ryel blushed deeper, and made no answer.

Edris laughed. "A few kisses with the girls, then? Some toyings and foolings behind the yats?" He savored Ryel's confusion awhile. "Well, that doesn't mean ruin. Good. Your virginity will add im-measurably to your power."

Ryel lifted his head despite himself. "What do you mean?"

"You have the Art within you, asleep but strong," Edris replied. "You betray it in your every action. Having watched you closely since I entered this yat, I have observed that you favor neither your right hand nor your left, but are double-handed as I am. That's a thing rare among ordinary men, but a clear sign of capacity for the Art."

Ryel felt himself enmeshed in Edris' eyes, that were a burning black in his pale face. Felt himself drawn, and changed, and torn. "What is the Art?"

Edris made no answer, but reached out and laid both hands on his nephew's head as if in blessing. His long fingers slid into Ryel's hair, and Ryel shuddered at the touch, but not because of fear; rather because it seemed as if he had longed for that contact all his

life. He closed his eyes, giving himself up to it. Then he heard Edris'
deep voice whispering in a strange tongue, not words so much as a
continued murmur like the storm-wind outside. Ryel clenched his
teeth, shivering.

The fingers moved like frozen slow currents through his hair.
But suddenly they turned to ice-knives, stabbing his temples so cruelly that his senses seemed to reel, and the air to blacken before him.

Edris' voice tore through the blackness, still speaking the gut-
tural tongue of the North. His fingers slid to Ryel's nape. "You were
marked for the Art, boy. It found you, and left its stamp. Forever."

"No," Ryel gasped. "Don't touch me. Not there."

But Edris' implacable fingers had found the hard lump of scar
tissue at the base of Ryel's neck. "Remember how you got this, lad.
Remember all of it."

At that command and that touch, the light returned—bright
sharp high-summer light. Ryel found himself alone in a green infinity of grass, alone save for his horse Jinn that grazed nearby. The air
was searing hot, so achingly ablaze that he winced at it, and sweated
from crown to heel. But on the horizon in every direction great dark
clouds were gathering fast. Shielding his eyes with his hand he
watched the lowering masses with increasing disquiet, wondering
how it was that they seemed to center on him. Slowly he turned
round about, watching the clouds scud ever nearer, the circle of
light shrink around him until suddenly there was no light left at all,
only endless roiling black. And out of the blackness flashed lightning, bolt after blinding rending bolt—

He would not remember more. He would not relive what came
next. He cried out until Yorganar pulled him free.

"Ryel!" Furiously Yorganar turned to Edris. "What have you
done to the boy?"

Edris met his twin's eyes, broodingly now. "Nothing but looked
within him, and seen what you never could. He can remain in the
Steppes no longer. His destiny must bring him to me."

"I'd sooner see him dead." And Yorganar forced Ryel to look
away from Edris and into his own eyes, which were so like to his
brother's, and yet so unlike. "You know what he is. I've told you often enough."

Edris' voice came deep as the snow outside, and colder. "Have you indeed, brother?" He turned to Ryel. "By all means tell me what I am, whelp."

Angered and still in pain from that terrible looking-in, Ryel rubbed the back of his neck and replied insolently. "You're a foul magician of the sorcerer-city of Markul. A charlatan and a fakir."

"And you're brave," Edris said. But Ryel involuntarily trembled at the cruel edge in the tall man's voice. "Brave but stupid. Anyone else using that tone with me would quickly regret he had, but to you I will only give better instruction. A wysard of Markul I am, yes. More accurately, a lord adept of the most powerful city in the World, compared to which Almancar the Bright is a cluster of huts, and its people simple savages—your pardon, sister. I am one of the Foretold, whelp, which means nothing to you now, but will soon, I promise you."

Ryel's mother turned her face away. "I knew this would come. But it came so soon. Too soon."

Edris replied gently, "I understand your sorrow, Mira. Of your three offspring, only Ryel survived infancy. But you will be consoled in seven months' time. For many weeks you've known yourself to be with child, but dared not believe it, much less speak of it."

"This goes too far." Yorganar reached for his sword. "Bad enough that you came here at all, but to jeer at her, and me—"

Edris remained unperturbed. "Put up your *tagh*, brother. It's a good blade, but mine's faster. Sister, you may tell him your secret at last."

Mira covered her face with her hands. "I feel the child within me," she whispered. Her hands slid down to her waist, and joined together just below her belt. "But I am afraid. So afraid."

Yorganar rounded angrily on first his brother, then his wife. "How is it you knew her secret? And woman, why did he know it before me?"

"Don't use that voice with her." Edris' own voice was dangerous. "What I know, my Art has taught me." He turned to Ryel's mother. "Mira."

At the sound of her name, uttered with such gentleness, she looked up. Never had she seemed more lovely to Ryel than at that moment.

Edris' eyes took hers deeply, in a way Ryel knew Yorganar's could have never done, and the boy felt lost and alone as he listened to the stranger's prophecy. "You will bear a daughter fair as daylight, and she will grow to beauty, and wed far above her fortune." Edris darted a glance at Ryel, then, and suddenly grinned in a broad white flash. "But you're mine, brat."

Ryel leapt to his feet. "Get out." He felt as if his heart would burst for fury and fear. "Go your way, and be damned to you."

Ignoring him, Edris turned to Yorganar. "Before I leave, first I would speak with my sister-in-law alone."

Yorganar stared, too amazed for anger. "You know you cannot."

Edris smiled. "Your laws were never mine, my brother—nor hers." Reaching to where Ryel's mother sat, he held out his hand. "Farewell, little star."

Mira said nothing in return, and turned her face away at the name he called her. But she put her hand in his, and Edris carried it to his lips and kissed it.

Ryel would bear no more. "Don't touch her!" Lunging forward, he forced Edris to face him. "Touch her again and I'll cut your heart out."

But Edris' dark eyes made Ryel's lifted fist fall helpless at his side. "You fool. You beautiful young fool. We will meet again, you and I, and soon, and you will ask my mercy on your knees."

Ryel's father shoved between them. "Out of this place at once, warlock, or—"

Edris held up a dismissing hand. "No threats, brother. This is the last that you will ever see of me, I promise. I only ask that you bid me farewell as we used to long ago, before we rode into battle together not knowing if we would ever meet again alive."

"I forgot those days long ago," Yorganar answered. But his voice came tight and strained.

So did Edris'. "I never could, brother. The reek of smoke, and the shouts, and the horses shrilling, and the swords clashing, and you and I so young and wild. The only thing I have forgotten is how many times we saved each other's lives, for they were countless."

With a choked cry of impatience, anger, and sorrow, Yorganar caught Edris in his arms, and crushed his cheek against that of his

brother's in the warrior's manner of salute and farewell, then kissed
Edris' temple in the Steppes way between men of shared blood.
Edris returned the kiss, and for a long moment they remained hard
embraced until Yorganar thrust free.

"There. You got what you wanted," he said, his words unsteady.
"You always did. Now go."

Edris blinked for an instant as if his eyes yet stung with battle-
smoke. "I thank you, brother, for remembering at last. Farewell."
He turned to Ryel then, and his infuriating grin flashed once more.
"To you, whelp, no goodbyes, for in a year's time you and I will
meet."

When Edris had departed, Mira stood dazed for a moment, then
pushed past Ryel and Yorganar and ran out of the yat, calling his
name. Ryel would have bolted after her, but Yorganar caught him.

"Let her go, lad."

"But father, she—"

"I said let her go." He stood behind Ryel, holding him fast by
both shoulders. "She has a right. And when she returns, leave her
alone about this." He shook him. "Do you understand?"

"Yes," Ryel said at last. "But it's wrong. She—"

"She is from another land than ours, with other laws. Even as *he*
is, now."

"I'll never be like him. I'll die first."

Behind his back Yorganar's voice—deep like his brother's, but
rougher—came musing and still. "You say that now, lad. But he may
be right—that you can be mine no longer." The great heavy hands
released him suddenly, with a terrible hint of a shove. "And perhaps
you were never meant to be."

A year later Ryel stood before the gates of Markul, and Edris
looked down upon him from the wall.

"So you've come," the deep voice rang. "Even as I said."

Ryel encircled his mare's neck with a weary arm, shivering in the
dank mist. "I've travelled more miles than I can count alone in this
wasteland. Jinn's nearly dead with thirst." Ryel himself was weak
with hunger, but he was damned if he'd ever let Edris know.

The hulking wysard uttered a word in some strange tongue. In that instant a spring of water bubbled up out of the ground at Ryel's feet. "There's for the beast."

Ryel leapt away from the water, and sought to pull his horse back from it. "No, Jinn! Don't drink." But Jinn would not be kept from the spring no matter how hard her mane was twitched.

"Let your mare be," Edris said. "The water will give her strength. Take some of it yourself—I know you're dry."

Parched beyond bearing though he was, Ryel would have sooner died than touch that water. The effort it took to turn away from the rilling clear stream used up the last of his strength. "And now what?" he asked, his voice rusky and trembling with the struggle. "Now that I'm here at your damned witch-fortress, may I not enter?"

The tall wysard shrugged. "What are you here for?"

Ryel was far too spent for rage. "That's for you to tell me," he muttered.

"I didn't hear you, whelp."

Licking cracked lips, Ryel repeated what he'd said. Edris seemed pleased. "Good. Such humility becomes you after your latter insolence. I will let you enter here, lad. But only you. Not your horse, nor your clothes, nor anything else you have with you. Naked and alone you must join the brotherhood."

Ryel clutched Jinn's mane, all his thirst, hunger and bone-weariness traded for this new pain. "No. I won't. My father gave me his sword that he wielded in battle, and this horse, the best of his herd. She's like a little sister to me. I cannot—"

Edris was inexorable. "Throw away your World-trash, brat. Unsaddle and unburden the animal, and let it go."

Ryel's hand shook as it stroked Jinn's side. "But ... I *can't*."

Edris made no reply, waiting with folded arms. During the silence Ryel at last did as he was commanded, because he had come too far to do otherwise. But he buried his face against Jinn's neck first, hiding his wet-eyed misery in her mane.

"Good," Edris said, as Jinn galloped away from Markul and was lost in the mist. "Now strip."

A desperate blush burnt Ryel's face. He had from the first observed that scattered all about in front of the towering wall were little heaps of belongings, garments and satchels and saddlebags. He had not known why. And now there were other watchers on the wall, some of them women.

"We all came naked into Markul, lad," Edris said, coolly merciless. "You've nothing we haven't seen before, believe me. Get on with it."

In furious haste Ryel unfastened his clothes and let them drop, kicked them aside and fell to his knees in the dust. Long he waited there with his head bowed. Then he heard the groan of creaking iron as the great doors swung open, pushed by unseen strength.

"Well?"

It was Edris' voice, nearby now. "I am here, even as you said," Ryel whispered, hoarse with wretchedness and exhaustion. "Make of me what I must be."

Edris seized Ryel's long black hair, wrapped it around his hand and yanked it back, forcing the boy to raise his head and show his face, now stained with dirt and tears.

"What shall be done with this young fool? Tell me, any of you."

Edris spoke in High Almancarian to the watchers on the wall, and was answered in the same tongue. "Send him back. He is but a little child," old Lord Srinnoul had said. "No one so young ever felt the Art within him."

"He has felt it since his birth," Edris replied. "I know this, because I have watched over his growing. And as for his youth, all of you remember that before him, I was the youngest ever to come to Markul."

"You were more than twice the age of this boy," Lord Ter had said. "Let him go back to his mother."

"I say no." Lady Serah's voice had come strong and clear. "Let him enter. We've need of new blood." Her voice warmed and teased, making Ryel heaten all over with acutest distress. "He's no hardship on the eyes, is he? Well grown in every respect."

Lady Haldwina shook her head, stirring her gray-yellow braids. "I beg you send him back, Lord Edris. We all of us came to Markul after our youth was spent—after we had lived in the World, loved, borne children, joyed and sorrowed. This poor lad is on the threshold of manhood—let him know the pleasure and the strength of it."

"He will know both to the limit, my lady sister," Edris said.

"But not in the World's way. This brat was born to the Art. And he's a pure virgin, too—or are you still, boy?"

Ryel trembled for weariness and hunger and rage and shame. "I am," he muttered.

"Excellent." Edris addressed the watchers. "You heard him. Think of what it means. But there is more."

Lord Ter leaned forward. "Tell us."

Edris, who had all this time stood with his hand twisted in Ryel's hair, loosened his hold. Then he said something in a tongue unknown to Ryel that made all the watchers exclaim and murmur. Many of them put questions to Edris, ever in that unknown tongue, and Edris made answer. At length the watchers were satisfied, and spoke again in High Almancarian.

"If he is as you say, let him enter," said Lord Srinnoul, "but it may be his death. Tell him that."

Edris looked down into Ryel's face. "He knows."

Ryel lowered his eyes to the dirt, where his bare knees quivered. "I am at your mercy, kinsman," he whispered. "I have come to you empty. Whether life or death awaits me, I no longer care."

Edris again put his hand to Ryel's hair, but gently now. "Good," he said, his long fingers smoothing the wind-tangled locks. "That's as it should be. Enter and welcome." For a moment Edris looked down at Ryel's forsaken World-gear, his wide underlip caught in his big teeth as he stared at Yorganar's sword. And to Ryel's mingled anxiety and joy, he reached for the weapon, unsheathing it to examine the perfection of its making. "My brother's *tagh*," he murmured, revery mingling with his admiration. "An uncommon blade, but heavy." Then a grin flashed over his face, and he shoved the sword back into its lacquered scabbard, slinging it over his shoulder. "We'll see how it does against mine. Come on, whelp."

Edris raised Ryel to his feet, and they went into the City together. As soon as they had entered the gates, Edris took off the great red-purple cloak he wore, and wrapped it about his young kinsman, and led him to his house.

How well I remember that day, Ryel thought. *Remember the wind of the plain, raw and cold on my nakedness, and the warmth of Edris' mantle as it enfolded me. But now ...*

He rose from his sleepless bed, took up the cloak, drew it about him, and went out into the night.

Never were the dead of Markul buried or burned. They were kept in the great tower at the southwest corner of the city, where they lay in rich robes, preserved from corruption by consummate Mastery. Some had lain there for nearly a millenium, yet to all seeming had died but that very hour. In a rich chamber at the tower's top, in wondrous state, were laid the bodies of all the First of Markul—save for that of Lady Riana of Zinaph, who had departed from Markul long ago and gone no one knew where. Every day since Edris' death Ryel had climbed the many steps of the tower, entered the cold room where his uncle lay, and stood over the inert figure, wrung with meditation. He stood there now in the undying Art-wrought radiance of torches that seemed to mock the lifeless forms they illumned.

Ryel pushed back the cloak's hood. The chill air shuddered across his naked scalp. "You would approve, *ithradrakis*," he said, using the Almancarian word that Edris had never in life acknowledged, his voice a numb echo on the stone walls. "I mourn you in Steppes fashion, head shorn and robes rent."

Edris lay unmoved. Half-open were his slant dark eyes, half-parted his lips. In the wide mouth the big teeth gleamed in something very like a grin.

I loved you, Ryel thought, staring down in numb anguish at the tall still form. *I would have died in your place. But it was I that struck you down. Show me how to bring you back, because I am at the end of my skill. I have attempted everything, even the forbidden spells of the Builders. Ithradrakis, dearer to me than father —*

And it seemed to Ryel that he would die, too, from the intolerable burning and stinging of his lightless eyes, the torment of unsheddable tears. He lifted Edris' limp dead hands to his forehead, and after that gesture of respect took his leave.

Returned to his house, Ryel sank down into the great chair that stood in the center of his windowless conjuring-room, and buried his face in his hands.

I am alone here, he thought. *Entirely alone.*

But even amid the most secret of his thoughts, the voice that had whispered to him on the wall spoke again, out of a swelter of oppressive air.

Ah, sweet eyes. What good to be greatest, if it be fool among fools? I that have shown you water can show you the World. Look here.

Ryel looked up, and found himself in a market-square of a city all unlike Markul. The buildings and towers of this place were of pale stone, alabaster and sweet-hued marble beautifully wrought. The wysard could see merchants' stalls heaped with rare goods, mosaic-lined canals alive with shimmering fish, throngs of people hastening to and fro under a sun so brilliant and hot that his eyes dazzled and his skin glowed. And he heard music, bells, peremptory voices.

"Make way for the Sovrena Diara!"

A long slender boat halted at the steps of a temple—the House of the Goddess Atlan, as the carving on the portals made clear. Half-naked slaves draped in jewels plied the oars, while soldiers in golden mail and ladies gorgeously clad guarded and attended a pavilion set in the midst of the deck. Ryel could discern a human form behind the translucent hangings—a woman's form, surpassingly beautiful. And when the curtains parted—

The vision vanished.

"Show me more," Ryel said, leaning forward, fighting for breath. "I saw her only for an instant."

Aha, the voice laughed. *She's changed since you last saw her, hasn't she? All grown up, now. Grown and ready for a man. Aching for one.*

Ryel shut his eyes, turning his thoughts from the vision, the pestering voice, the room around him. But he could not hold back memory, that flooded his mind yet again.

"You called me."

Often had Edris srih-summoned Ryel to his house, to impart some bit of lore or other. But now for the first time he drew aside the curtain that veiled his Glass. "Look hard here, whelp. You know this man, I think."

Ryel looked, and saw a cavalcade of horsemen riding at an easy pace over a great sweep of flower-spangled grassland. The leader caught the eye and held it—a tall man with features most purely

Almancarian, dressed Steppes-wise, but in silk and gold. "I've never forgotten him," Ryel said, feeling his blood warm and quicken as he spoke. "Mycenas Dranthene, brother to the Sovran Agenor. He came to Risma when I was thirteen, and watched me during the races at the horse-fair, and gave me my dagger."

Edris' voice held a grin, one Ryel didn't like. "Maybe you recall the rumors about the Sovranet Mycenas and your grandmother Ysandra."

Ryel shook his head vehemently. "I'll never believe them. They dishonor our house."

"Hah. Spoken like a true Steppes lout. That hearsay would make the Sovranet your grandfather, and *you* heir to the Dranthene dynasty, albeit by many a remove."

"I'm not listening." For a time Ryel studied Mycenas and his entourage and their wonderful horses, but then his eyes fixed on one sight alone. "Tell me who that boy is, riding next to the Sovranet."

Edris seemed surprised. "Boy? What—ah, I see who you mean. I don't know, whelp. One of Mycenas' servants, probably. Some page or other."

"He's dressed too well for that."

Eldris grinned, all too meaningly. "Maybe he's a special favorite—*very* special. Maybe the Sovranet's tastes run to—"

"Don't say it." Ryel waved away the enormity of the implication, furiously. He'd discovered the truth, to his infinite relief. "It's not a boy, but a girl."

"Ah. Really? Enlighten me as to what makes you so sure, whelp."

"Her hair. It touches her saddle-bow, and some of it's in braids. Braids with jewels in them."

Edris gave a great bay of a laugh. "And what about those beckoning curves in her shirt and her breeches? Don't tell me you didn't see *them*."

Ryel had, but he'd never let Edris know.

"I'll give the little wench this—she knows how to ride."

Ryel nodded full assent at Edris' observation. She was admirably firm in the saddle, this girl—firm and supple and fearless. Overly fearless.

"That's too much horse for her," Ryel frowned.

"I have to agree," Edris said. "Those Fang'an geldings are as wild as full-stoned stallions. Mycenas should know better than to put his own niece in such danger."

Ryel's eyes widened. "*Niece* ?"

As if the word were a malign spell, the horse curvetted and reared. A great outcry went up among Mycenas' entourage, and all rushed to the girl's rescue, but she kept tight in the saddle and impatiently waved away every offer of help. The animal at last calmed, and the ride resumed.

"Strong legs for a lass so young," Edris said, coolly approving. "And that Steppes rig shows them off uncommonly well, wouldn't you say?"

Ryel ignored the question. "She was afraid," he said. "I could see it. But her pride was even greater than her fear."

"The Dranthene are notorious for pride, if nothing else."

At that remark Ryel turned about to accuse his kinsman. "You knew who she was. You knew all along."

Edris gave a bare nod. "And now you do, finally. About time you had a sight of the peerless Diara, old Agenor's daughter. She's visited Risma every year in Mycenas' company since she was twelve. She's sixteen now, and ready for a man from the looks of her."

Ryel felt a surge of regret and anger. "She and I could have met, had I never come to Markul."

"No doubt you would have," Edris tranquilly agreed. "And you'd have been an ignorant unlettered churl stinking of stable-reek, and she'd have passed you by without a second glance. As it is—"

"As it is I'm buried here," Ryel muttered. He yanked the curtain over the Glass, covering the image. "I didn't need reminders." He would have left the room, very swiftly, had not Edris blocked the way.

"I didn't show you the Dranthene princess to torture you, whelp—much though you may enjoy thinking so."

"Then why?"

"As with everything else I show you, for your instruction."

Ryel eyed his uncle bitterly. "And what *have* you taught me, except to prove yet again that I'm a prisoner here? I've been living in cold fog for half my life almost, but it's springtime in the World. The Steppes are covered with flowers, and the sun is shining down on them, and a beautiful girl I'll never know is riding through those

flowers, under that sun. And laughing. I haven't laughed since I
came to Markul, not once—but you wouldn't have noticed."

This Ryel said and much more, as his kinsman stood listening
with remarkable patience. When he'd at last made an end, Edris
calmly enjoyed the silence awhile before speaking.

"Well, brat. I can't say it hasn't been hard for you—and it's going to get harder, believe me. But if it's any comfort, you're very
likely not destined to end your days within these walls."

"What do you mean?"

"You'll learn."

Ryel had heard those two words endless times during his years in
Markul—long years full of danger, cold and, very often, pain. He
felt anger rising in him, but the anger was so familiar that he despised it.

"I'm going to attempt the Crossing," he said.

"Oh, really? When?"

"You'll learn." And Ryel flung out of the room, expecting Edris'
jeers to embed his back like flung knives. But he heard nothing, and
his door-slam resonated in the hollow of utmost emptiness.

Suddenly the voice threaded into that emptiness, snide and insinuating.

You asked for it, young blood. Look.

Once more Ryel was in the midst of pale lovely buildings, amid
music and brilliant light and spangled water. The curtains of the carrying-chair parted, and the Sovrena of Destimar came forth. "By every god," breathed Ryel. Beyond that he was speechless.

Diara's slim form was veiled in film upon dawn-tinted film of
gossamer silk, her face concealed by a half-mask encrusted with jewels. But Ryel could easily discern past those provoking veils that she
was far fairer than the riches that covered her.

Eighteen years old, the voice continued mercilessly. *Beneath her
silks, all the answers to men's riddles: nothing more slender than her
waist. Nothing softer and sweeter than her breasts. Nothing smoother
than her back, straighter than her legs. Nothing more tight and wet
than —*

"Enough," Ryel rasped, dry-mouthed.

It seemed then that Diara looked directly at him, her gaze at once imperious and inviting. But beyond that Ryel saw something else behind the mask, something that disturbed him—a desperate pleading that froze out his desire. Yet only for an eyeblink, until her jewels flashed and glittered under the white sun with unbearable intensity, forcing him to close his eyes. When he opened them again he was alone, in cold darkness dispelled only by a single candle.

Yes, the voice at his elbow oozed. *Light is hard to bear, after years spent in dank fogs and shadows. And lust is even harder ... or is it, eunuch?*

"Leave me," Ryel snapped. "Leave me and never return." And he said a spell-word of dismissal, a strong one, but the voice only laughed.

I'm no srih-servant to be commanded. Nor can you so easily rid yourself of yourself, young blood. But enough of visions. Time now to get your hands full of the World. The World you have been locked away from for a dozen weary years.

"I cannot return to the World." The wysard blinked burning lids, thinking of the beautiful girl who could never look upon him save with horror. "I cannot. Not with these eyes."

The World does not see with the Art-brotherhood's acuity, the voice replied. *It will behold you as you once were.*

Hope wrestled down disbelief. "Explain," Ryel commanded.

Only one learned in the Art can discern an Overreacher.

Ryel leapt from his chair. "How is it you know that? Tell me!"

A long while he stood waiting. But he knew by the quality of the air, by a sudden lightening of the atmosphere, that whatever had spoken had departed to whatever place it came from.

Chapter Two

Ryel slept little and badly after that day. Even though the voice did not torment him again, it had destroyed his powers of concentration and his desire for study. The wysard found himself wasting that most precious of his possessions, time. He would sit for hours at his great window that opened onto the Aqqar, watching mist succeed mist, waiting for he knew not what, anxious in his heart for reasons he could not explain. No human form came out of the mist during his watching, nor did he expect it.

His impenetrable eyes rested on the scattered clusters of garments and belongings, most of them wonderfully rich, left behind by those who had been taken into the city. By far the humblest one was made up of the common gear of a Steppes horseman. Such was the Mastery girding Markul that despite the eternal damp, each of these objects was as whole and unweathered as the day he had flung it from him, as indeed was everything left by others.

Were I to believe what the voice said, I could don those clothes again, Ryel thought. *Belt them about me, pull on those boots, toss that bag upon my shoulder and leave this place even as I came. Leave behind the learning of the Art, I that have already learned more than any man living, and take up the World's way. The world of clear light, and blue water, and golden towers —*

He half-rose from the window-embrasure where he sat, but another thought made him return to his place, and lock his arms around his knees.

"The voice wants that," he whispered. "Wants me to venture forth alone, and without doubt wishes me harm."

He rested his chin on his knees, and stared as far into the fog as he could, and remembered his first years in Markul. From the beginning he had been fortunate in having his kinsman Edris as his teacher. No blood-ties united the celibate wysards of the City, and newcomers were by custom given shelter and instruction by whoever it was that first saw them from the walls—not always a fortuitous circumstance. The first year had been hardest. Ryel had been required to put away all recollection of his past, to force his mind and body into the complete calm and mental readiness requisite for the second year's learning—difficult enough for a grown man, but far harder for a boy. The second year he had begun to experiment with and inure himself to the many drugs used by the Art-brotherhood to channel concentration and heighten perceptual acuity. And he learned his first spells, those that would harness the servant-spirits of the Outer World, an urgently necessary but dangerous test of will that had ever proven the winnowing-threshold separating live lord adept from mere dead aspirant.

Ryel had resisted this crucial step, but not out of fear. Even as a little child he had been deeply skeptical of those tales in which fakirs commanded the air for whatever they wished. What had seemed impossible to him then was in no way more plausible now. "It can't happen," he had said. And Edris had replied with the most contemptuously resonant of snorts.

"Spoken like a hard-headed ignorant yat-brat. Look around you, boy. You know full well that none of this was brought here by mules and carts. But what if it had been? Would you have thought mules magical beasts?"

Ryel shrugged as he blushed. "I'm only saying that it doesn't seem possible to create material objects from nothingness."

Edris' scorn was profound. "You're a fool, whelp. When you threw off your clothes outside the walls, you were meant to strip your mind fully as bare. In Markul the possible and the impossible are one and the same. Yet even in the World everything is a miracle, if viewed closely—the wind in the air, the blinking of your eyes, a seed's progress to a fruit. The Mastery of Air is no more or less miraculous, no more or less commonplace. But apparently you were too dull in the World to wonder how the stars got into the sky—or how you got into your mother's womb."

"I'm not as dull as you like to think," Ryel said, turning away at his kinsman's last words, remembering how from earliest childhood he would escape into the Steppes night while all else slept, running far from the yats into the deep fields, there to lie with his back to the breathing grass and his face to the flickering infinity overhead. As a child he had known no greater delight than those rapt communions that leapt to ecstasy at every touchstone streak of meteor. But as he grew older the joy ebbed, giving way to aching awe, ineffable hunger, solitude absolute and godless where each pinprick shimmer melded into a burning white weight just above his heart, intensifying with every star that fell.

I have not known the stars in two years, he thought. The remembrance of everything else he missed seemed to envelop him like Markulit fog, chill and desolate.

Rough gibing woke him. "Where're you woolgathering now, whelp?"

"Far away from this place," Ryel replied, every word snapped.

Edris shook his head, impatient. "I've been too easy on you. You're not learning fast enough."

"I can't learn any faster."

"You mean you don't want to."

Ryel lifted his chin. "I know by heart the spells that tame srihs."

"Then use them, fool."

"They shouldn't work," Ryel replied, stung and angry. "Not by the World's laws."

Edris snorted again, even more contemptuously. "Damn the dullard World. The Art takes imagination, lad—something you've shown precious little of, I'm sorry to say. You have to not only accept the impossible, but also make it happen. That's what the meditations and the drugs of the first couple of years are for—to loosen your mind, open it up, free it from fear and doubt. You've learned all that, but you'll never move on to the next step as long as I keep feeding you. A few days' fasting, and you'd learn srih-Mastery soon enough ..." To Ryel's deep perturbation and resentment, Edris' long eyes lit in mocking malice. "Now there's a thought. I'll just quit feeding you. Find your own dinner tonight, brat."

Ryel went hungry for three days. During that time he endured not only starvation, but Edris' taunts and wavings of food in his face, which he stonily ignored. However, by the dawning of the fourth day he knew by the lightness of his head and the famished tremor of the rest of him that he must either progress to the next step of the Art while he still had the strength, or submit to having his uncle throw him scraps and call him idiot. Goaded beyond all misgivings, he called up the last of his strength and strode to the book-table in the middle of his room, knocking aside the scrolls and volumes, cursing his stomach, the Art, Markul, Edris, everything. With peremptory exasperation he barked out the necessary mantra, then commanded a full Steppes breakfast with *chal* hot and strong. When these things appeared, he felt no astonishment, and scarcely muttered thanks to his unseen servitors as he grabbed a piece of bread and tore off a vengeful bite.

"So, brat—you finally came round." Edris leaned in the doorway, grinning. "Good job, lad. " Uninvited he came in, examining the food with a critical eye. "Not very fancily dished, but everything looks fresh." He sampled the food with approval. "And not a trace of poison, either. You must have done it right. Srihs are like horses—if you don't show them straightway who's master they'll throw you. The only difference is you might survive a toss from a horse."

Edris said that full-mouthed, and Ryel for a vicious moment wished his Art less, and his srihs venomous. "My thanks for your fatherly concern." He put a bitter stress on the adjective, one that made Edris stop chewing and swallow hard.

"Listen, whelp." His two great hands clamped down over Ryel's shoulders, his dark slant eyes probed Ryel's like thorns. "I wouldn't want a hair of your thick head so much as frayed. Believe that. But you've got to learn, and fast."

Ryel struggled to free himself, unavailingly. "Why should I hurry? Am I not to grow old here, like all the rest of you?"

Edris' warning shake made Ryel's teeth clack. "Watch it, brat. I'm not so much a graybeard that I can't keep you in line. It may be that neither of us will stay here forever. It may be that your Art is meant for the World. But even if you end up on your back in the Jade Tower, you're going to learn everything I can teach you first."

"I won't." Ryel wrenched himself from his kinsman's grip and kicked over the table, scattering everything. "I want to go home. I want to—to look at stars. I'm leaving."

Edris only laughed. "Try getting the gates open."

"I'll slide down the damned walls if I have to."

"Not a chance, lad." The big hands caught him again, and tightened beyond any escape. "You're staying here. And you're learning. You're going to learn the Art faster and more cleverly than anyone has since the First built this City. I'll see to it." A long time he looked upon Ryel's face, for once without irony. "But you won't have to live under my roof or by my rules any longer. You've shown today that you can take care of yourself. Markul's full of empty houses—choose one for your own."

Three days ago Ryel might have greeted that news with overt joy. Now he merely gave a curt nod, as one grown man to another. "I already have."

Edris was amused, but for once tried not to show it. "Where?"

"Not far from this. It's the one built above the wall, looking westward."

"Ah. Lord Aubrel lived there—and died there, out of his mind and by his own hand."

Ryel shrugged away his shudder. "It's well-placed and large."

Edris grinned. "Considerably larger than this, you mean. Well, I had elbow room enough until you came along, whelp, and I won't mind getting it back. You're welcome to Lord Aubrel's house—no one's crossed its threshold since he was carried out lifeless over it. You needn't worry about its being haunted, but I'll bet the dust is a foot thick."

Ryel shrugged again, confidently now. "My srihs will clean it."

"Well said." For a silent while Edris seemed to brood, then his eyes fixed not on Ryel's but someplace immeasurably far."You're stronger than you know, lad. Stronger than I'll ever be." That grin again, more ferociously jeering than ever. "And too foolish by much to fear anything. So order us some fresh breakfast, and after it we'll go on to the next step."

Ryel had learned the next step, and the next, and all others after. He learned quickly, without particular effort. The hard part was overcoming revulsion and fear, emotions all too frequent in Art-dealings. His initiation complete, Ryel might have followed Edris' example and Markulit custom, and devoted all his study to the Mastery. But he chose instead to concentrate his Art on the study of humankind. Many of the adepts of Markul had been notable physicians in the World, and from them Ryel learned surgery and herbal medicine. He could at need set a broken limb, cure illness, counteract poison—and more.

"You're probably the only male in this city still capable of delivering a baby," Edris had said, when Ryel was in his fifth Markulit year. "The men here who used to be doctors have long forgotten everything you've been learning from Serah Dalkith and her friends. It's that pretty face of yours—the sisterhood tell you things about their bodies' workings that the rest of us never had time to understand, and now have no use for. But you've wasted enough time in World-physic."

"I've often wondered that you ever let me learn it to begin with," Ryel replied.

"It'll have its uses, maybe. But it's high time you turned your studies entirely to the Art. Things are happening, whelp. Happening fast."

Ryel was confused by Edris' tone, vaguely alarmed. "What do you mean?"

Edris did not reply at once. "None of us has ever equalled the Builders in skill, but then again none of us ever expected to. You're going to have to prove the exception. You're young, fairly strong, and not too stupid. It's up to you, whelp."

"*What* is?"

Edris didn't answer—not directly. "People have been dying too fast in this City, and not by accident nor the wear of years. Their srihs turned on them. We took Abenamar to the death-tower only a few days ago—he was far from a fool, and not ten years older than me. And not long before that, Colbrent and Melisende. Whenever one of our brotherhood dies, his srihs go on to serve other adepts, or at least that's the way it's always been, until lately. Now they simply disappear. I can feel it, as if the air were growing thin. Someone—or something—has it in for us. I want you to find out why."

Ryel shrugged. "That shouldn't be hard."

Edris gave a laugh-grunt, scorningly. "You're well pleased with yourself, brat. But for your better instruction—and to somewhat temper your conceit—you've got a rival. Someone just as clever, if not more, and completely free of any inconvenient moral scruples."

Indignantly amazed, Ryel lifted his chin. "A rival? And who might that be?"

"A brash young wonder named Michael, up in Elecambron."

"How long has he dwelt there?"

"Not long. Six years, I think, which would make him about twenty-seven now."

"So he's older than me," Ryel said, shrugging as best he could. "But six years in Elecambron isn't much."

"It is if you came there with well-educated wits and a battle-hardened body, studied the Art with your entire attention and almost no sleep, and didn't piss your time away playing quack."

"Why did no one tell me of Michael before?" Ryel asked, half in disbelief. "Why did *you* not tell me?"

Edris' smile was mostly grimace. "I didn't want to perturb your self-satisfaction. But he's famous in Elecambron, is Michael. He's skilled enough that he can veil his Glass, so I've never set eyes on him. But from what I hear he's an ill-tempered, arrogant young brute. " Eldris half-smiled in ambivalent reminiscence. "It runs in his family. His father and I were friends, long ago in my warrior days. They called him Warraven." Edris' long eyes slitted with memory. "One of the deadliest bladesmen in all the North—a fact I know only too well, because my left ribs bear a deep remembrance of his skill. When I arrived in Markul and learned to command the air, the first thing I ordered my srihs to do was steal his cloak, just as I had them bring my sword as soon as I learned the trick."

It was an old Steppes custom between friends to exchange some garment—most often a shirt, but frequently enough a cloak—as a sign of their bond. Ryel himself had done so with his play-brother Shiran, before leaving Risma. "You must have admired this Warraven very much," he said aloud.

Edris half laughed. "I did indeed. He damned near killed me. And I've no doubt whatever that his son's inherited his sword-skill, with the Art's help to strengthen it."

Ryel had to fight down both envy and unease. "Does Michael know of me?"

Edris gave a curt nod. "He does. And he's not overly impressed, from what I hear. You're nothing but a mere Steppes lout, after all, and he's descended from one of the noblest lineages in the Northland. There's another even greater thing I could tell you about his ancestry, but it can keep. You'd only feel more at a disadvantage if you knew."

Ryel flushed. "I hope Michael and I meet someday. Then we'll see who's strongest."

Edris gave a scorning head-shake. "He'd eat you alive, brat, if you were to meet him now. But I'll at least do what I can to help you hold your own with him in a sword-bout. Get your blade, boy, and meet me in the courtyard."

Minutes later they faced one another in cold mist, on chill flagstones, their robes and sleeves tucked up and tied back for ease of action, their feet unshod for surer movement. It was ever Edris' wont to go barefoot even when snow drifted thick upon the top of Markul's wall, but Ryel had not yet acquired that extremity of control over his flesh. To forget the icy rough rock beneath his naked soles, the young wysard fingered the hilt of the sword that Yorganar had given him in his thirteenth World-year—a Kaltiri blade of great worth that had drawn blood in battle countless times. The Rismai neither made nor carried swords, preferring the bow, the spear, and the dagger; but Yorganar had wished that his son learn the warrior's art of his homeland, and to that end instructed him as thoroughly as he might in the little time he had. When Ryel left for Markul a year later, Yorganar had given him stern advice.

"Don't go soft in that sorcerer's roost. Edris knows a sword's use as well as me, if not better—make him teach you some of his skill."

They spoke man to man in the cold gray of dawn, for Ryel's mother had retired to the yat with Nelora, unable to bear the torment of parting from her only son. Mounted and ready, Ryel twined Jinn's mane in his fingers, trying to warm them as he struggled for words, using the most formal of the Rismai dialect. "You have given me great gifts, my father—this horse that is the best you own, and the sword you carried in war.

Little Nelora at that moment escaped from the yat and ran staggering toward them, bawling with baby abandon. Yorganar picked her up, hushing her with a tenderness he had never shown Ryel.

"Hold your noise, wee lamb." He tossed the child in his arms until Nel quieted and smiled. Addressing Ryel again, Yorganar harshened. "Those are not gifts. Nelora will grow up as a Rismai woman should, and have no need of a sword. As for the mare, she was yours from the day of her birth, and I am no back-taker."

It's better this way, Ryel thought. *I'm glad he loves Nel, at least.* Reaching out, he stroked the child's wild curls, marvelling as he always did at their bright gold gleam, so rare in the Steppes and so praised; the touch felt like a blessing. "Farewell, small sister." Then Ryel turned to Yorganar, all haltingly. "My father, I will miss you."

Yorganar held Nelora closer, not looking at Ryel. "Edris will take my place. Has he not already?"

Ryel had no reply to that. For the past year he had remembered Edris every night as he lay awake, and dreamed of dark towers when at last he slept; had ridden the plain and climbed the dead fire-mountains and played *kriy* and wrestled with his play-brothers, knowing in his secret heart that he would never grow to manhood among them; had been a devoted son to his mother, and a loving brother to Nelora; had kept out of Yorganar's way, save when they fought with swords.

"Farewell, Yorganar Desharem," he said, then bent from the saddle and kissed him for the first and last time in his life, on the temple in the Steppes way between male kindred, swiftly lest he be pushed away. Wheeling Jinn about, he sent her into a gallop with a touch of his heel, and felt the swift wind blow the tears out of his eyes into his streaming hair.

"Wake up, whelp."

Ryel blinked, torn from his revery. Edris stood waiting, his own sword drawn and ready—a Kaltiri *tagh* like Yorganar's, slim, double-edged and silver-bright, its hilt fashioned long for two-handed combat; like Yorganar's, but far richer and deadlier. Most wonderful of all, it was incredibly light, as easily wielded as a willow switch. Yorganar's sword felt like a log of lead in comparison. Ryel had been permitted to handle this exquisite weapon only once, but forever after had coveted the way its hilt-ridges took his grip like a firm hand-clasp, the fearful beauty of its glass-keen blade etched with an inscription that Ryel could not read and that Edris would not translate.

"I want your sword," the boy-wysard said, feeling Yorganar's great tagh maddeningly clumsy in his hand.

Edris' cropped head gave a fierce scorning shake. "You'll have to kill me first."

"You've come close to being killed lots of times, from the looks of it," Ryel said, at once defiant and daunted. "You're covered with scars."

"Grown men gave them to me, boy."

Ryel knew that Edris had in his early manhood soldiered in Northern wars, and become a member of an arcane cult of warriors known as the Fraternity of the Sword. The inscription on Edris' blade had been conferred by that order, after deadly combat; that much Ryel knew, but no more. "Tell me what those runes say."

"Never, brat. Come on."

They squared off and saluted in one of the Kaltiri ways—not the salute of enemies bent upon death, nor of friends vying in strength, but of a warrior testing his squire—a low bow from Ryel, and almost none at all from Edris, and then blades lightly crossed once, twice, then drawn apart slowly—and in that lingering last moment, battle swift and strenuous. Soon Ryel felt all his blood grown hot, heard himself panting as he slashed and lunged.

He knew his kinsman's strength only too well. Fifty World-years had thinned and grayed Edris' close-shorn dark hair, and deeply etched his outer eye-corners, but none of those years had shrunken or softened the lean muscles that clung to his hulking height. Now the disarray of combat revealed the long stark-sinewed arms and legs, the broad chest, that the trailing amplitudes of Markulit robes at all other times concealed, and at the sight Ryel felt newborn weak and naked. Furiously Ryel redoubled his attack, all in vain. Edris only laughed at him, and with his tagh's flat swatted Ryel across the side of the head, very hard.

"You'd need Mastery to beat me, brat. Do your worst."

Delirious with rage and pain and humiliation, Ryel shouted an

Art-word, all his fury balled into it. He had never forgiven himself
for what came next. His blade sheared across Edris' throat, cutting it
clean through.

"*Ihthradrakis —*"

Edris tried to speak. No sound came but a horrible wordless rasp
as he clutched at the wound. Blood welled up between his fingers,
spilled down his chest, drained the bright battle-flush from his face.

Ryel forced his kinsman's hands away, replacing them with his
own. The hot blood pulsed under his desperate palms, leaving no
time for anything but as many words of Mastery as he could remember and rattle off lesson-like, terrified lest none of them should
work, knowing that he had no right to utter any of them, that they
were many levels above his learning, yet knowing too that any mortal art was more useless still. And with those words he mingled others of his own making, desperate mantras never learned from books,
but surging forth from that hidden place within where his secret
strength lay.

Only when his tears trickled into his mouth-corners and made
him gag did he realize he was crying. He could smell Edris' blood,
there was so much of it—a metallic savor of rust—and the fear-
soured reek of his own body; feel the chill damp stones gritting his
bare knees, the raw mist-laden wind freezing his face. Under his encircling arm Edris was slipping, growing limp. *You can't*, Ryel
thought, all his own blood panicking. *Not this way.*

Edris' head lolled heavily against Ryel's shoulder, its eyes shut
hard, its lips snarled in a lifeless grimace.

No, Ryel thought. *Not while I live.* And scorning that life he Art-
willed his strength into Edris' dying body, uttering each word with
such fevered concentration that when he fell silent he could barely
breathe for exhaustion. But his kinsman remained motionless.

"Gone," Ryel whispered brokenly. "Gone—" he closed his own
eyes, sick with desolation. In his heartbreak he began to make the
keening moan uttered by the Rismai in their worst despair as he
rocked back and forth cradling his kinsman's dead weight, a mourn-
ing-cry he'd forgotten for years.

But in that torturing moment he felt a stinging pat across his
cheek as startling as a full-fisted blow, and Edris' heavy inert body

give an impatient twitch. Ryel started, looked down, cried out. Edris' long dark eyes were open and gleaming, and his wide mouth grinned, and his deep voice mocked.

"In the name of All, quit squealing, brat. And hold still."

Ryel had already frozen. He was mute as well, but Edris didn't appear to notice.

"Not bad Mastery, whelp. Presumptuous, dangerous, and stupid, but good of its kind."

Ryel felt as weak as if half his own blood had been drawn. He couldn't speak, and didn't want to cry anymore, had no reason to now, yet the tears still fell. And for the first time in their lives together he felt Edris embrace him and hold him close, making him sob all the more.

"Shh. Quiet down, lad." Edris' long fingers raked Ryel's black locks, and his lips touched the thudding wet-haired fever just above Ryel's left ear. "Well done. First kill me, which so many have tried to do and failed, and then bring me back. Clever work."

Ryel heard his voice leap and crack. "Forgive me."

"Hah. Not in a hurry I won't. You had to resort to the Art to give me that cut—an unfair advantage."

"Treacherous, you mean," Ryel muttered. "I despise myself."

Edris shook his head. "Don't. I asked for it. I wanted to see how good you were in all your skill, Art and swordplay both. You're an indifferent fighter, but I'll have to admit you're turning into a pretty fair wysard."

Ryel felt his breath coming fast. "You mean you let me wound you?"

Edris shrugged. "It didn't hurt that much."

"But my uncle—the cut was mortal."

Edris gave a laugh. "Damned right it was. I'd have died had your Mastery been less."

Ryel trembled. "You'd not have saved yourself?"

"I'm not sure I could have, lad." He gave Ryel an impatient shake. "Quit snivelling. It's unmanly."

Ryel quieted, and for some minutes he and Edris rested against each other on the courtyard flagstones. *Ah, ithradrakis,* Ryel thought as he rubbed his wet cheek against the gore-stiffened hair of

Edris' chest. *How could I love you with my entire heart, and nearly kill you—*

"You're shivering," Edris said abruptly. "It's raw out here, and our sweat's grown cold and we're reeking dirty. Come on." He got to his feet, and pulled Ryel to his.

Ryel stared at the place he'd cut. "Are you in pain?"

Edris considered a moment. "Not much. Hardly at all."

"There's a scar."

Edris fingered the place where he'd bled. "Yes. A good big one." He wiped his hands on his clothes. "What was that name you called me? The Almancarian one."

Ryel bit his lip. "Ithradrakis."

Edris seemed not to hear as he threw his cloak about him. "I need a drink of something strong. Come on." He strode away, but Ryel watched him long before he followed.

An indifferent fighter, Ryel thought as the memory trailed away into the mists. *I was that, my uncle, then. But you taught me more in the next seven years. Much more. All of your warrior's art, which was great, I learned. And it has made me strong, stronger in body than anyone in this City; but what good to measure my strength against the nerveless impotence of these creeping dotards? And what good to have learned the surgeon's art to no purpose, practicing on corpses? To have a birther's skill in this childless place? To know all the mysteries of pleasure—for I have learned them, as thoroughly as any amorist—and never hold a woman in my arms?*

That last thought made him clasp his knees more tightly, and press his forehead against them until pain came to match that of his next memory.

Something like a woman I indeed embraced, that very night after my duel with Edris—a creature more beautiful than any woman alive could hope to be, which should have put me on my guard. But I had been hot with the knowledge of my strength, and restless with hungers I had no name for, and —

He forced his thoughts away from the memory of that night, but only to remember other beauty, real and breathing beneath its jewelled mask and diaphanous silk. Tormented, he hugged his knees harder, and ground his forehead against them until he winced as much from his body's pain as his mind's.

A light hand on his shoulder made Ryel start, even as a voice he loved calmed him again.

"Lost in dreams you look, young brother."

Lady Serah Dalkith stood at his side gazing down at him, her face unflinchingly gentle as her beryl-green eyes met his empty ones. "Knock though I might, you heard naught. But I made bold to enter—all the easier since your door's never locked."

"Never against you, my lady sister." Ryel released himself, and laid his hand on hers. "I'm glad of your coming." The wysard spoke the command-tongue to the air, and instantly a laden tray appeared at his side, with wine and the sweet delicacies Serah loved best in precious vessels of crystal and gold. Ryel poured a glass of wine for each of them, and they gazed out at the mist as they sipped and talked.

"Yon's the frock I threw off twenty years gone," the lady said, pointing a smooth bejeweled forefinger at one of the cloth-heaps beyond the wall. "Purple silk and gold embroidery still unfaded and untarnished. And I could still fit into it, I do assure you, were I to wear it now."

"It'd become you well," Ryel said, again admiring Lady Serah's Northern looks—beauty tall and fine-boned, hair like a fox's pelt thrown back from a high forehead and hanging over strong shoulders. The pelt had silvered along the temples, but the lady's form retained its slender elegance, even as her face kept its bold hard beauty, its vivid lips and brows. And Ryel had always enjoyed the lilting tang of Lady Serah's voice, its Northern nuances. Whenever he heard it he envisioned places he had never seen save in books and dreams—Serah's native land of Wycast, and its neighbors Ralnahr and Hryeland—cold lands of rough moss-grown crags, towering pines and aspens, snow-fed streams and waterfalls, wide skies of deepest blue and white-feathered clouds.

Lady Serah chose a sweet and nibbled it daintily. "What be your thoughts of, brother?"

"Of Northern lands. Places I'll never go."

"Then strange it is that you should be so knowing of their languages. Not only Hryelesh that we now are speaking, but even Ralnahren, known to none but the wildest of highland folk."

"I was taught them from earliest childhood."

"Luckily for me. No one else in this City save you—and Lord Edris, when he lived—could hold converse with me in my mother tongue."

"Reason enough to learn it," Ryel said.

"But not the only one." She rested her arms on her knees, her chin on her arms. Her face grew brooding. "As I said, brother, with Steppes courtesy you greet me, and like a true bannerman of Risma never would you think of asking me the reason for my visit. Well, the truth is that I myself had a visitor today."

"An unwelcome one, it would seem."

"Srin Yan Tai it was," Serah replied slowly. "She called me to my Glass this morning—rather earlier than I prefer. 'Twas of you we spoke."

Ryel had heard much of Srin Yan Tai over the years from Lady Serah and others. Lady Srin had come from the Kugglatai Steppes to Markul, but had left the City many years past to dwell in the mountains overlooking Almancar. "How could she know me?" he asked. "We never met."

"All your life has she known you," Serah answered. "She charged me to give you a message."

Ryel waited, then prompted. "Tell me, then, my lady."

"According to Lady Srin, she must acquaint you with dire foretellings of events long in forming and soon to take place—events involving you, my brother, and the rest of the Foretold."

Ryel had drunk only half a glass of wine, but now it felt like an entire bottleful. "The Foretold. Edris always said he would instruct me concerning them. He never got the chance."

"For your loss I feel deeply, Ryel." Serah's voice was always soothing, always like music he loved, but never more than at this moment. "Lord Edris had been my friend from the moment we met. "

"I still can't understand how he died," Ryel said. "He was as strong in body as in Art."

For a long moment Lady Serah was silent, and spoke with all but whispered reluctance. "Srin Yan Tai believes that Edris was murdered, brother."

Ryel started, but was too numb to feel it. "Murdered? But how? By whom?"

"By *what*, you mean," Serah slowly replied. "Srin Yan Tai believes the killer was Dagar of Elecambron."

Ryel could not speak for a long time, and when he did it came out raw. "But Serah, that cannot be. Lord Dagar died more than a hundred years ago."

Lady Serah's ironic lips curled, but not in a smile. "Did he indeed? Srin Yan Tai maintains that Dagar exists in a place between life and death, between this World and the Outer one." She lifted a bright-ringed hand against Ryel's protest. "Yes, Markul teaches that death of the body is death of the rai—death entirely. And Elecambron has for a thousand years done all it could to disprove us, to no avail. But nevertheless one cannot deny that many of the Art-brotherhood—yourself the latest, *my brother*—have stood on the edge of existence, and sensed the shadow-land between being and unbeing."

Ryel nodded, but reluctantly. Both Markul and Elecambron believed in the existence of the *rai*, the vital force said to animate the corporeal form. But Markul held that death of the body inevitably meant death for the rai, while Elecambron put full conviction in the rai's immortality. The Markulit Art was in the service of life, and to that end the adepts of that City made the Mastery their chief concern. But for cold Elecambron the after-workings of death were its focus of study, and the Crossing its highest aim. A very few of the Markulit brotherhood had attempted the Crossing, but only when very old, and never without some terrible cost to body or mind.

"Yes," Ryel whispered. "I was there."

"And you returned from it, thank luck. But most adamantly does Srin Yan Tai insist that Dagar has long dwelt in that chartless realm, disencarnate yet vitally malignant. She believes that in those secret reaches Dagar's power is great, and is steadily increased by the energy it robs and takes unto itself from those emanations we of the brotherhood harness for our daily use. She is sure that Dagar is the cause of the decline of our powers, and I am persuaded that she is right. Furious and vengeful Dagar ever was, and if he continues to draw his power from the Outer World, I tremble for what might be. Especially since Lord Michael of Elecambron is his sworn servant, if what Lady Srin says be true."

Ryel started. "But that can't be. I've heard much of Lord Michael's pride, but of his greatness too. He would never serve a daimon to work wrongdoing."

"Given fit persuasions, the noblest soul might swerve," Lady Serah replied. "Would that I or some other of our brotherhood might have turned him toward the Markulit philosophy. But he veils his Glass, and can neither be seen nor spoken with."

"I know. I've tried."

"Had you done so any time recent, you'd have lost your labor. Lord Michael departed Elecambron fully a year ago."

Ormalan sorcerers routinely trafficked with mere men, and the enchanters of Tesba on occasion returned to the World. But so infrequently did those of the two greatest Cities, scarce once in every decade, that Ryel was as much perturbed as surprised. "Michael has left? But why?"

"For no good, I am only too sure. But Lady Srin will tell you more."

"I will contact her through my Glass, and speak with her," Ryel said.

Serah contradicted him with a vigorous shake of her fox-haired head. "You'll not succeed. Quite insistent she was that she would have a face to face encounter with you or nothing."

Ryel recalled the invasive unknown voice, the vision of Almancar. He reached for Edris' cloak that lay near, crumpling its warm scarlet cloth in his hand. "Then she will have to meet me here. I will never leave Markul."

"Never is long, my lord brother." Lady Serah rose to her feet with a rustling of raven-black silk. "But best that I go now. Time you require to consider the matter of our talk. Have I leave to visit you again? Fear not, we'll speak only of trifles, I promise."

"Whenever you wish and with pleasure, my lady sister."

They bade farewell, and Ryel turned back to the mist, and reached for his empty goblet.

"Again," he said in the command-tongue, and watched as the rich vintage welled up from the whorled crystal stem like a ruby spring, dark and fragrant. Seldom if ever did the wysard drink more than a single glass of wine at a time, but his conversation with Lady Serah had unsettled his wonted calm.

"Dagar," he murmured, the name bitter on his lips. "Dagar, most beautiful and most base. He that no wysard of any City dared or deigned to call brother." *You died, Dagar,* he thought. *There's nothing left of you. Edris always said Srin Yan Tai was half mad-woman.*

He lifted the glass to his lips and drank. But all at once he was aware of a sudden oppression of the atmosphere, a stifling heaviness of the air. With a weary groan he waited for the ever-intrusive voice to torment him yet again. But then he heard a sigh—not the voice's, but a woman's, and not within his head, but behind him. Ryel turned, and stared, and felt his fingers freeze around the goblet's bell.

"Mother."

A woman attired in a silken gown of Almancarian fashion, her heavy black hair falling in mingled tresses and plaits almost to her waist, stood in the middle of the room—a woman neither old nor young and agelessly beautiful.

Ryel leapt up, heedless of the goblet's crash. Although a dozen years had passed, he knew her, scarcely changed since the day he had left Risma. But surely his mother would never have stood thus unseeing, unresponsive to his voice.

Ryel dropped to his knees. "My lady mother. I implore you to speak to me."

She did not reply, nor even look his way. Instead she paced distraught to and fro, clutching her body with both arms as if entranced with grief and pain. Then she caught sight of the wysard's Glass, that hung on the wall of an inner room. As if gathering her resolution with great effort she swiftly approached it. Ryel rose and followed, knowing now that it was useless to call her.

Mira Stradianis Yorganara stared into the Glass. To Ryel's astonishment her reflection stared back. Ever keeping her eyes on the mirrored image's, she flung back her hair and began one by one to rip away the brooches that fastened the front of her gown. Then with a desperate wrench she tore apart the silken cloth. Ryel would have instantly looked away, having never forgotten the Steppes law that demanded death from any grown man who laid eyes on his mother's nakedness. But the horror revealed in that first eyeblink held him appalled. Next to the reflection's perfect right breast hung a bruised bagful of pus, livid and foul. Ryel cried out in horror at the sight, but his mother did not turn around. She only stared into the mirror, her beautiful face now drawn and pale, her dry lips trembling. Then she hid her face in her hands, and vanished.

Ryel stood numbed, incapable of movement, crushed by the atmosphere's weight. "You caused this," he whispered into the stifling air. "You wrought this lie." And he waited in silence, but not for long.

I do not lie, the hated voice smoothly said. *The woman's cancered.*

Ryel struck the cold unyielding surface of the Glass. "You poisoned her!"

I assure you I didn't, young blood. As you might have noted, she's far beyond the skill of any doctor—but perhaps not beyond the Art of the greatest wysard of Markul. The greatest living, I should say.

Ryel remembered what Lady Serah had imparted to him, what Srin Yan Tai had foreseen; remembered, and forgot to breathe. "Tell me your name, daimon."

The voice laughed at him. *Patience, sweet eyes. Rather than rudely questioning, you should thank me for giving you the chance to reach your mama in time. Not that she has much time left. For my own part, I hardly care whether the woman lives or dies. You've already been the death of he that you so cloyingly called ithradrakis, dearer than father—now's your mother's turn.*

Never had Ryel felt so helplessly enraged. "Go and be damned, slave of darkness!" he shouted. As if in complete obedience the air lightened, and he was again able to breathe freely. Drawing a starved draught of air, he sank down in front of the Glass, that now reflected nothing.

"I can't lose you, too," he whispered. "I will not."

He had felt guilty sorrow two years before, when he had learned of Yorganar's death—a death such as every Steppes bannerman

prayed for, swift and without suffering and in the full accomplish-
ment of his years, his neck cleanly broken by a throw from an
overspirited horse. For Edris he had shrieked and thrashed until
Lady Serah came to rub his temples with oil of mandragora, uttering
frantic spells until he finally quieted and slept. And if his mother
were indeed sick and died through his neglect, he would not be able
to survive his grief. "It will kill me," he whispered.

The air thickened and slowed.

Such extravagance of sorrow, the hated voice sneered. *Such filial
devotion. Your mama would be proud.*

Furious, Ryel did not reply, but leapt to his feet and went to his
bedchamber. The voice pursued him, teasingly.

Ah, we are angry. We refuse to speak.

Ryel clenched his teeth, and stared into his mirror, and muttered
a word. At once his shaven head began to darken, covering itself
with thick hair, straight and black. When the hair reached well past
his shoulders, Ryel said another word that stopped the growth.

Very good indeed, young blood, the voice cooed. *Much better.*

Still ignoring the voice, Ryel uttered a word that faintly bearded
his smooth face.

Excellent, breathed the voice. *Most virile. Why this charming
metamorphosis?*

"You know why."

Where will you travel?

"You know where."

The voice grew cloyingly, mockingly sweet. *The Aqqar is wide,
and Risma far. You may not get to your dear mama in time. But I
could help you. I can—*

Ryel spat at the Glass. "You can go back to the hell you came
from. I won't need your help."

A laugh, hysterical and shrill. Then the oppression lifted.

Naked one came into Markul, and naked one was constrained to
leave it. Ryel would be able to take nothing with him that he had acquired in the City—no books or talismans, none of his fine robes or
other rich possessions, not even the plain gold rings in his ears and
on his fingers. Nor did he greatly care. But it wrung him to have to
part with Edris' mantle, and Edris' sword. He gathered the cloak to

his heart in a long embrace, rubbing his cheek across the warm nap, then set the garment by. He next reached for the sword that had become his at Edris' death and slowly unsheathed it, reading character by exquisite character the words that ran like scrolled fire down the brilliant double-edged blade.

"Keener than lover's hunger, / Sharp as a king's despair,
Fell as a wysard's fury, / Coward and cruel, beware!
Turning to water the wicked, / Heavy as deadman's land,
Lighter than air am I lifted, / Fire in a hero's hand."

Those verses were Ryel's doggerel approximation of the distichs written in the hidden language of the Fraternity of the Sword, a Northern cult of great antiquity. Edris had become a Swordbrother during his years as a warrior, when he fought as a mercenary of the Dominor of Hryeland against the White Barbarians. In accordance with the Fraternity's commandment he had forever after kept its ceremonials and its speech a secret even to Ryel. The young wysard had only divined the Fraternity's language by accident in his tenth Markulit year, while reading the history of the first lords of Elecambron. To his surprise their ancient runes had proven virtually identical to those on Edris' sword. He would have told his uncle of his discovery, but an inexplicable reluctance, a dislike of admitting himself an infringer into hard-won privilege, had continually prevented him.

Ryel raised the blade in both hands, touching his brow to it. The cold steel stung like a wound. Sheathing the tagh slowly, he lapped it in the cloak and laid it at the foot of his bed. After a final mirror-glance at his new self, he left the room and strode out of his house, leaving the door unlocked, and swiftly descended the black stone stairs that zigzagged level by level down to the western gate. A cold drizzle had begun to fall, but he did not feel it. Softly though he trod, nonetheless the quick ears of the Markulit brotherhood heard, and many looked out their windows to watch the Overreacher pass. Some left their houses and followed, sensing what was to come.

At the western gate Ryel stood, and uttered the opening-spell. With a recalcitrant shriek of metal stronger than any steel the great portals turned on their hinges, and at that noise so seldom heard a throng began to gather, watching for what would next occur, questioning Ryel to no avail. Lady Serah was among the crowd, and she alone did not ask why he was leaving. Indeed, she said nothing, but only looked upon him with disquiet and sorrow.

Ryel felt himself gazing back in the same way. "Since I must take nothing with me from Markul, allow me to present you with these, my lady sister." And he unfastened the golden circlets from his ears and drew off his finger-rings, giving them to Serah. Then he took her hands in his and touched them to his brow. She held his tightly as her beryl-green eyes looked into his, no longer with their wonted irony.

"So. You took my advice after all."

The wysard shook his head. "I have no wish to find Srin Yan Tai. Another reason calls me away, one far stronger."

Lady Serah did not ask what that reason might be. "I fear for you, my brother," she murmured.

"Don't. Only be so kind as to look after my house until I return."

"Since I've no idea when that will be, I'll seize my chance for this." Cat-quick, she slipped her arms around his neck and drew him down to her, kissing his mouth. "I've wanted to do that for years." Smiling with her old deviltry, she ran a swift hand over his bearded chin. "I like your new looks, by the way."

Ryel smiled in return. Then he began to ungird his robe, but paused abashed. Lady Serah at once understood.

"Come, you gawkers," she said to the watching crowd. "We'll climb upon the walls and watch our young brother's going, even as twelve years ago we witnessed his coming."

The Steppes modesty that Ryel had learned as a boy he had never outgrown despite all the knowledge he'd gained in Markul, and he blushed to strip before a watching crowd. Thankful for Serah's discretion, he waited until everyone had begun to climb the many stairs to the ramparts, then cast off his Markulit garb in haste.

He turned and passed through the gate, naked as he had entered twelve years before. The endless mist felt suddenly and unbearably icy on his bare skin as the wysard stood outside his City for the first time in twelve years. He at once went to the heap of clothes that had been his, and opened the saddlebags wherein were carefully folded other Steppes garments, larger than those he had cast off so long ago.

"You will grow," his mother had told him when he left Risma as a boy of fourteen. "Therefore I have made these clothes to fit the tall man you will become." And she had embraced him, and he had dried his tears in her hair as he whispered that surely he would return to her someday …

Shuddering with cold, Ryel dressed as quickly as he might in the clothes he found still fresh in the saddlebags. Shirt, leggings, long-skirted coat—everything fit as if made to his measure, even the riding-boots that had been so loose when he set out on his journey. Warmth of both home-loomed web and remembered love enveloped him, but nevertheless he could not help another twinge of chill. A Steppes bannerman of considerable means he now looked, but a true Rismai brave went armed and cloaked, and he was neither. His dagger lay yet unrusted in its sheath, and this he hung on his belt, but it seemed little protection against the predators of the Aqqar Plain, even as his coat seemed insufficient proof against the rawness of the cold, Art or no Art.

Lady Serah, who for a time had left the wall, now reappeared and spoke, somewhat flushed and out of breath. "My lord Ryel! Among my goods nearby you is a purseful of gold coin and jewels, which is yours as my gift. You'll be needing them in the World, believe me." Then she gave that flashing grin of hers, the one that made her look so young. "And these things too you may find use for, I'm thinking." She tossed a mulberry-colored bundle down from the wall. Ryel caught it, and with a thrill of joy found Edris' great cloak wrapped around his sword.

"That was ill done, woman," Lord Wirgal snapped to Serah Dalkith. "You know the laws of Markul—the boy may take nothing of his from our City."

She tossed her fox-haired head. "What I gave Lord Ryel were the erstwhile possessions of Lord Edris, beloved and mourned by us all—or nearly all."

Lord Wirgal glowered under gray brows. "Equivocating female, how dare you—"

"Let be, old fool," Serah snapped back. "Never will you leave this place, Wirgal, but die babbling in your bed."

During their quarrel Ryel slung the tagh's belt baldric-wise over his shoulder in the Steppes way, then donned the cloak. Gazing up at Lady Serah, he bowed low in the brotherhood's most reverent obeisance. "I will never forget this kindness of yours, sister."

"Thank yourself rather, for never locking your door," Serah replied smiling. But now her lips trembled.

Suddenly others wished to give Ryel parting-gifts, perhaps stung by Serah's words to Lord Wirgal. "Young lord, over there is the baggage I left more than fifty years ago," cried Lord Nestris, "and it is full of Almancarian robes wonderfully rich, and of your measure, and still as fresh as the day they were made. I pray you take as many as please you."

Lady Haldwina, too, raised up her voice. "And among my havings are a case of medicinal balms, and phials of healing essences—take them, and welcome!"

Unwieldy Lord Ter spoke next. "Over yonder are my things— bottles of water and wine and brandy you will find, and food too, all unperished. Take them, and spare your Art's strength thereby."

Many other lords and ladies of Markul offered Ryel whatever he wished to choose from the possessions they had been constrained to relinquish at the gates. Soon Ryel's saddlebags were laden with gifts and his pockets as well, but one last thing of seemingly little use he also took—Jinn's halter of gold-embossed leather, that he wished to keep as a remembrance of his beloved mare now forever lost. Thanking his many benefactors once again and bowing a last time to Lady Serah, he shouldered his baggage and set forth. When he was some distance from the City he turned about, and saw that everyone still watched him, and he waved. Then he observed Lady Serah reach into the pouch hanging at her belt, and take out what seemed a ball of amber. Breathing on it, she threw it far from the wall. Midway in its flight the little sphere became a bright gold butterfly winging its way toward Ryel like a windblown flame-flicker amid the cobwebs of mist. As it flitted and played about him the wysard smiled, and waved a last time to his Art-sister. Then he faced westward again, and strode on.

Chapter Three

With Serah's butterfly playing about him Ryel trekked westward, until he knew that the City at his back would seem only a somber child's strange toy dropped and forgotten. But when he next looked round, he found that Markul had been completely engulfed by mist, and when he turned back again he discovered that the butterfly had vanished. Alone in the biting fog he stood for a time gazing about him, feeling most solitary and bereft. He thought of the contemplative tranquility he was forsaking, the long silent hours of study. Seen from the outside for the first time in a dozen years, the great walls of the City seemed no longer a prison as it all too often had in the past, but a sanctuary. Outside those walls and beyond the fog lay a World whose pleasures and dangers Ryel had read of in a hundred histories, and experienced barely at all, and longed for constantly. But now the pleasures seemed empty, and the dangers mortal.

"I'm going back," he said, challenging the mist. But although he waited for the atmosphere to thicken and the voice to speak, nothing happened.

"You lied," he said. "She is well."

Complete silence in reply. Something in its inexorable density made Ryel murmur imprecations and once again turn west, and walk.

No roads led to Markul, and too few aspirants came there year by year for their trails to mark the land. But those truly desiring to find the City never lost their way. Ryel well remembered his own first traversal of the Aqqar, and how much easier the actuality had seemed at fourteen than the very prospect did now.

That was because I had Jinn with me, he thought. *Jinn to talk to as I rode and to watch over me over me as I slept, and Edris, feared and beloved, awaiting me at the end of the journey. Now only unknowns draw me on.*

For a considerable while the wysard walked untired, following the path of the fogbound sun. But after several hours the saddlebags weighed heavy on his shoulder, and he stopped to rest. Sitting down on a slab of rock and opening a flask of brandy, he swigged and ruminated.

"There's got to be an easier way," he said aloud, newly aware of how much deeper his voice had grown since that first Aqqar journey, and how it had never lost its Steppes tang despite all the years in Markul. Hearing it emboldened him. "It'll take me ages to reach Risma afoot. What if I tried that spell of Lord Garnos, the Mastery of Translation?"

But even as he spoke, he laughed at himself. What if, indeed. Not until Ryel was very old in the Art would he dare to attempt anything so risky as a translation-spell. And at any rate, that spell of Garnos' was a lost one, like so many others of his. But a fool's trick for amusement's sake could do no harm—a trick such as Ryel was fond of trying in those days long past when he was a mere famulus … and Edris wasn't looking. Accordingly Ryel uttered the words to make his saddlebags dance for him, which they should have done with as much nimble alacrity as was possible in their packed state. But they only shuffled listlessly a moment before sinking down again like a fat skatefish on a sea-bottom. Feeling both sheepish and disquieted Ryel once more uttered the spell, this time with complete seriousness and concentration, but the saddlebags stayed sullenly put.

Something, the wysard thought slowly, *is very wrong.*

He hadn't packed *that* heavily. The problem was too much Turmaron brandy, no doubt. Like all Steppes folk he had small tolerance for strong spirits. Moreover, he had walked for miles, the day was darkening fast, and rain had begun to fall, light but cold—high time to make camp. The wysard spoke some command-words into the air, expecting both shelter and fire.

Nothing appeared. Used as he was to complete and lavish obedience to his requests, Ryel was too amazed to feel anger.

Surely mere distance from Markul cannot be causing this, he thought. *Could it be that Dagar has drained the spirit-energy from the air around my City, as Srin Yan Tai maintains? No. Never. My Mastery would be strong whether in Markul or at some inaccessible end of the World.*

To test that, he lifted his face to the rain's chill drip and shouted a word that in less frustrating times he would have whispered, and that carefully. To the wysard's intense gratification a wisp of fog whirled into a spiral, and touched ground five feet from where he stood. The spiral eventually took on a wavering man-form, feature-less save for long eyes like glowing amythest, and spoke in a voice blurred and sullen, now running its words together, now stopping short.

"Leavemealone."

Ryel ignored the request, and instead gestured to the empty ground. "Shelter. And make it comfortable."

A great soundless flash lit the night, and subsided to reveal a yat fit for a wandering prince, with a porch large enough for ten people, and a blazing fire under it.

Ryel at once installed himself amid the cushions heaped before the fire, and held his hands out to the warmth. "Good. Very good, Pukk. Quite close to my desire."

The wraith quivered on the point of dissolution. "Iwillg onow."

Ryel lifted his hand. "Wrong. Stay."

A long hesitation. Then, "Un usualre quest."

Pukk's tone was emotionless and distant, as ever, but its words sharpened the chill of the night. *I am alone and outside my City for the first time,* Ryel thought with a pang of disquiet. *And my powers are not what they were in Markul—a temporary weakening without doubt, yet one that this daimon must not perceive.*

But Pukk's preternatural senses detected every uneasy emana-tion, every prickle of human flesh. "Youf ear. Andnowon der. I amstron ghere. May bestron gerthan you."

Pukk was infallibly insolent, and Ryel had always taken a tense pleasure in their encounters. The most powerful of all the spirits of air, Pukk alone was capable of semi-speech and quasi-embodiment. It had been the death of at least a dozen lord adepts in both Markul and Elecambron. But Ryel had never allowed himself to fear Pukk—never until now. Steeling his self-command, he used all his Markulit training to keep his skin from sweating, his heart from racing.

"You don't want to try me, Pukk," he said, very coolly. "Since there's no one else fit to wait on me, I'll trouble you for some dinner."

Pukk shimmered in fury. "Ic ouldpoi sonyou."

Ryel lifted his chin, meeting the srih's glowing eyes with its own empty ones. "I think not. I might destroy you first."

Silence, save for the rain—far quieter, it seemed to Ryel, than his own breathing. Pukk's lambent violet eyes became slits, and then blinked. At that moment a steaming trayful of delicious-smelling food materialized at Ryel's side. "There. Eatitan dchoke."

The palpitating moment had stilled, and the frisson of fear evaporated like a rag of mist. *I have my own strength*, the wysard thought as his blood warmed again. *My inward Mastery that owes nothing to the Outer World. Strong Mastery that this srih senses, and fears.*

"You'll never kill me with your cookery, Pukk," Ryel said aloud, quite calmly now. "You forgot the bones and the venom. My infinite thanks." Suddenly too hungry for fear, he turned all his attention to the tray.

The amythest eyes of the srih glowed disdain and injury. "Iwillg onow." And as Pukk spoke it started to fade.

"Wait," Ryel said with his mouth full. "Tell me about Dagar first."

With a furious smoky shudder Pukk intensified, but did not reply.

Ryel, well pleased with uncommonly exquisite Steppes cuisine, urged without asperity. "He was a hard master?"

Pukk replied with more than a shred of contempt. "Hard erthany ou."

Ryel sat back, interested and amused. "Where is he now, communicative and garrulous servitor?"

"Dagard well sinthe Void."

"Do you mean the shadow-realm of the Outer World, from whence come you and the other servants of the brotherhood?" the wysard prompted.

"No."

Startled by that rusky monosyllable, Ryel leaned forward. "Then it is a place apart from both the Outer World and this?"

"Yes."

"What else exists in the Void?"

"Otherra is."

"*What* other rais?" the wysard demanded, his vehemence stark. "Rais like Dagar's, bent on harm?"

Pukk never admitted ignorance. It merely said nothing—as now.

Unsettled as he was by his servant's silence, Ryel felt his blood heaten with hope never known until now. "The rai survives the body after death," he murmured. "It survives."

Pukk heard, and replied almost immediately. "No." Observing Ryel's speechless infuriation, it continued grudgingly, "Abo dycanb eseparat edfromit srai. Bot hwills urv ive."

"But how can that occur?" Ryel demanded.

Pukk made no answer.

"Dagar's body was destroyed," Ryel said, angrily now. "Burnt to ashes in Elecambron. I read it in the Books."

Pukk seemed to incline its head. "Yes. But therai ofDag arre mains." Then slowly, softly, alarmingly, Pukk whispered, "Dagar'sp ow erg rows. Hewill grows trong er. Indark nesshedr awsst rength."

For once Ryel was confused by Pukk's idiosyncratic syntax. "Dagar draws strength in the darkness? Meaning that he is powerless during the day?"

Pukk gave a reluctant quiver of assent. "Itwill notal waysb eso. Morew illcome. Soon."

"Why has Dagar not taken you?"

Pukk guttered under the insult. "Iamstr ong. Stron gestof myk ind. Nottobe take nuntilall elseistaken."

Ryel felt his heart beating too fast, and could not calm it. "And what if all else *is* taken? What comes after?"

The purple eyes blazed. "Itwill havey ou. As itss *lave*." In that last sneering syllable Pukk began to fade.

Ryel leapt to his feet. "I command you stay! You feckless ectoplasm, if you dare—"

But Pukk had vanished, all but its eyes. In another moment

those eyes gave a malignant scornful flash, and were extinguished by the rain. A few minutes later the princely yat had dwindled to a miserable tent, and the ardent blaze had shrunk to flickering smoke.

"Damn," Ryel muttered, furious and alarmed. He hugged his cloak around him, and listened hard. Only the lulling fall of skywater came to his ears. At least he'd be able to sleep, if the rain held. The wolves and night-serpents for which the Aqqar was universally ill-famed kept to their lairs during wet weather.

"I've roughed it worse," the wysard assured himself aloud. But he knew to his discomfiture that it had been very long since he last had. Sheltering in the folds of Edris' cloak he with great difficulty found a dry spot inside the tent and flung himself down, overmasteringly spent. But Pukk's words kept him restless where rain and cold could not.

Uncertain sunlight woke him, and he rose on an elbow, blinking. The tent was gone, and the fire. Only a little heap of soggy cinders marked his erstwhile camp, but at least it wasn't raining.

Ryel sniffed, groaned, and cleared his throat. His breath vapored on the chill air. "Chal. At once."

None appeared.

Quite deliberately he asked again, but with the same result. Dagar might not be powerful in the day, but Pukk had been right: the spirit-energy of the Aqqar was sucked dry. After last night's colloquy Ryel was disinclined to summon Pukk again, but he had no other servants in this place—only his Mastery, meant for higher aims than the body's needs, and his own ingenuity, not particularly scintillating just now.

"I would be with you now if I could," he whispered to his mother in a sleep-roughened voice. "But I have no way. And it'll take long to reach you, every day bringing you more pain. If only I had the Art."

As if in answer to that wish, a whickering snort resonated from very close by. Ryel started up to find an animal grazing less than twenty feet away. Had it been a fabulous monster all horns and warts, the wysard could not have been more astonished. But it was a mare of the true Steppes breed, neat-limbed and lovely, worth its weight in matched pearls.

"This *is* a dream," he whispered. The horse heard him, and lifted its head to look his way with great dark wondering eyes. At that gesture, so graceful and apt, Ryel caught his breath.

"*Jinn* ?"

The horse's ears twitched, and its dark eyes assessed the wysard warily under thick-fringed lashes, but without fear. Very slowly Ryel got to his feet. He was trembling, but not from the dawn cold this time.

"Jinn. I know it's you. But how?"

By this time he had his hand on the horse's mane. Very gently Ryel stroked the pale shimmering forelock. In doing so he ran a finger over the cocked left ear, seeking a little nick at its base. He found it, and jerked back as if bitten.

"No. It can't be."

It couldn't, not after so many years. Nevertheless the horse was warmly real, its breath vaporing on the raw Aqqar air. Real, and undoubtedly fleet and tough if her likeness to Jinn went further than mere semblance. Slowly lest he frighten the animal away, Ryel went to his saddlebags and took out the halter. "I never dreamed I'd have a use for this, here in the wasteland. Could you get used to it again ... Jinn?"

The name worked like a spell. The mare stood motionless, giving only a snort or two as Ryel tossed the saddlebags onto her back and fitted the halter onto her head. Reaching into his pocket, the wysard brought out a bag of dried fruit.

"Here, little one. Apricots—your favorites, remember? They're a bit on the leathery side, and I'd say a word to freshen them, but it wouldn't work now. Don't you want them?"

The horse apparently did not. After a tentative sniff, Jinn turned her head away.

"Very well. I won't force you," Ryel said. "But let me do this, at least." And he stroked Jinn's satin mane, and hugged her about the neck.

Although he had not ridden for a dozen years, the wysard vaulted without effort onto the mare's back and sat easily despite the lack of a saddle, his Steppes horsemanship unforgotten.

"All right, little one. Let's have a run, and see if you're as fast as your namesake was."

He touched a heel to her side, and the mare leapt into a gallop that no whip in the world could have prompted, and that surely no other mount in the world might equal. Ryel felt his hair stream out behind him, and in the fulness of his joy he began to sing a Rismaian ballad forgotten by him until that moment, shouting the words to the wind.

The day passed in an eyeblink—far too fast, in fact. Tirelessly Jinn raced across the infinities of green, never slowing her pace for an instant. At last Ryel forced her to a halt lest he kill her.

"This isn't right," he said, more disquieted than pleased, now. "Miles and miles gone by at a dead gallop, but you're not lathered even a fleck. You don't seem to need to eat or drink—or satisfy any other natural urges, for that matter. I'm starting to think you aren't real."

Jinn gave a whinny that sounded indignant, but Ryel was beginning to feel strong unease. He expected in the next moment for the air to close in chokingly around him, and the persecuting voice to shrill about his ears like an evil bug, and the horse to transform into something unspeakably monstrous.

For several taut heart-taxing minutes the wysard awaited the worst as Jinn watched him with great questioning eyes. At last Ryel allowed himself to calm, and put out a steady hand to stroke the mare's bright mane.

"Someone sent you," he said. " Someone who knows my memories. Someone who wishes me well. But who could it be?"

Whatever Jinn's arcane powers, speech was apparently not one of them, and Ryel had no time to ask whose Art-imbued agency had intervened so wonderfully in his behalf. He remounted, and rode.

But even if Jinn never tired, Ryel did. At sunset he made camp in the simple way of a Steppes bannerman, with no other shelter than his cloak. By now he was well out of the Aqqar. The mists had thinned, and at last he was amid open air. With a World-horse the journey would have taken many a weary day, but Jinn's swiftness owed nothing to earth, for which the wysard was inutterably grateful. That night Ryel looked up at the sky and for the first time in twelve years saw stars glimmering among the ragged clouds. He did not sleep that night, but kept his eyes on the flickering sparks, and waited for the dawn with hunger in his heart. As he stared, the sky lightened as if on fire, and he turned his head and saw the sun, and his eyes dazzled and burned.

That same day he found a trail and followed it sunward, tracing the path to a caravan-road he remembered well, riding ever south-west. It was under bright midday that he at last saw the banners of his people, deep blue with a triple star of silver, fluttering and snapping above the horizon's curve. Beyond the banners stretched a soft green plain, immensely vast, studded here and there with little conical hills. Far beyond that plain the white peaks of a range of huge mountains, the Gray Sisterhood, cut a jagged swath between earth and heaven.

My land, Ryel thought as his heart leapt. *My great green land.*

Those far-flung little hills had once been live volcanoes spitting fire many thousands of years gone. Each cinder-cone bore the name of a Rismaian deity, and in their hollows the phratri sheltered their horses from the winter winds, sure of divine as well as natural protection. No river flowed through Risma, but scattered spring-fed ponds reflected the swift-changing clouds. At the edge of one of these basins stood the springtide encampment of the Elhin Gazal, its scattered yats echoing the shape of the cinder-cones, smoke rising from the peaked roofs as if from live fire-mountains.

His blood aleap at the sight, Ryel would have driven his heels into Jinn's sides. But there was no need, for Jinn had seen the yats as well and plunged into a gallop that mocked all other speed she'd shown.

A sentinel had noted Ryel's approach, and now drew his bow. Well aware that only two words would save his life, the wysard forced Jinn to a skidding halt and drew a deep breath.

"Ryel!" he shouted. "Ryel Mirai!"

The wysard waited, his hands lifted clear of his weapons in token of his peaceful intent, as the warrior overcame his apparent surprise and cantered up. *I half know you*, Ryel thought, his recognition joyous and amazed. *You draw your hood about your face, but I know your eyes. Of all lucks, I had not hoped for this.*

They were now a spear's length apart. The hooded warrior spoke first, in the common Almancarian that was the trade-tongue of the Steppes.

"The name you shouted so proudly belongs to one many years gone," he said.

"Gone, but now returned," Ryel said. I greet you, Shiran."

The warrior's eyes widened, but only for a moment. "Many of the Rismai are named Shiran."

Your voice has changed, Ryel thought. *As mine has.*

"Shiran is indeed a common name on the Inner Steppes," he said aloud. "But in all the Steppes there is only one Shiran Belarem Alizai, and he and I once raced our first horses on this same stretch of ground. But he used always to wear a bow-guard of heavy gold, a treasured heirloom. Why does he not wear it now?"

Frowning brows at that, and a searching stare. Then from behind the hood the voice came rough. "Your eyes are strange."

Ryel felt the blood drain from his face like water into hot sand. *No*, he thought. *Oh, no. He sees it. Sees the blackness, and —*

"Yes," the sentinel said. "Strange. Not like ours." But as he spoke he took his hand from his dagger-hilt, and his voice grew calmer, sweetened with something like laughter. When he next spoke it was in the Rismai dialect, although formally, as befit men newly acquainted. "There used once to be a boy with such blue eyes, here in the camp."

Ryel blinked, but replied in the same language. "Was there indeed?"

The sentinel nodded. "A pale weakling he was. I used to jeer at him, until he grew strong enough to make me sorry." The cowl fell free, then, to bare a brave face all in smiles. "And now will I greet him in the same way I said farewell those many years gone." Shiran bent from the saddle and caught Ryel about the neck, pressing his right cheek against that of his friend's. "Our faces were smooth when last we took leave of each other like this—and now we meet again grown and bearded. Long years, play-brother."

The wysard returned the embrace with all his heart. "But I came back."

"You took your time. Have you returned to stay?"

"For a little while."

"You will find some things changed. Your sister, most."

"I have no doubt," Ryel said. "When I left, she was only a little child."

"She has grown into a woman since, play-brother—too fair a one, if you ask me. Half the braves of the encampment are at each other's throats for her sake—which is just as she likes it."

"Who does she favor? You, I hope."

"Hardly." But then Shiran ceased smiling, and looked away. "I do wrong to throw away your time this idly, Ry. You should see to your mother at once."

Ryel remembered the voice. The cruel taunting. "Then she is ..."

"In deep need of all the physician's skill you learned in Fershom Rikh. I am sorry you had to learn it, but better from me than another. Though I would ask how you knew she was—"

"I can't stay," Ryel said abruptly, already turning Jinn's head toward the yats.

Shiran nodded understanding. "May your doctor's arts help her. And when we next talk, may I hear of her cure."

"You will, Shir." They parted, and Ryel rode on to the encampment.

He had forgotten how rough life was among the yats. Forgotten the dirt and the din, the compacted miasma of meat seared by fire, of hot spices, horses, human sweat, the gritty reek of dust and smoke. The noisy hordes of children, and gangs of truculent dogs. Markul had taught him the luxuries of peace and cleanliness, however sparely he had elected to live there, and now he could not help wondering why his mother chose still to dwell among the Elhin Gazal when she might freely return to her native city of Almancar, the fairest in the World. Ryel felt a wrench of sorrow for that delicate spirit suborned to a dullard husband, a rough people, a harsh land.

He had recognized his family's yat-compound at once, pitched at some distance from the rest of the encampment and looked after by servants working hard at their various chores. Then Ryel's breath came fast, for he saw that the largest yat's entrance framed a woman, tall and girl-slender. Like a queen enthroned she half-reclined in a chair, instead of sitting upon a carpet in the Rismai fashion. Her night-hued tresses, only a little touched with silver, were arranged in the Almancarian fashion of many plaits, and her garments were Almancarian likewise, gleaming silk and fine embroidery falling in a thousand narrow folds. She was more fair than many another woman half her age, but her cheeks were pale and her eyes and lips were taut with pain. She lifted her face to the sunlight as if it were the last she would ever feel.

Ryel flung himself off his horse and fell to his knees before her, pressing the backs of her hands against his forehead to receive their blessing. "My lady mother." He kissed her fingers, that were fully as cold as his own, and breathed the slightly bitter fragrance that clung to them. *You're drugged,* he thought. *Drugged strongly with hrask, which means that your pain is great, but your doctors good.*

At first she had recoiled, breathlessly startled. But now she gazed down at him, uncertainty giving way to recognition. "My little son," she said wonderingly, in the high tongue of her native city. "My boy-child, now grown so tall." She reached out and laid a hand upon his head, caressing his hair. But her fingers trembled, and her voice was as faint as her smile. "Ah, Ry, I longed for this. At the sight of you my heart beat so strong—"

She gasped, and fainted. Ryel leapt up and caught her in his arms, carrying her inside the yat. He found his way at once to the curtained chamber that was hers and set her upon her bed, kneeling at her side as she opened her eyes again.

Despair clouded her gaze. "Too late, Ryel. Too late."

"I know you are sick, my mother," he said, taking her hand in his. "I have come to cure you."

Mira blinked away tears as she shook her head. "I am beyond any physician's cure. But how did you know?"

"I saw your malady in a vision," Ryel replied. "Because of it I am here."

"To no avail. The sickness has spread too far, now... and the pain. But soon both will end, and I will be free." Tenderly she regarded him, but with aching sorrow. "How glad I am, to have had this sight of you before my d—"

Ryel could not bear to hear any more, and murmured a word that made Mira fall into sleep. Then he fastened shut the hangings of the entrance, returned to his mother's side, and again knelt. All around was silence, for the dense hangings and layered carpets muted every sound within the yat and without. Ryel lit the lamps, and then, keenly feeling the chill in the room, he piled more *kulm* into the little tiled Almancarian stove, one of several that heated the various chambers of the tent-dwelling. He next threw in a handful of dust—feia powder, taken from Lady Haldwina's gifts—and at once a heady scent, not sweet but redolent of summer's earth, impregnated the air. In her sleep Mira breathed deeply of it.

"Good," Ryel murmured. "Let it take you." *It's taking me as well*, he thought. *Blocking out the World, leading me deep into my mind's widest reaches, to my real strength.*

Outside was strong daylight with Dagar not yet abroad, if Pukk was to be trusted. But Ryel did not greatly care either way, for he would rely on his Mastery to work his mother's cure, not the services of his srihs. He cradled both his mother's hands in his own and bowed his head over them, pressing the cold fingers against his brow.

"Give unto me the death within you," he whispered. "The death that thinks it owns you. Give it to me, and let me make it suffer."

He uttered a word, and felt his being slip away from his body; and suddenly he was slammed into icy blackness sharp as knives. Excruciating as the pain was, it was yet worsened by Ryel's realization that he'd felt it once before. This was not his first time in the emptiness: he had stood in the same place almost two months ago, and he had never felt such horror or such fear before as then.

But I'm not afraid now, he thought. *It can do no more to me than it has done.*

There in the echoing abyss he stood on a narrow bridge that linked him to his mother body and mind. Naked and unarmed he stood, knowing he must not look down, but straight on into the blackness. In that moment he was mindful of the half-mocking words of Edris.

"Here's a little rhyme for you, whelp—never forget it," his kinsman had said. "'If there be doubt, the Art will find it out.' Any flinching, and you'll fail. Always. Either give it your all or leave it alone."

Half-mockingly spoken, yes. But behind those dark eyes Ryel had seen a sternness that made him tremble. "I will," he had replied, firmly quelling his fear, facing his kinsman with lifted chin and steady gaze. "I will."

And now Ryel faced the blackness with the same level defiance, with his entire determination, his complete self committed to the fight. Swiftly and boldly he spoke the needful spells, those that would destroy the cancer and restore the corrupt flesh to wholeness. His words reverberated a thousandfold before silence suddenly enclosed him, heartlessly cold. He stood breathless, straining like drawn wire.

And then it came.

His skin—the invisible integument of his disembodied being, not his shell of flesh now left a million leagues behind—began to tingle, then burn. And then the cancer engulfed him in a crawling swarm of fanged and clawed clots of slime. Taken aback by the onslaught, Ryel struggled appalled.

I can't fight this. It's too strong. By every god —

Strangled by overwhelming doom he thrashed and writhed, but all in vain. The foul tusks and fiery talons rent and tore him until he could no longer shriek, but dropped throttled into the abyss.

Chapter Four

O<small>UT</small> of the blackness the voice he
loathed came like a kick.

*So, sweet eyes. You're not invincible after all. What was it you said
to her—'give your death to me, that I may make it suffer'? You arrogant imbecile.*

Even though he lacked material form, Ryel still ached and
smarted bitterly. But he had another's pain to think of. "Is she
alive?"

Yes, damn her.

"And healed?"

To my inutterable disgust, yes.

"Then my Mastery prevailed," Ryel murmured, dazed with tri-
umph.

The voice was furious. *Your Mastery*, it sneered. *Fool and double
fool—I saved your idiot skin. Your sorry Art was only strong enough to
rid the woman of her cancer. Without me, your heart would have
stopped forever. You might thank me, fool.*

Ryel was too startled—and crestfallen—to feel any gratitude.
"You helped me? But why?"

*I have my reasons, and you'll learn them soon enough. But you
throw your life away as fast as I can save it. And for what? That an old
woman might grow yet older.*

Ryel smiled. "Good."

*A woman who by your dirty land's laws should have been worm's
meat long ago.*

Disembodied though he was, Ryel shook at that. "Why? For
what cause?"

The voice laughed, sly and greasy. *Guess it, my arrogant beauty.*

The wysard comprehended, and grew furious. "You lie. My mother has been blameless all her life. She is—"

The voice howled, giggling. *A whore! As cunning a trollop as any of her city's brothel-quarter. Edris did not need to force her, oh no. She slipped between his sheets all willing, under the very roof where her husband snored oblivious. And the bastard fruit of their bed-sport became Markul's youngest lord adept, Ryel the Pure. How do you think you could have grown so great so young, fool, had not a wysard made you? But now that you're speechless and gaping, get back to where you belong.*

Ryel opened his eyes. Still he was on his knees at his mother's side, holding both of her hands. But now her fingers were warm, and his cold.

He could not speak yet, but only whisper. "Mira."

His mother was yet far in sleep, but her pain-worn pallor had given way to the beauty he remembered from his boyhood, and that all the Steppes had marvelled at and sung of.

How fair you are, Ryel thought. *Mira Silestra, beloved of Edris Lord of Markul, mother of his son —*

His eyes burnt, his body ached to the bone, his wits gyred. But he could not rest. Not yet, not until …

Releasing his mother's hands, he unfastened the brooches clasping the bodice of the gown, and unlaced the opening of the linen shift. He breathed freely for the first time. The cure was complete. His mother's flesh was as whole and sound as in the days he drank life from it. With a physician's calm Ryel completed the examination, and fastened again the brooches and laces, but that once done, he buried his face in his hands to cool his eyes' burning, and clenched his teeth to calm his heart.

Ah, Edris. Dearer to me than father and my father indeed, why did you never tell me? Why did I never divine the truth when it stood so plain? When I knelt at your feet before the walls of Markul, and felt your hand so harsh and gentle in my hair?

He went to the window-flap, untied and lifted it. A chill night breeze caught him full in the face. The sun had set in the last hour, and now only a blood-red bar of dying light forced a swath between blackness and blackness.

"You're out there," he whispered, speaking to his father's murderer. "I feel you, Dagar." But amid the darkness of his rage and his sorrow drove a burning doubt, for he realized that the unbidden voice which haunted his thoughts had never spoken to him save in the night.

A turbulence outside the chamber made him turn away. Summoning all that was left of his strength, Ryel rose and drew aside the curtain. Standing before him was a beautiful youth in riding gear, high-colored and bold-featured, with light long hair and upslanting eyes of violet-tinged heaven-blue.

He knew her, but still had to make sure. "Nelora?"

"High time you came home, brother," the girl at once replied, entwining her hands in his, gazing up in mingled joy and reproach. "Why did you stay so long away?"

I can understand why Shiran worships you, the wysard thought. Aloud he said, "I had to learn my art. Such learning does not come quickly, and cannot be interrupted."

Nelora lowered her eyes. "No healer yet has been able to help our mother, save to give her sleeping-draughts and pain-allays. The tabib Grustar has said that—" she bit her lip and blinked—"that she has not long before—" She turned away, but Ryel took her by both shoulders and turned her back.

"Look at me, little sister. Grustar I remember from my childhood, and never knew him a fool or a liar. But my skill is greater than his. Our mother is well again, because I healed her."

Nelora stared at him helplessly wide-eyed, her belief now stretched to breaking. Ryel felt for her. She was, after all, very young, and had come near to being orphaned, and now here was a complete stranger claiming not only her mother's cure, but kinship.

Mira herself, suddenly between them, turned that terrible moment to rejoicing. "Believe him, daughter. For too long I've been kept from this, and this." She drew her two children close. "No more tears, my eaglets, ever again. Tonight we'll revel."

That night they were joyful. Shiran was asked to the feast with his sister Yalena, as was the clan chief Khirgar, and many others. During the celebration Ryel saw how Shiran wooed Nelora with a thousand unavailing attentions, and how Khirgar barely spoke to Mira but ever gazed on her with looks yearning and awed. And the wysard thought of Diara, Sovrena of the City of Gold. But most of all he remembered Edris and the years he had spent with him learn-

ing the Art, and those innumerable instances of kindness and sever-
ity far surpassing any mere kinsman's care.

I was blind, ithradrakis, he thought. *Blind as I was that night you
came to the yat and kissed my mother's hands, and looked into her eyes
far deeper than Shiran is now looking into my sister's.*

Sometime after midnight the guests had departed and Nelora
had staggered yawning to her bed, but Ryel and his mother still sat
together upon the deep cushions scattered over the carpet, close to
the open yat-flap that let in the moonlight.

"It's grown cold," Ryel said. "Let me get your shawl."

Mira shook her head. "Only lend me your cloak awhile."

Ryel did so, draping the red-purple folds about his mother's
shoulders. Mira smiled her thanks. "How well this holds your
warmth."

"Just as it once held my father's."

Mira filled her glass again, but her fingers trembled on the gob-
let-stem, and some of the wine dropped wet rubies upon the gem-
tinted rug. "How did you learn? From Edris?"

"No."

"He kept his promise. I half hoped he would not." Mira's lips
quivered on the goblet-rim. "I wanted to tell you. I might have told
you tonight."

"Mother—"

She looked up at him, deep into his eyes, for the first time in reproach. "But when would you have told me of Edris' death? No, say
nothing now. I have known for two months almost, and wept all my
tears out. Only the pain is left, which in many ways surpasses a
cancer's agony."

Ryel drew back, amazed. "But how could you have learned?"

Mira fixed her gaze on the black sky outside the tent. "Three
months ago I was riding out to the grazing-lands with Nelora, when
suddenly it seemed that a shadow passed, and something sharp and
chill drove into my heart like an arrow so that I fell from my horse.
And then I looked round and saw Edris as he had been at our first
meeting, young and wild in warrior's gear. And he lifted me up and
held me in his arms, and kissed me, and I was joyful. But as he kissed
me his lips turned deadly cold, until I cried out. And when I next
opened my eyes I was here in the yat, and Nelora was at my side

with the tabib Grustar. And I understood what the vision meant, and fainted yet again." She drew a deep unsteady breath. "It was Edris I loved, Ryel. Always. Only after Yorganar and I were wed and Edris had departed for Markul did I wonder that my husband no longer had any wish to dance, nor any skill at music. That he had lost those wild graces of laughter and of wit, and no longer looked into my eyes with that comprehending tenderness that ever made me tremble..."

Awhile they were both silent, mother and son. Then Ryel spoke, half unwillingly, "My heart-name for Edris was always *ithradrakis*."

"'Dearer than father.'" Mira smiled with pleasure. "So you have not forgotten your language lessons in the palace tongue of my city."

"All that was taught me, I remember," Ryel said, returning the smile. "Every beautiful word—like *ilandrakis*, 'dearer than brother.' And *silestra*, 'as fair within as without'—always my name for you."

"I never thought I deserved it."

"More now than ever."

Mira stared into the candles' flickering faint radiance, and spoke in a whisper. "I wish I could ask you how Edris died. But I cannot bear to know he ended his life in pain."

"He did not," Ryel said. And he despised himself for the lie, especially because his mother was so quick to believe it. "But nonetheless he was killed by a force of evil, Dagar by name. A thing neither alive nor dead, seeking to return embodied to the World. And since Edris' death I have been tormented by a voice within, goading me with taunts and scorns."

Mira's color waned. "Is it ... is it the voice of the daimon?"

Ryel gave a weary sigh. "I'm beginning to think it only too possible, but Dagar is beyond reach of my vengeance. And whatever the voice may be, it warned me of your illness, and helped me to heal you. For that I am grateful. But I won't be led any further. I'll remain here with you for a while, and then return to my City." He stood up. "We'll speak more of these things, but at another time. The hour's late, and you should rest."

They stood together silently for some time, hand in hand. Then Mira spoke. "I owe you my life, little son."

Ryel touched his lips to her cheek. "I but gave back what I received, Mira Silestra."

"Blessed am I in you." Mira returned the kiss, then took off Edris' cloak and wrapped it about Ryel's shoulders with the same care she had always used in his childhood. "I'll not need this again. Sleep well."

But Ryel slept little that night, kept awake by memories of the day, and thoughts of the future. Almost as he expected, the air closed around him, stifling and silent, and the voice spoke, very sweetly this time.

So. My brave lad has found out his father, and forgiven his erring mama. Now what will he do?

"Return to Markul," Lagan answered in his thoughts. "As soon as possible."

Oh? And what about Almancar?

The wysard stiffened. "Nothing calls me there."

Really? Not even pretty little Diara?

Ryel did not reply. The voice persisted, sweeter still.

Do you remember how in Markul I said the girl would go mad for you? I meant it. Even as we speak, all Almancar is bewailing the incurable insanity of its Sovrena.

Ryel felt his chest constrict. "*Damn* you," he whispered aloud.

The voice sneered and giggled. *Yes,* it hissed. *Clear out of her mind she is. Tearing at her tender body with demented hands, besmearing herself with her own shit, shrieking obscenity and drivel. An interesting sight, should you care to see it.*

Ryel struggled up on his elbow. "You lie, daimon."

Did I lie about your mother?

"Is the Sovrena's madness your work—Dagar?"

A shrieking peal of scorn in reply. *Soon, sweet eyes. In Almancar.*

The air lightened and cleared before Ryel could speak again. For the rest of that night he lay motionless and open-eyed.

The wysard knew the dawn when it came. In Markul the silence of the air had been complete save for the wind and the rain, but the Steppes were never still. Wild beasts and camp-dogs and babies had moaned and mewled and howled in the night, and now the birds were awake, crying far overhead. Ryel rose, dressed, and went out into the morning.

The sky hovered between night and day, dark overhead yet glowing ever brighter on the eastern horizon. Some little distance from the yat his sister Nelora was sitting crosslegged on a rug with a trayful of chal and sweets at her elbow, her eyes on the gathering light. She was wrapped in a horseman's greatcoat, and her fair hair streamed out beneath a fur-lined riding-cap rather too large for her. Ryel approached, and sat down at her side.

"A good morning, sister."

"If you say so." She smiled at him, but Ryel could see her cordiality was strained. He understood, and smiled back in much the same way. Since they met they'd adopted the intimate form of the Rismai dialect, used among siblings and other close kin. He had always used it with Edris.

"You're up early," he said.

"Couldn't sleep," she replied, a little shortly. "I was thirsty."

"You drank wine last night."

She sighed. "Too much. My head aches like a broken toe."

"It's most unseemly for a Steppes maiden to drink to excess."

She tossed her head, then winced. "None of your lectures, brother. I only did it because I was so glad to see you. Have some chal—it's still hot."

Ryel filled a cup with vaporing brew and wrapped his hands around it, glad of the warmth. But when he drank, he grimaced. "Agh. There's *frangin* in this chal."

Frangin was the strong liquor of the Steppes, made by the Kaltiri Kugglatai from the tart green berries of the thickets that covered part of their lands. The Rismai seldom touched it, save in times of great joy or great sorrow. "You're incorrigible," Ryel sternly informed his sister. But he drank again, finding himself actually liking the mingled savor of harsh and smooth. He next turned his attention to the chal-tray, and gave a little start of pleasure. "My *krusghan!*"

"You're welcome to it," Nelora said testily. "I was going to play something, but it made my head hurt."

Ryel set his chal-cup aside and reached for the Steppes flute, running reminiscent fingers over its polished ebony and joinings of carved jade. "When I was a boy, wherever I went this went too. A thousand songs I've played on it." And he lifted it to his lips, softly sounding a remembered tune. But at the first notes Nel gave a dismal dog-howl.

"*Don't*, brother! You'll split my skull." She shuddered, pulling her cap down over her ears, closing her eyes tight. "Be a sweet tabib and heal me. The frangin isn't working."

Ryel shook his head. "It's better for you to suffer, and repent."

Nelora glared through a wince. "You didn't say that to our mother."

The wysard felt his smile slide away. "Enough. Take off that hat and lean your head toward me." And Ryel massaged his sister's temples with the tips of his fingers, combing her long fair tresses with his fingers. "Your hair's exactly like Jinn's mane," he said, gently now. "It's so thick I could hide an egg in it."

Nelora's mouth-corner quirked. "I'd rather you didn't, but my thanks for the compliment."

"I remember how folk came from far and wide to gaze upon you when you were a baby." He gave the pale wild locks a last caress, but as he did so he thought of Diara Dranthene's night-black jewel-twined braids. "How's your headache now?"

Nel cocked her head, warily considering. "I don't have one. How'd you do that?"

Ryel smiled. "Magic."

His sister smiled back. "I believe you. Here's your reward." She popped a sweet into his mouth. "Remember?"

Ryel let the delicious almond-sugar and apricot preserve melt on his tongue a little before answering, deep in recollection the while. "It's *lakh*. I used to steal it because I could never get enough, back when I was little."

Nelora nodded patiently. "Our mother tells me as much every time she makes a batch. That's why I brought some out here, just for you."

"How did you know I'd be up so early?"

"I knew, big brother. Were I home after being away for a dozen years, I'd not waste time abed, but rise early to see my charming sister." She noticed his face then, and her own became concerned. "You're pale, brother, and your eyes are sunken. It looks as if what little sleep you got was bad. You're shivering, too. Here, have some more chal."

He drank and grew a little warmer. "I'd like it if you called me Ry."

She smiled, entirely this time. "Then I will ... Ry."

The wysard looked skyward, into the waning stars. "We're up far before the sun."

"Not much before," Nelora said as she pointed eastward. "Look, over there at the very edge of the world—light at last. It's just like what the poet says in the epic—'And surging up from the sea's bed, driving forth darkness, cloud-lathered sun-horses scorched the world-rim'."

Ryel recognized the quotation, and nodded approvingly. "You're remarkably learned. But I hadn't thought to find my little sister so manlike, in a horse-tamer's boots and breeches. Many another girl would fear the talk of the old women, and keep to the yat."

Nelora swung her bright locks back from her blushes. "I care nothing for the clack of hags, brother. It's never been deemed a shame for a girl of the Three Stars to be a horse-tamer, if her spirit and her strength be equal to it. Speaking of such, can I borrow that mare of yours for a run? I swear I'll be gentle."

"You swear too much as it is. And Jinn's been wrung hard these past few days. Let her rest awhile." The last thing Ryel wanted was for Jinn's inexplicable powers to be discovered. Before Nelora could protest or plead, he changed the subject. "Where'd you get that bracelet you're wearing?" But he already knew the answer.

Nel cast an annoyed glance at the gleaming wide band of heavy gold. "It's not a bracelet. It's a bow-guard."

"And an heirloom of Shiran's family," Ryel said sternly. "Unless you consider Shiran your betrothed, you're required to return it."

She bristled. "I don't obey Rismai law. I'm half Almancarian, like you. I'll never wed in the Steppes, especially to that illiterate bumpkin Shiran."

"Then who would you have?"

"The most wonderful man in the world, of course."

"And who might that be?"

"The Sovranel Priamnor, brother to the Sovrena Diara."

Ryel couldn't decide whether to laugh or frown, because he had heard rumors of the Sovranel during the feast in his mother's yat. "From what I gather from hearsay, the Sovranel has not ventured outside his palace for the past five years."

"Well, and?"

"It's said that he was stricken by a disease caught in Almancar's brothel-quarter, and nearly died of it."

Nel's lip curled in scorn. "Vile slander."

Ryel persisted. "Shiran says the Sovranel might once have been the handsomest man in Destimar, but now he's a disfigured eunuch, and looks like an old white monkey."

This information only elicited a half-contemptuous, half-pitying smile. "Shiran's such an ass." A storm overtook Nelora's blue eyes, then, sudden and fierce. "I *hate* the Steppes. We could be living in a great city, in the mansion where our mother grew up, instead of a tent in the middle of a sea of weeds. Just think of it, Ry. Don't you wish *you* were in Almancar this minute?"

"No," Ryel said slowly, remembering with a twitch of loathing the lying words of the daimon. "I don't."

The wysard firmly refused to believe the voice that had haunted him with tales of the Sovrena's madness. As if in compliance, it left him alone. The next two days the wysard spent in the encampment enjoying being his mother's son again, and a brother to Nelora, and renewing old acquaintances among the phratri. He also helped Grustar in doctoring his people's various complaints, none of them life-threatening, to his great relief. He spent time, too, in currying Jinn until she gleamed like new gold, and fitting her with a saddle worthy of her beauty.

The second afternoon he rode out alone. There was a place he had to revisit, a place he had shut out of his every memory, if not his dreams, for sixteen years.

The day had started fair, but by noon the sky began to darken with clouds, and from afar off Ryel's quick ears could hear the deep growl of a coming storm. The noise made him quiver with an emotion part expectation, part unease. Markul's weather had been always the same—eternal fogs and mists and drizzles unrelentingly chill, the seasons distinguishable only by their extremes of rain or snow. But the Steppes were notorious for wild winter winds and devastating spring storms. The storms were the worst: to be split in two by lightning was no unusual death among the Rismai.

Ryel sniffed the air: it was full of danger. How often as a little child he had huddled in the yat when the great tempests shook the grasslands, feeling helplessly unsheltered in his frail tent. But as he grew he learned to love the lightning-bolts in all their terrible forms. The shattering straight rods, the delicate branching fire-veins streaking out in all directions, the dragon-leaps of light high up, now hidden in the clouds, now flashing forth—these he had watched for and thrilled at.

But now he had reached the fire-mountain he'd sought—a little grass-covered hollow-cored cinder cone that thousands of years past had been a volcano spurting liquid fire. It was named Banat Yal, after the Rismai god of the air. Reining in, Ryel dismounted, then began the brief ascent to the top. Every step became increasingly difficult, not so much from the climb's steepness as from the weight of memories. The wind was rising, and the sky's blue had been utterly effaced by clouds dark as night. Under that rumbling shadow Ryel stood on the rim of the fire-hill, looking out to the endless sweep of green.

The air became heavy with storm-threat. Harsh winds tore at Ryel's clothes, and the wysard clutched Edris' cloak tighter about him lest they strip him bare. And then a great brand of blinding light shot down from the darkness, hitting another fire-cone not at all far away. Ryel winced, waiting for the thunder-clap. At once it sounded, with deafening force.

Only a fool would stay out in such weather, but Ryel put his faith in the old saying about lightning. It couldn't hit him again— not here. Accordingly, he stood his ground. But recollection, not the storm, made him tremble.

Fourteen years ago a storm identical to this had shook the Risma plains, and Ryel had rushed to this same fire-cone drenched and breathless, hoping to shelter in its bowl. But the lightning had blasted down all around him, and the electricity in the air had lifted his hair from the back of his neck. He'd only managed to struggle to the hillock's rim when something hit him from behind with a tremendous shove, sending him hurtling down the bowl's shallow slope into the pit. Over and over he tumbled, never feeling the glass-edged cinder-rocks tearing his clothes and skin. His only sensations were the rending throb at the nape of his neck, and the agony rattling in his spine. But then he became aware of the wind, so strong now that he felt himself pulled into the air, caught up in its terrible whirl. His clothes whipped about him, flew off in rags, became part of the spinning debris. With blank horror Ryel realized that the next thing torn to pieces would be his body.

When he discovered he was still alive, he was lying naked, stretched prone in a pool of mud. The storm had subsided to cold needles of rain. He had never hurt worse. He put his hand to the back of his neck, and with sick dread felt throbbing warmth oozing under his fingers. When he touched the gaping lips of the lightning-wound, he fainted yet again.

Then he dreamed a very beautiful dream. In it a tall figure swathed in long robes came to where he lay, lifted him up out of the mud, and carried him away from that place of pain, singing all the while some lovely quiet wordless song, soft and deep. Ryel had never felt more sheltered from danger, or more grateful for his deliverance. Tears of joy warmed his cheeks.

"Thank you," he whispered. He never expected any reply, but one came.

"It was meant to happen, whelp. Now rest, for you need it." The voice was vibrantly low, like thunder, but Ryel wasn't afraid any more. Not when the voice was so sorrowing, and so gentle. He only smiled, and felt darkness steal over him again like a soft enveloping blanket.

When he again awoke he was home in his yat, his mother and Yorganar bending over him in an anguish of worry. He couldn't have been asleep long, because he was still covered with mud, still bleeding, still naked. But the terrible wound at the back of his neck had somehow closed up as if cauterized. All that remained was a knot the size of a sparrow-hawk's egg that the tabib Grustar diagnosed as a bad bruise. Ryel had decided never to tell anyone the truth, which he himself was far from sure of. In time the knot's swelling subsided to a mere lump not much bigger than a grape, which Ryel's long hair hid from view. It never went away, nor for a long time did the pain. Even now, years later, Ryel winced at the memory-prodded twinge deep in the base of his skull.

"Were you here, ithradrakis?" he wondered aloud. "Was it you that saved me?"

He had never asked Edris that question while his kinsman lived.

It couldn't have been possible, at any rate—not possible that Edris should have materialized for his help. But when he had come to Markul and learned a little of the Art, Ryel often recalled his encounter with the lightning and the whirlwind at the age of twelve. Often he wished he might experience it again, and through his Art derive some use or knowledge from it. But Markul's weather was unchangeably dull, year upon year of fog-bound damp.

And at any rate, weather-witching was a lost Art. Only the Highest had ever possessed it. Folk of the World believed that power over the weather was the commonest wysardry of all, even as they deemed shape-changing and thought-reading and mind-moving to be likewise common attainments among lord adepts of the Four Cities. Nothing could have been less true. Such things took innate talent, immense concentration, and untold study to achieve. But now Ryel stood again on the lip of that epiphanic fire-hill, under a dark sky close enough almost for touching, and never had he felt more strong or more sure of his Art. He raised his face to the boiling black clouds, and felt first one huge cold drop hit his cheek, then another his eyelid, and then too many more to count, masking his face with dripping chill. He spread his arms to the storm, called it to him.

And it came.

Roaring and crashing it came, enveloping him in wind and lightning and torrent. He knew no spells to harness the wild power of that tempest, but made up a Mastery of his own, crying it into the downpour—mere meaningless syllables, mantras that pulled his Art's strength into a blinding white ball and hurled it into the storm. And the storm wrapped around it, and became a whirlwind.

Ryel never stopped to consider what he'd wrought. Still shouting mantras he felt himself being lifted and taken, but this time he directed his course with his thoughts. The storm's blackness engulfed him wholly then, and he very probably lost consciousness at some point, because when he next became aware of the world around him he was standing upright within view of his mother's yat, even as he had wished. The first thing he did was ascertain if he were still clothed, and unhurt. He was both, to his more than mild astonishment.

A steady rain still fell, and no one was outside. He hadn't been seen, thank—

"Ry! Where in the name of All did *you* come from?"

Turning about, Ryel saw Shiran very close by on horseback. Despite so much water pelting around him the wysard's throat dried up, making him mute.

Shiran didn't seem to notice. He rode closer, shaking his head in bafflement. "I looked around and there you were."

Not knowing how to reply, Ryel made an attempt at a shrug. "Right. Here I am." But he was concerned about Jinn. He'd paid no attention to her once he'd begun climbing the fire-hill. What had happened to her since? What if she'd—

"I found your mare," Shiran said, as if answering his thoughts. "She was wandering out in the fields there." He jerked his thumb over his shoulder.

Ryel blinked. "When?"

"Just now. I was on my way to tell you." Shiran's initial amusement became concern. "What happened? Did she throw you?"

Ryel nodded. It was easier than an explanation. "Where's Jinn now?"

"Tied up behind my yat. Come on over and get dry. I'll give you some chal—or better yet, frangin. You look as groggy as if you just dropped from the skies."

The wysard glanced up at the pelting clouds, and smiled. "Next time I'll work harder on my landing."

On his third day among the Elhin Gazal the wysard rode out with Shiran to the fields where the Yorganarem horses grazed. The herds had long been looked after by some of Rismai's most expert horse-breeders, men who had been Yorganar's comrades for many years, and nearly all of whom Ryel remembered from boyhood. For two days the wysard lived among horses and men, spending his waking hours in the saddle and his sleeptime on the ground. Ryel greatly enjoyed himself, and much admired the best of the Yorganarem herd, in particular the great buff-colored stallion Suragh.

"He's Windskimmer's handsomest grandson, Suragh is," said Belar, a Kaltiri warrior who had served with Yorganar during the Shrivrani wars. "He'd make a fit suitor for that pretty little mare of yours, Ryel Mirai. I've seen him ogling her, believe me."

"Jinn's somewhat young yet for a lover," Ryel replied.

Belar shook his head in emphatic denial. "Their offspring would be priceless. Your Jinn has the blood of Windskimmer in her veins, that much is clear to see. From their looks she and Suragh could be brother and sister."

"Rather close kinship for mating," Ryel said, more than a little doubtful.

Belar smiled forgivingly. "Not a bit of it. Look at the royal house of Destimar, if you care to see how incest improves the blood line. Be mindful that the Sovran Agenor's parents were brother and sister. The Rismai would punish such mating with death, but I'm an old soldier, and have seen somewhat more of the world than our yat-folk. The Dranthene line is purebred, and merits praise."

Shiran frowned, scandalized. "It is against the law of kind."

Belar only chuckled in answer. "Some laws were meant to be broken. And from the manner in which Diara of Destimar is sung of and languished over, I think many would agree with me."

Shiran would have spoken sharply to the contrary, but at that moment a horseman approached them, galloping hard. Belar's quick eyes squinted in recognition. "Aha. There's my kinsman Mirib, just back from Almancar. I hope Count Tesandrion decided to buy our horses." He lifted his voice in greeting to the newcomer. "What word from the City of Gold, cousin? Are we rich?"

Mirib dismounted wearily. "Richer than ever. The Count paid all we asked."

Belar gazed on his kinsman with bewilderment. "Then why look so glum?"

When Mirib did not answer, Ryel did. "I know why," he said, his breath coming fast. "The Sovrena Diara is ill."

They all turned to stare at him, Mirib the hardest. "How did you learn?" he demanded.

"I heard rumors on the road from Fershom Rikh," the wysard lied. "She was said to be in great danger. But tell me the rest."

Mirib drew a long breath. "It's worse than mere sickness. They say now that a demon torments her." Amid black silence he addressed Ryel. "No one knows how to cure the girl. The Sovran has called in the realm's best doctors, all to nothing. They say she'll die soon if no help comes."

Proudly independent though the Steppes folk were, they shared a deep loyalty to the imperial house, and real fondness for the Sovrena Diara. The princess was all but worshipped among the Rismai, as Ryel had amply learned in his short time with the phratri. Everyone looked heart-stricken at Mirib's words, but the wysard knew with helpless certainty that no pain could be sharper than his own.

"I have to get back to the encampment," the wysard said. "At once."

Belar divined Ryel's intention, and shook his head. "You're a good tabib, Ryel Mirai. But if you think to journey to Almancar for the Sovrena's sake, surely you'll lose your labor."

"Or your life," Mirib dryly added. "The Sovran Agenor has punished with death some of those doctors who've failed to heal his daughter. And—" he lowered his voice—"it's said that he has begun to welcome sorcerers from the witch-cities to use their black arts upon her."

Everyone listening murmured in revulsion and made warding-off gestures, save for Ryel.

"I can't stay," he said, barely able to bring out the words. Whistling Jinn, he vaulted onto her back.

Shiran scrambled for his own horse. "Wait! I'm coming, too."

But Jinn far outstripped Shiran's great gelding, and reached the encampment even as the caravan from Almancar was telling its news. As the wysard leapt from the saddle, his mother hastened to him.

"Ry, they've said that the Sovrena—"

"I know," the wysard said. "I must leave for Almancar as soon as may be."

"But surely there are many physicians who might—"

"Many might try," Ryel said. "I alone can succeed."

Mira put her hand to her heart, close to where the cancer had been. "I fear for you. Surely your enemy means you harm, and lures you onward."

Ryel let out a resigned breath. "No doubt it does."

She took his arm. "Don't go."

Gently he freed himself. "I must. Every moment the poor girl endures as a captive is more than I can bear."

She understood, or thought she did. "Ah, Ry. If you're in love with her—"

"I'm not." He glanced at the sun. "If I leave now, I'll have six hours of daylight."

But the wysard could not leave until his gear was gathered, and his mother had filled Jinn's saddlebags with more than enough provisions for his journey, and Nel had begged to ride with him. Only an hour later, every minute of it grudged, was Ryel mounted and ready. During that time Shiran had arrived to add his farewells to the others'.

"The trade-road lies nearly straight northwest to Almancar, as you know," he said. "Good luck to you, play-brother. I only wish you weren't going alone."

"I myself wish it, too," the wysard replied. "But no one could keep up with Jinn."

"*I'd* try," Nelora muttered. Ryel reached out and ruffled her long light locks.

"I see you're still wearing that bow-guard, little sister."

Nel cast an impatient glance first at the massive gold bracelet on her wrist, then at her suitor. "It weighs like lead. But Shiran insisted I keep it."

"You're luckier than you know, imp."

Mira laid a light hand upon Ryel's knee. "So. I lose you yet again."

He felt her trembling. "Not for long," he said gently. "I promise you."

"When will you return?"

Ryel caught her hand, warming it in his, and bent his brow to its back. "Soon. Very soon."

"Not *too* soon," Shiran said with a brave attempt at a grin. "Almancar's pleasures will take up at least a little of your time—and I can think of no better place to spend some of your reward than in the Diamond Heaven."

Nelora shot him a glance of purest scorn. "As if *you* were ever in that harlot's haunt." While Shiran looked foolish, Nel reached out and drew Ryel down from the saddle until her lips touched his ear. "When you see the Sovranel Priamnor, tell him of me, brother Ry. And give him this." She kissed his cheek, close to the mouth. Before Ryel could reprove her, Shiran dealt Jinn a smart slap on the rump that sent the mare flying.

Chapter Five

Even Jinn's speed was too slow for Ryel's liking, now that he knew he could harness the weather to take him where he wished. But the skies were at present cloudless, and none of his Art could make them otherwise.

"I haven't the skill," he said to himself. "And the air's drained all but dry thanks to Dagar, save what nature provides—which hasn't been much of late."

Which was probably all to the good. The fact that he could rely on his own Mastery to summon the forces of the air was exhilarating, yes, but sobering, too. Ryel was fully convinced that he had done something very dangerous, no matter how strong he felt. It was enough now to enjoy the clear unbroken beauty of the skies, so wonderfully different from the perpetual murks of Markul.

The moon had come up full on the second night of Ryel's journey, bright enough to ride by. But the wysard had elected from the first to travel only by night, that Jinn's preternatural speed might be less observed. He only halted at his own desire—as now, to draw breath awhile.

Anyone looking upon him with World-eyes beheld a young Rismai brave superbly mounted and armed, dressed with that warlike elegance for which the Steppes was famed, and enviably unencumbered. But one thing Ryel much regretted having left behind: his krusghan, the music of which would have given him solace at this moment, and offered thanks to the moon-bright loveliness of the World around him.

Ryel stretched, shrugging off his coat, whistling a Kugglatai air between his teeth. The night was warm—the first real warmth Ryel had known in years. Long silver-rimmed shreds of cloud fleeted northward over the dark land, casting wraiths of shadow on the rise and fall of the treeless hills.

Ryel rode to the top of one of these and looked about. At the limit of the northwest distance he discerned a faint irregular line, gleaming white—the Gray Sisterhood that divided the plains of eastern Destimar from the savannah and seacoast of the Zallan west. He knew their names: Tanwen the Maiden. Wilful and untrusty Dolgash. Baltaigor the Kind, with the pass into Zalla that was clear even at winter's worst. Winlowen, hardly more tender, and her twin Tryphene. In their midst Kalima, eldest, tallest, most murderous— and somewhere among her crags, Lady Srin Yan Tai. Long did Ryel look at them, his eyes moving from one to another. But as he looked, his thoughts began to take him elsewhere, far from the road to Almancar.

He had parted from Edris and returned to his house to bathe away the grit and sweat of their all but fatal duel. Sinking into the vaporing water with a long sigh of pleasure, he closed his eyes, ready to give himself up to serene meditation. He was still a little drunk from the brandy he and his uncle had shared, which was all to the good.

"Shall I scrub your back?"

At that voice and its question, both startling, Ryel bolted up, sending water flying. A woman stood silhouetted in the doorway, her hair a silken gold corolla, her body's outline exquisitely visible under the transparent folds of her gown.

She laughed. "I've startled you."

Beautiful though she was, her voice was grating and shrill, and her laugh set Ryel's teeth on edge. The wysard said the words that banished malignant daimons of the Outer World, but she did not disappear.

"How did you get in here?" he demanded.

"Your door was unlocked."

"What do you want?" he asked angrily. But his anger was for himself, because his voice wouldn't stop breaking and his pulse wouldn't calm.

She laughed again. "I'm but newly arrived in Markul. I was told that you were the greatest of this City's adepts, and I have come to learn of you. But it seems I've not chosen my time well." She turned as if to leave, silhouetting her side view. At that sight Ryel felt his mouth go dry.

"Wait. Stay." Reaching for a vial on a nearby table, Ryel poured some of its contents into the water, which instantly turned the opaque turquoise of a mountain lake, hiding his nakedness. "Come in."

With deliberate grace she entered the many-mirrored chamber, increasing her beauty sixfold. She unfastened the diamond clasps at her shoulders, and the gown dropped to the floor. Then she slowly turned about as she took the pins from her hair and let it flow like white molten gold down her back. As Ryel watched, tranced with amazement and desire and drink, she slipped into the water, supple as an otter, and pressed close to him.

"You're hot, Ryel," she whispered. "Hot and hard."

He seized her, pulled her close. "And you're—" he started as if burnt. "You're—cold. You're like ice."

"Warm me, then. Fill me with fire."

But he had none. "The water's ... freezing." It chilled him to the soul, despite the thick bed of embers glowing just under the crystal. He struggled out and threw on his robe, staring down at the woman in the water—and saw that now the water was no longer opaque turquoise, but a crystal that concealed nothing.

She stretched to the full, luxuriously. As she did so the water began to bubble and steam. She arched her back, and her breasts broke above the boiling water-line. Lifting her knees, she opened them wide to the steam, tauntingly shameless. "Is this too hot for you?"

At the joining of her legs she glowed white gold and hot wild rose. Under the crystalline water the fine silk hair waved like a sea-creature's around the soft split of flesh. Her perfume rose on the silver mist of the bath—a strange fragrance made of a hundred scents of which Ryel could not name even one, half of which repelled despite the heady seduction of the rest.

He loathed her, but couldn't bear his hunger. "Get up, damn you."

She only laughed. "Make me."

Braving the boiling water, he roughly lifted her out. Her weight took him aback—dead weight, slippery and burning hot, so hot he could not hold her long. Carrying her as fast as he could into the next room, he dropped her onto his bed, dripping as she was. All the while she laughed that infuriating laugh, and to stop her mouth he kissed her. The thrust of her tongue in his mouth came like a jolt from some malignant fish, and her lips clung like leeches to a wound. Twining her arms around his neck, she pulled him down with irresistible strength, rolling him under her. As he lay breathless and ribsore from the clutch of her knees, her hands ripped his robe open. Under her clutching fingers his stiff flesh throbbed as if flayed with white-hot knives, and he gave a groan.

"Do it," he whispered, clutching her hips to force her down upon him. "Fuck my life out."

Her changeable eyes had turned complete black. She laughed like a madwoman, and lowered her body to engulf his. But suddenly her laughter changed to filthy cursings, and her knees' grip loosened, and Edris' voice came like the boom of a storm.

"Get off of him, bitch."

Seething with frustrated lust, Ryel struck at his uncle with all the strength he had left, but Edris shoved him away like a tiresome child and caught the woman around the throat, dragging her from the bed.

"Who sent you? Tell me the name, hell-whore."

The woman shrieked with laughter, and lunged for Edris' eyes. He seized her wrists, and for a little while they struggled, she far the stronger, until Edris shouted out an unjointed string of syllables that Ryel had never heard before. At first the woman's beautiful features contorted with fury, but then her face went blank, and her prismatic eyes rolled upward, and she dropped with all her weight. The sharp crack of bone brought Ryel fully to his senses at last.

"You killed her," he stammered.

Edris rounded on him, grippng both his shoulders. "You damned fool, Ryel. Do you have any idea what danger you were in?"

Ryel was more furious still. "You *killed* her. You murdering bast—"

The back of Edris' swift heavy hand knocked the words from his mouth. "Quit squealing, and wake up. Fool, she was already dead."

Ryel was utterly numb save for his throbbing cheek. "No. She couldn't have been ..."

"Dead, I tell you. A stinking corpse, animated by a malignant srih. Doubtless sent by one of Elecambron, for no Ormalan has this kind of skill, and we of Markul scorn such fakery."

Dazed, Ryel replied ashen-mouthed. "But ... but why would anyone do this?"

Edris snorted, angrily scornful. "You're slow, whelp. I can think of quite a few uses for some fresh young seed drained from Markul's darling boy."

Suddenly marrowless, Ryel sank onto the bed's edge, staring down at the woman's sprawled silent form as Edris' voice hammered away at him.

"Answer me, fool. Did you enter her?"

Ryel shook his head, bitterly shamed. "You gave me no time."

"Couldn't you tell what she was, fool? Didn't any of your training alert you?"

Ryel shook his head. He felt his lips twitching, and bit them hard.

"What of her hot and cold, fool? Her changeable eyes? Look here." Edris lifted one of her eyelids, revealing pure white and deep lapis-blue. "This is the real color."

"They were like opals. But then they turned black. All black."

Edris seemed to quell a shudder. "I saw it. That should've been enough to stop anyone but an idiot like you." For some moments he contemplated the white nakedness with impassive deep scrutiny. "Barely an hour dead. And young—twenty-five at most. It's hard that she should have ended thus."

"Who was she? Who sent her?"

Edris reached for a blanket and covered the dead form. "I think you're going to have to be careful from now on, lad. If anything in the least untoward occurs to you, I want to know of it at once. This scheme wasn't expected to go awry."

Ryel shuddered at the dank thinness of his robe. "Tell me who—or what—could have done this. And why."

"It was her lover killed her, for his master's sake," Edris replied.

"Tell me his name, and his master's."

Edris turned away. "I don't remember." But his pallor all asweat showed that memory served only too strongly. Ryel seized his arm, hard.

"You lie. It was Michael, wasn't it? Tell me!"

The tall man shook him off like a bug. "Don't plague me, whelp. But keep your eyes open. Damn it, you'd better."

Often they had quarreled during the past four years. But now Ryel heard fear vibrating beneath Edris' anger for the first time, and it awed him. "Even as you wish, my uncle," he murmured. "I'll be watchful, I promise you."

Edris drew a long breath, and his next words came with his usual irony. "See that you are, whelp. Now, what about this corpse? We should burn it."

"No," Ryel said instantly. "Her death was not of her own making, and she was a sister in the Art. She belongs in the Jade Tower."

Edris seemed impressed, although faintly. "Have it your way, whelp." He took up his fallen cloak. "We'll have her taken to the tower tomorrow. For now, get some rest. She'll keep." He made no attempt to smother a yawn. "I'm going back to bed." He would have turned, but Ryel caught him by the shoulder.

"Edris, wait." He hesitated. "You—" He dropped his eyes. "You took a great risk."

"Let go of me, brat."

But Ryel would not be kept from taking Edris' hands and bending his brow to them. "I will always be somewhere in your debt, ithradrakis."

At the Almancarian word Edris made no reply, and pulled his hands free, but then he laid one of them on Ryel's head in a hurried embarrassed gesture, half caress, half blessing. "You'll repay me someday, Ry. Let's see if you can stay out of trouble for the rest of the night at least."

But when Edris had left, Ryel dressed in warm robes, then calmed himself with some minutes' intense meditation. He gathered up the corpse, now much lighter in his arms than it had been, and carried it to his surgery, laying it out on the granite slab in the middle of the cold windowless room. Since the srih had departed, the flesh gleamed white as marble in the lantern-light, too coldly inert for any lust, but its beauty finally glowed clean and whole.

Despite his Art-driven dispassion, Ryek could not help feeling deep sorrow for this unknown woman, done to death so young. *You were of rare intelligence,* he thought as he rolled up his sleeves. *It shows in the refinement of your face. The daimon that mocked your lost soul with its lubricity spoiled your charms worse than any disease. Had your lover known how much, he'd have never given you over to death. For your sake someday I will find out who he is, and what master he serves. But not now.*

He bent, and touched his lips to the smooth white forehead. Then he took up a scalpel, and began an incision from the navel down.

Ryel shook that memory from him, along with his skin's crawling, and spoke sharply into the air of the night.

"You sent her. Didn't you, Dagar?"

No voice answered him. Awhile the wysard waited. Then, observing that the hour had advanced and he was utterly alone on the great road, he pressed his heel to Jinn's side. The horse leapt into a tearing gallop, and Ryel was borne away as if he gripped a whirlwind between his knees.

The next night Ryel spent alone in the desert surrounding Almancar, encamped in the arcaded portico of a ruined mansion. Well within sight the city glowed vast and silent. Above all the other buildings the palaces of the imperial Dranthene towered in the midst, raised upon great platforms of stone. Not a single wisp of cloud flecked the sky, and the risen moon wrought fair alchemy on the gleaming spires.

The city was so near that he could see lights in the windows of the gate-towers. He might easily have ridden the few miles remaining in his journey, but he required time in meditation to gather his strength for the morrow. With his hair tied back and naked to the waist he sat crosslegged before his chal-fire, savoring the unaccustomed pleasures of the night's warmth on his skin, and steady silver radiance. As he had since leaving Risma, he made his camp like a simple bannerman, knowing that it would only too probably be useless to call upon his srihs for any service. He was in fact pleased with himself for requiring so little for his comfort, for so quickly readjusting to the life of the Steppes. After long riding, plain horseman's rations tasted fully as delicious as any banquet commanded from the air, and Edris' cloak made the softest of couches. Tranquilly the wysard sipped his chal, giving his mind over completely to the task ahead, and to she that had drawn him here.

I wonder why I care so much, he thought. *I saw you only once, in a daimon-sent vison, and even then you were masked. Why have I come to your help, when I might have returned to my City? It's not as if I loved you.*

"I know you do not. I would not wish you to."

A beautiful voice, soft and low and sweet, had spoken in answer to his thoughts—spoken in the most melodious language in the World, the palace tongue of the City of Gold. But Ryel snatched up his sword and leapt to his feet nevertheless.

Out of the shadows glided a slim form, white and black under the moon—a human form, but translucent. "Lay your weapon by," it gently implored. "I cannot harm you. I would not."

Wary and trustless Ryel regarded the apparition. "What are you?" he asked, using the same language as his sudden visitor, but far less gently.

The slender spectre glided closer, until it stood opposite the wysard's kulm-fire. Ryel felt his pulse fail.

"Not you," he whispered. "Not again."

The Sovrena Diara looked on him with surprise. "Again?"

He sensed rather than saw her in the faint gleam of moon and fire, discerning that now she was clad in a single film of diaphanous white without a single jewel, and that her black hair fell unplaited to her elbows, her face unmasked. All this he could discern only if he beheld her indirectly, as one views certain star-clusters in the night sky, yet as the stars her beauty gleamed fair and bright, and as with stars Ryel stood awed and wondering.

But she was speaking. "How did I seem, when you saw me last?"

"You were masked," Ryel somehow managed to reply. "But only the upper half of your face."

"A rich mask?"

"Yes. Covered in jewels."

"Ah. Yet another insult." Her voice was weary and sad, now. "Only the courtesans of the Diamond Heaven wear masks, Ryel

Mirai. My captor mocks me, cruelly as always. Shows me how much his slave I am, and to what further debasements he destines me."

The wysard felt the night's heat in his face, and cold anger to his fingertips. "Tell me all you know of your captor, my lady."

She sighed. "I only know that he gives me no rest. Even now he torments me, there in the palace. Makes me tear and bruise and starve myself." She looked toward the silver towers. "So immeasurably distant I feel from everything."

The wysard took an involuntary step backward, even as his sword fell from his numbed grip. "I address your rai."

She inclined her head, still with her regard fixed on the far towers. "Yes, Lord Ryel. My spirit-self, enclosed in a wraith of my human form."

The night air continued warm, but the wysard felt a chill sweat break out on his chest and back. "Who sent you? How is it you know my name?"

She turned again to him. "I was told."

"By whom?"

"A woman, with powers like to yours."

Ryel came closer. "Serah Dalkith? Srin Yan Tai?"

Diara let him approach, until they were only a few steps apart. "I do not know."

"Why have you appeared to me?"

"I send a message," she answered. "You are not here for my sake, Ryel of Markul."

"For whose then?"

"The World's. Be assured that my captor has designs far larger than the torment of a helpless girl, but nonetheless he delights in giving pain no matter what the degree, and for a long time has lacked that pleasure. Thus he does not miss my spirit's absence now, so rapt he is with my body's torture."

Fury cramped Ryel's insides. "I will not let you suffer another instant." He reached for his shirt, but with a swift gesture she halted him.

"You cannot come to me, Ryel. Not now. You must put yourself in readiness. Tonight you must meditate on the Analects of Khiar."

The Analects were strong precepts against fear. Ryel had last murmured them to himself three months ago before attempting the spell that had wrought his eyes' darkness and his kinsman's death. "What would you know of Khiar?" he demanded. "How—" Racing possibilities made his blood leap. "My lady—are you one of the Foretold?"

She seemed to shake her head. "No. But my brother Priam is. For the past five years he has for private reasons lived in seclusion, never leaving the Eastern Palace. But tomorrow he will join my father in the selection of a physician, and he will choose you." She caught her breath as if in pain. "You will see horrors, Ryel. I am afraid of how how my captor will use me, and ashamed—" She wrung her hands, and turned her face away.

He reached toward her, uselessly. "Most exalted, if I could only—"

"You cannot ... Ry." She said his name so softly that he more felt than heard it, sensing it envelope him like some exquisite scent, some dearly remembered music. "I am glad you do not love me, so glad. My captor would exult in turning that love to loathing, or would kill me outright to give you greater pain, and himself more sport." She trembled. "I do not wish to die, Ryel."

He inclined his head, wrung by the desperate supplication in her voice. With all his Art's strength he willed himself to forget the beauty of her face, the moonlit ravishments revealed by her shift's gossamer. "I promise never to put you in the slightest danger, most exalted."

"Thank you, a thousand times." But then it seemed her voice smiled. "What a pity."

Ryel looked up, astonished. "My lady?"

She *was* smiling. "It's really too bad. You're so handsome." Her regard slid to his shoulders, his chest, his arms, every glance an appraising caress. "And you look very strong."

He felt himself reddening all over, but somehow replied calmly. "All of my strength is yours, most exalted."

"Is it? What a pleasant thought." But then her smile faded, and she paused as if listening. "I must return lest my captor suspect."

Ryel had never felt more helpless. "I would do anything to help you here and now. Anything."

With infinite thanks she regarded him. "You are kind and good. It is a great power in you. But my captor knows of it, and will do all he can to warp it to his own uses. Have no fear for me at this time, however, for I will have a respite at dawn. During the hours of daylight my captor leaves me, and my entire being rests unconscious and free of torment until dusk. Tomorrow my father holds audience of physicians an hour after noon in his palace, and I would have you enjoy my city until then, for its beauty will give you strength."

The wysard bowed. "I will not fail, most exalted."

"Don't call me that. Call me by my name."

"If you wish it ... Diara." He tasted it on his lips like a kiss.

She, too, seemed to feel it. "Until tomorrow ... Ry."

She faded until the night claimed her. Ryel stood unmoving for some time, sternly compelling his memory to blankness. But although with extremest effort he succeeded in blocking out every unique quality of spirit that had drawn him to Diara during their encounter, no effort of will could vanquish the desire aroused by beauty veiled only in a nebulous film of seeming silk. He ran his hands over his arms, cruelly gripping the bare flesh, but the pain only more sharply reminded him that he was male, and fully grown, and save for one terrible time entirely unknowing of pleasure with a woman. And it seemed to him that he had at last discovered the realm of joy only to stand on its threshold quivering and cold, longing for warm limbs yielding to his body's blind need, a mouth wet and searching under his—any limbs, any mouth. His sex oppressed him, and he reached downward not knowing whether he meant to chasten or assuage. But suddenly the night blackened about him, tightened in a strangling squeeze, laughed low and sly.

Oh, young blood. We're hot tonight, aren't we?

The wysard's arms fell to his sides, and he tried to swallow, uselessly. "Get away from me, daimon."

Who were you thinking of, sweet eyes?

"No one."

Not even the delicious little Sovrena?

"I have no feelings for her. You torture her for nothing."

Oh, not for nothing, the voice snidely giggled. *It's been very amusing. But if you care as little as you say, then why are you here?*

"Because I cannot stand idly by and witness suffering that only I can alleviate."

So selfless. So heroic. Like your dead father.

Ryel leaned against a broken pillar, dazed by comprehension. In the same moment he stood straight, and glared into the darkness. "Tell me how you killed him, Dagar."

I will—after you and I meet.

"You don't deny your name," Ryel breathed. "It *is* you. The scourge of Elecambron."

And of the World, soon, the voice purred. *No need for me to conceal my identity now that I've brought you this far. Guess why you're here, sweet eyes.*

Ryel felt the night like solid ice around him, lightless and haunted like the most secret depths of the sea. It had all come together: the voice that had haunted him in Markul, Diara's torturer, Dagar—all one and the same entity, tripartite malignance. "I know what you want," he said.

The daimon giggled again. *Do you?*

Ryel stilled a tremor of revulsion. "You won't get it. You're not strong enough."

But I will be, young blood. And you know it. This meeting is only meant to improve our acquaintance. I've been longing for you, beauty. We'll be together soon. Very soon, now. Sweet dreams, beauty—sweet and wet.

Before Ryel could reply, the dense air thinned, freeing the moon. Clenching his teeth and closing his eyes, the wysard lifted his face to the silver light, forcing his breath to steady slow rises and falls, focusing his entire concentration on the white glow filling the desperate immensity behind his shut lids. When his pulse had at last slowed and his body warmed to the night, he seated himself again at his fire and jabbed it back to life, and with fierce effort turned his thoughts to the Analects of Khiar.

Great Almancar was walled high and strong in massive blocks of pale-rose granite carved in fantastic representations of men and beasts that told of the First Life, when the gods dwelt on earth as brothers with the mortals they had created from air and water. Of these first people the Almancarians claimed descent, and considered themselves set apart from the lesser race of earth and fire that came after. Such had Ryel read while yet young in Markul, and now remembered as he approached the southern gate and watched the wall's carvings leap to life in the first rays of dawn.

All around the city was desert and wasteland, dotted with scattered ruins, but once there had been orchards full of fruit, and great estates of rich men, very long ago. It was said that a wysard wrought that desolation—a sorcerer who demanded in marriage one of the imperial daughters and was refused. In revenge he had cursed the land around the city, and made it barren with his Art. But he had no power over the Gray Sisterhood where the jewel-mines were, and because of those mines Almancar's folk were the world's richest. Caravans came and went at every gate, bringing provisions and luxuries into the city.

The city was far-famed as a place of wonder and delight. It gleamed in rich soft colors that caught the light of the sun and threw it back in pride. Many thousands of people dwelt in Almancar, and swarms of visitors came from the world over to barter or gawk. The city's rich—and they were many—dwelt in the gold-towered mansions of the First and Second Districts. Its temple quarter was said to be the most magnificent ever built by hands. In the midst of the city, their proud spires aglow in the never-clouded sunlight, were the palaces of the Dranthene, buildings proverbial for their beauty. But most noted—or, to some, notorious—of all was the Diamond Heaven, Almancar's pleasure district, where the joys of the flesh were celebrated with religious fervor in the name of Atlan, goddess of desire.

Yet Ryel knew from talk around the Rismai fires that this paradise was governed with an iron hand, and not always wisely. Any theft exceeding the value of a gold piece was punished by death without trial at the hands of the Sovran's soldiers, and any quarrel put down by the same means. Moreover, the Sovran's ministers were exclusively nobles and merchants, not many of them able or clever councilors, who made no secret of despising the folk of the Fourth District, who worked the jewel-mines of the mountains or toiled at every dirty chore within the city.

Nevertheless Ryel did not think of the dark side of Almancar's fabled splendor as he entered the city gates with his senses calmed and open. Mindful of the instructions given him the night before, he set side all thought of trials and dangers to come, immersing himself instead in the beauty around him. Almancar's loveliness revealed itself facet by flawless facet as Ryel passed through broad avenues paved with tesselated marble, lined with interlaced trees that gave shade from the burning sun, intersected by canals where mosaics of gold glass and colored stone glimmered beneath water clear and sweet as the morning air. Poverty, squalor, meanness, and misery seemed to have no existence here, where every citizen went dressed in fresh silk and precious ornaments

What a wondrous place this is, Ryel thought, remembering the words of Diara as a surge of fresh energy filled him. *What a beautiful, perfect place.*

But the wysard soon became conscious of curious and not entirely approving glances directed at his road-weathered Steppes gear. Ignoring those looks he progressed to the great market-square, where he breakfasted on delicacies offered at the many stalls. Exploring afterward, at length he came to the horse traders', where his practised eye assessed the animals and found them excellent all, but none as good as his own mare, who attracted much attention.

"That's a fine animal you've got there, bannerman," said one of the horse-dealers. "She deserves to be ridden by none but some great prince decked in silk and gold."

Ryel ignored this veiled reflection on his appearance, his attention drawn to another market being held in a building uncommonly elaborate, with a clientele surpassingly bedizened. "What do they sell there where so many rich folk go in and out?"

"The most precious merchandise in all the city, bannerman," the trader replied with a meaning smile. "Exclusive goods ... for exclusive buyers, as you see. Not the sort of thing a Steppes brave of your sort would be interested in."

"What do you mean?"

"It's the slave market." The horse-merchant laughed, too meaningly. "Most of the items for sale are well worth the looking at—especially those destined for the Diamond Heaven." He reached out to stroke Jinn's mane, a gesture the horse evaded. "She's a true beauty, this one. Would you perhaps consider—"

"Not for any gold," Ryel said. "My horse is as free as I am."

The dealer laughed. "Not to offend you, bannerman, but in Almancar your horse might fetch a higher price than you would. You'd understand, if you cared to stroll among the slave market's offerings."

"I don't." Seizing Jinn's reins from the horse-dealer's hand, the wysard turned away.

After that Ryel rode distraught and saddened despite the beauty of the city and the fairness of the sun that lit its towers. His shift of mood made him sensitive to the disquiet among Almancar's citizens and among the many visitors from foreign lands come to trade and marvel. For all the animation of the markets, gloom and misgiving hung like faint but acrid smoke over Almancar and its fabled magnificence, stinging the eyes, casting a pall over the constant sun.

As if in response to his mood, the wysard found the city's buildings diminishing in splendor, and the broad straight streets narrowing to tangled lanes. The deterioration seemed to affect even the people around him. The City of Gold's rich folk were of unalloyed Almancarian blood, while their slaves were of many lands. Now Ryel found himself amid a people of mixed heritage, whose Almancarian features mingled with those of countless other races. The city's wealthy and their slaves were sleekly groomed and magnificently arrayed, but the folk Ryel now found himself among wore plain garments of coarse stuff that only too fitly set off bodies and faces marked by unremitting drudgery. No one seemed to be any way in want, but their sense of privation and their resentment were very real, to judge by the hostility with which they eyed anyone richly dressed.

Ryel would have stopped someone for directions, for clearly he had lost his way. But all at once he heard an extraordinary voice cry out, a voice so like Edris' that it nearly stopped his heart.

"Death! Misery, and shame, and death to this city of dust!"

Ryel instantly turned toward the voice, and saw that a man stood alone in the midst of the square—the first madman dressed in the first rags the wysard had yet seen in Almancar.

"Death is upon this city!" the madman shouted. "Death armed with steel, death with fangs of fire! Already it clutches at the soul of the Sovrena Diara, who lies raving in her own dirt up in Agenor's palace of gold! Diara, child of sin against the law of kind!"

He spoke the common tongue with a strange accent but complete fluency. Hardly had the lunatic begun to harangue than people emerged from the taverns and shops and leaned out of windows to listen, and soon an ever-increasing throng of muleteers and jewelminers and tavern-wenches had gathered about him. Ryel had fully expected them to mock and gibe, but they did neither. Rather they hearkened earnestly, and even murmured approval from time to time. Marvelling that anyone would seriously attend the ravings of one so obviously deranged, the wysard bent from the saddle to question one of the crowd.

"Who is he?"

She answered with curt impatience. "He is the teller of truth. Be silent, and listen to his wisdom!"

Taken aback by her vehemence, Ryel stared into the girl's face— a child's face, gaudy and weary, with painted eyes that shone in desperate adoration and worship as they gazed on the ragged prophet; a face yearning for revenge on the destroyers of its innocence. Shuddering, the wysard turned and considered the mad loud orator more closely.

The seduction of the man's address Ryel had instantly remarked, even before the first sight of him. His voice had all of Edris' timbre and depth—the resemblance had made Ryel's blood leap—and was even more resonant and melodious. One's immediate, all but involuntary reaction after hearing that voice was to look round for the speaker, even as Ryel had done.

Once attracted, the eye widened, blinked, and lingered. In Almancar the Bright, where even the poorest went wholly and cleanly clad, this man stood out starkly. He was barefoot, and wore a single trailing garment of dirty black wool full of rents that bared his arms to the shoulders, but there was something deeply impressive in his destitution. When his features chanced to relax, one might readily discern that under its grime his face was of a forceful harsh handsomeness. Like his face, his head was shaven, baring to advantage the fine bones of the skull and the well-shaped ears lying close to it, and giving great expressiveness to the heavy dark brows. Grim and squalid he undoubtedly was, but his lean form was tall and well-made, and he held himself arrogantly erect. At one point as the prophet gestured his rags parted over his back and revealed powerful shoulders seamed with red stripes, the mark of whips that he bore as proudly as a lord might jewelled orders.

Theatrical, Ryel thought, unwillingly impressed. *Very effective in its way. This is no mere street preacher, not at all. He's hardly older than me—little more than thirty—and plainly he's of birth far beyond that of the people he addresses, and of great and subtle intellect. But anyone not blind may see that this man is arrogant and violent, as remote from humility as he is from humanity. And strong—very strong.*

Scorning to acknowledge his empire over his listeners, the street evangelist lifted the deep male music of his voice yet louder.

"She will meet her end in shrieking torment, and drag countless lives and souls down with her! For her sake hundreds have come to attempt her cure and all have failed, and many have died for their failure at the command of your senile impotent Sovran! Thousands have babbled worthless prayers to false gods, imploring mercy from senseless blocks of stone! But the Master will avenge this blasphemy against His greatness, and the line of the Dranthene will die with the Sovrena and her lust-cankered inbred brother! Almancar the Whore with its pride, this cesspit of luxury with its jewelled strumpets and drug-stunned minions and debased slaves, will burn to stinking ash, and the ash scatter to nothingness!"

Ryel had had enough. "You lie."

The wysard had spoken very quietly, but everyone turned to stare at him. The prophet swiftly whirled about, and his fierce eyes—eyes without white or iris, dead black eyes—sought Ryel's. Jinn shyed in sudden terror, and even Ryel could not help a thrill of shock.

You're no madman, he thought amazed. *You're of the Art-brotherhood, an Overreacher like myself. You're—*

"Michael!" one of the crowd shouted. "Curse the fool, Michael!"

Ryel's blood leapt as the wysard demagogue's empty eyes burned into his. *You,* he thought. *You, my brilliant unruly rival, Lord Michael of Elecambron. But why are you here, far from your ice-encircled City? Surely we meet thus for a reason, but what could it be?*

The ragged prophet knew Ryel in the same instant, and took a step backward at the sight of the Markulit wysard's eyes and the black emptiness only he among all that crowd could discern. Then he laughed, baring keen teeth jarringly white against his face's dirt.

Laughed as if he'd been waiting long for this moment, and meant to use it cruelly.

"Other hands than mine, hands invisible perhaps, will avenge me for your insolence, Steppes gypsy," Michael sneered. "As for myself, clairvoyance enough I have to know what brings you to this place, and what success you will enjoy. Go and try to save Agenor's daughter, since you have come for that. And watch her wither and burn, slave to the Master that strikes hard and slumbers not, before your Overreaching eyes!"

Ryel held his ground unmoved. "Strong must this master be, if you deign to serve him."

Michael grinned with fierce teeth terribly white. "You will learn His strength, and serve as well. All will serve the Master one day. But your road lies not here in the Fourth Ward, home to worse than slaves. There's your way, through the streets that sell bright vanities to spendthrift fools, toys beyond the reach of these poor children, orphans of Agenor's indifference. Get you gone by that road, and tell the Sovran and his son that their damnation waits them, after that of their darling girl." His hard bare arm shot forth, and his filth-rimmed finger pointed eastward.

Long did their eyes lock, Markulit's and Elecambronian's, black upon black. Then Ryel bowed low in the saddle. "For your instruction I thank you, Lord Michael," he said, with all the respect due to a great brother in the Art, no matter how bad. The people who had begun to jeer him looked at one another in confusion, and back to the dour prophet so incongruously yet with such strange fitness ennobled by the wysard's word. "I am glad of this encounter. It may be we'll meet again."

Michael did not return the bow save by the faintest inclination of his shaven head, and he spat in the dust afterward. "Ill met you are to me, Overreacher, now and forever. Begone, take your road."

Chapter Six

Michael's directions were accurate, to Ryel's mild surprise. The wysard successfully threaded the maze of constricted streets and emerged into a region of wide avenues and great arcaded mansions. The houses slept under the burning heat of the sun, their latticed shutters folded, but as he passed Ryel could smell the spiced aroma of midday feasts, hear music and soft laughter and the chimes of crystal and silver wafting through the tracery. With a twinge of hunger that went far beyond the body he remembered the Steppes, never more distant from him than now. He thought with fresh regret of his mother who might have dwelt in a house such as these around him, and of his sister Nelora who longed for such a life. Most of all he thought of the unhappy folk of the Fourth District, inexorably debarred from this luxury so arrogantly flaunted.

Then as he emerged from beneath an archway the wysard confronted the palace, a vast edifice raised on a high platform of gold-flecked dawn-violet stone approached by long wide ramps. No wall encircled the building, but guards even more magnificent than those at the city gates were stationed at each incline and portal. Above the platform the imperial palace rose in dazzling splendor of all that man might create, given the most extravagant imagination and endless wealth of gold and gems. But Ryel marveled most at the gardens that covered and overflowed every roof. Under the fiery sky shimmered lush trees thick with fruit, vines laden with rare flowers, all spangled with fountain-spray fairer than diamonds—the fabled paradise that Ryel as a child had made his mother describe again and again to brighten the barren emptiness of the Steppes at least in imagination. Growing to manhood in Markul he had sometimes stared out at the dank infinities of mist and remembered those stories, and contemned them as idle tales meant only to beguile a restless yat-brat. Now he inwardly asked his mother's pardon.

In normal circumstances no personage less than a great noble would have been allowed entry to the palace of the Sovran of Destimar, but the desperate illness of the Dranthene princess suspended all protocol. Anyone claiming a physician's credentials, no matter how mean-seeming, was admitted into the presence-chamber with few questions, only the obviously deranged being turned away. While some led Jinn to the palace stables, others swiftly ushered the wysard through ramped hallways to the Sovran's presence-chamber. There Ryel found that the number of doctors awaiting the Sovran's appearance was few despite the prospect of dazzling reward—barely twenty in all. Most of them were dressed with exceeding richness, and Ryel bitterly regretted not having donned one of his Almancarian robes before entering the palace. Then he noticed that by far the most bedizened of all the throng were wysards. He at once recognized a pair of flashy Ormalans with their inevitable attendant familiars—in this case a nasty-eyed white cat and a lizard almost as big—and observed three Tesbai even gaudier still, wearing their characteristic enormous hats. These five he avoided with lowered eyes lest they discover and cry out against the Overreacher in their midst, but they paid him no heed whatever, save to eye his Steppes garb with cursory scorn.

Ryel kept his distance for another reason: cats were detested by most Rismai as being the harborers of bad spirits, and he had seen very few in his life. But he would never forget having hugged one as a little child, rapturous with its soft purring tabby fur, only to almost instantly feel his eyes swell shut, his breathing strangle. For two entire days afterward he had lain miserably gasping and sneezing, his face swollen like a soaked sponge. But even worse, his mother could not come near him until his garments had been burnt and his body washed clean of all feline contamination, and the yat's hangings taken out and aired. After that incident Yorganar had trained his dogs to tear to pieces any cat they found.

Now music sounded, and the little throng of would-be healers gave way as the sole ruler of great Destimar approached, borne high in a palanquined carrying-chair on the shoulders of his guard, preceded and followed by attendants and soldiery. Ryel was at first much impressed, for Agenor Dranthene was a gorgeous sight in his imperial finery of purple, scarlet, and gold. At second glance the wysard observed how the stiffly projecting shoulders of the Sovran's billowing cloak failed to disguise his age-bowed back, while a wide many-wrapped sash did little to bind in his corpulent girth. His entire inert body seemed a great mound of glitter from which protruded two limp fat-fingered hands barely visible for their rings and bracelets, while atop this gleaming heap the Sovran's unmoving unblinking head appeared to be part of a badly tinted second-rate statue, its hair dyed an unnatural and glossless black, its face's weak features bedaubed with garish painting. Ryel had observed in his travels through the city that it was customary for upper-caste Almancarians of both sexes to make use of cosmetics, but never this thickly plastered. It was only too obvious that a skin-surgeon's skilled yet futile handiwork had attempted to confer a semblance of youth, and succeeded only in producing a ghastly mockery of it—especially since just beneath the tautly-pulled chin hung two others wobbling full of fat. The wysard with wry amusement further noted that among the jewels encircling Agenor's swollen neck were many amulets and charms surely meant to confer bed-prowess, good digestion, swift recovery from alcoholic excess, and relief from piles.

Suddenly the heap of jewels stirred, the plumes of the lofty crown quivered, and the painted mask twitched. The Sovran sat upright and outraged, sniffing the air. His reddened lips grimaced to reveal bad teeth, and he shrieked.

"Get that—that monstrosity out of here! *Now* !"

Every attendant stiffened, and blankly stared about them. The soldiers looked from Agenor's trembling finger to the thing it pointed at, and found the offending object arching and glaring on the pale Ormalan's shoulder.

"Kill the filthy thing," Agenor gasped as he blurted a sneeze, sending his chins juddering. At once the guardsman so commanded tore the cat from its owner despite its deeply-dug claws, then flung the screeching creature out the nearest window. A frantic moment

the luckless beast grappled the air before its yowling plummet. Order thus restored, Agenor sank back again into his cushions, peev-
ishly wiping his streaming eyes and nose on his silken sleeve. As if
this were a sign, all of his entourage save for the guardsmen genu-
flected in various degrees of abasement.

A militant hiss scorched the wysard's ear. "You forget yourself,
fellow."

Alerted by the soldier, Ryel glanced about and saw that all the
would-be healers were likewise on their knees, and some even more
servile on all fours. Yet no lord adept of Markul, much less a Rismai
of the Elhin Gazal, would so demean himself, and Ryel only
watched with impassive disregard as the guard who had spoken now
half-drew his sword.

"How'd *you* get into the audience-room, Fourth District dog?"
the soldier snapped. "Bow down or be cut down."

Ryel's sole reply was to second the guard's gesture and lift his
chin in defiance. With petulant exasperation the Sovran Agenor
peered at the wysard through the great table-diamond that hung
from his neck on a chain of gold. "Kill the intruding fool," he said
at last with faint disgust and utter indifference, far less energetically
than he had ordered the dispatch of the cat. But from the doorway a
voice rang out, sweet and clear as Diara's but commandingly male.

"Soldier, I order you to stop."

Thus speaking, a young noble strode swiftly forward—clearly a
great lord despite the sober plainness of his dress and lack of atten-
dance, for everyone in the assembly bowed more deeply as he approached, and the guard at once thrust his sword back into its
sheath.

The austere young man turned to the gaudy old one, his voice
now edged with a hint of accusation. "Father, I thought we had
agreed that I would join you this day in choosing a physician for my
sister."

The Sovran glared squintingly down at his son, forgetting Ryel
completely. The wysard seized that opportunity to eclipse himself in
the crowd. "Aware as we are of your habit of sleeping until the hour
of noon, Sovranel, we had no wish to interrupt your slumbers."

Contemptuously as this was said, Priamnor Dranthene bowed

unmoved. "And I thank you for that indulgence, because I believe it has shown me how the Sovrena my sister may be healed."

While Agenor snorted and the watching throng murmured, Ryel covertly studied the newcomer. He knew Diara's brother at once. The Sovranel Priamnor was perhaps twenty-five years of age. His unadorned robes of dusky blue-purple silk were closer cut to the body than was typical of extravagant Almancarian court dress, revealing the shoulders' unpadded breadth, the slim waist outlined rather than enforced by the silver belt, the straight carriage turning middle height to tallness. Not a single jewel or amulet did the Sovranel wear, which permitted undistracted scrutiny to dwell wholly on the singularity of the face and hands. These, Ryel noted with surprise, were not the wonted Almancarian white, but the bronze of one who lived much in the sun. Moreover, Priamnor's night-colored hair was shorn close to his head and his face was clean-shaven and unpainted, both likewise contrary to Almancarian custom. The smooth visage drew its beauty, which was great, as much from the keen intelligence of its expression as from the pure regularity of its features. The wysard marveled at the glowing violet-tinged blue of those eyes, all the bluer for the dark lashes that edged them and sun-darkened face in which they were set. Ryel marked how even Agenor himself flinched under that calm appraising stare.

"Explain what you have said, Sovranel," Agenor said as he glanced away.

Priamnor turned his attention from his father, searchingly scanning the little crowd. When he spoke, it was with manifest reluctance. "I saw my sister in a dream this morning."

The Sovran shrugged. "What of it? We not only dream, but see visions too, sometimes."

"But I do not, father," Priamnor evenly replied. "Which leads me to think that this occurence may be of import."

"The gods work arcanely, even through the most hardened of skeptics," Agenor said, though without conviction. "Tell us what you saw, but be brief."

"I saw my sister as she was when in health," Priamnor said. "I spoke with her, and from her lips learned who might heal her."

Agenor's own lips, raddled and weak, quirked mirthlessly. "So—

the cynic atheist now puts his faith in portents. And who does this vision of yours suggest as the Sovrena's healer?"

"I was told that he would be among this assembly, father."

"Then find him, if you can," Agenor said. "But for this moment we will make use of our own judgment." The Sovran lifted his quizzing-diamond to his watery eye. "We will have these," he loudly and abruptly said after a momentary inspection of the most flamboyantly clad contenders, and with an imperious spike-nailed finger beckoned the two Ormalans, who approached with leering smiles and bent-kneed bows. "Tell us your names and your stations."

Ryel did not need to learn either. He knew their kind. Both were base scum, offscourings of the least of the Four Cities; both addicted to a variety of drugs, obvious from their glassy and protruding eyes—drugs very probably administered by clyster, the Ormalan method of choice for swift stupefaction. The one seemed not a little sorry for the loss of his cat, but the other's joy was gigglingly manifest.

"Your slaves Rickrasha and Smimir are we, most worshipful," she grinned. She was a plump Turmaronian, citron-skinned and gap-toothed. As she spoke, she patted the oversized chameleon that squatted on her shoulder staring at once toward the ceiling and at the Sovran with its yellow balls of eyes—eyes little different, Ryel remarked, from its owner's. "Great adepts and healers, we. Thousands of cures. Thousands of testimonials." And she brandished a great sheaf of documents.

Agenor bestowed a brief glance on the certificates. "Adepts, you say? That is well. And where from?"

"The great and marvelous city of Ormala, most worshipful."

At the mention of that place only too well known to the World, the Sovran's train murmured alarm. But the ruler of Almancar nodded cool approval from the height of his carrying-chair.

"Wysards, then. Good. You will possess far more skill, and we hope will enjoy far greater success than any of these tiresome little quacks." And he cast a disdainful sneer upon the disappointed throng of aspirants before turning back to the Ormalan sorcerers. "But we warn you—others of your brotherhood have tried and failed."

Smimir gave a smirk. His Northern looks had a rattish cast, and were framed by limp locks of greasy brass-tinted hair. "May I ask who made the attempt, most worshipful?"

"A witch from the city of Tesba."

Smimir and Rickrasha exchanged sniggers.

"Most worshipful," said Rickrasha between chortles, "I regret to inform you that Tesba was never known for its greatness. I'm not surprised that it could not produce a healer for your daughter."

The Sovran's mask-face did not smile. "There was an Elecambronian, too, that failed—or rather, we did not allow him to try. He attempted to drug the Sovrena with some deadly concoction ... for which we had him summarily put to death."

Smimir paled to tallow, and Rickrasha to chalk. During their abject silence Agenor Dranthene gestured listlessly to Priamnor. "Now make your own choice if you must, Sovranel."

Priamnor did not reply. His jewel-blue eyes had alighted on Ryel, having examined and rejected all other contenders. The crowd parted as he approached the wysard, and the two of them stood face to face. For the first time the Sovranel smiled.

"*Keirai.*"

At that smile bestowed with such grace, and that greeting uttered in High Almancarian, Ryel felt a strange yet pleasurable sensation, almost a shudder, travel down his back—a sensation heightened by the celestial scent that wafted from the prince's garments, ineffably sweet. He had first smelled that fragrance the night before, in the desert with Diara—and Priamnor resembled his sister uncannily, save that his features were more strongly planed and inarguably male. "*Keirai d'yash,*" the wysard replied, bewildered and enthralled.

But even as he spoke, he felt his face afire at his error. High Almancarian was a language at once exalted and intimate: a ceremonial tongue between strangers, a gentle secret one between friends. In his reply to the Sovranel Ryel had involuntarily used the most familiar form of address, a form reserved by law only for use between kinsmen of the blood imperial. His was a grave error if not a capital offense, and the Sovran Agenor was enraged by it.

"How dare you address one of the Dranthene thus, you scum of the Dog's Ward?" the bejeweled old man hissed, his painted face aflame. "We will have you—"

"He has committed no crime, father," the Sovranel broke in, smiling reassurance at Ryel as he spoke.

Agenor stiffened. "No crime? Is this fellow known to you then, and of your rank?"

Priamnor bowed his head. "He is, father. In my dream my sister described him so accurately that I recognized him at once. As for his rank, the folk of the Inner Steppes bow down to no one, and consider themselves equal to any station no matter how high."

Agenor glared through his quizzing-diamond at Ryel, his neck craning as much as it could under his chins. "Steppes?"

Priamnor Dranthene nodded. "From his dress and his manner—not to mention much of his looks—this man is clearly not of our city, but comes from the southern reaches of bold warriors and fine horses." He turned to the wysard. "Am I not right?"

Before Ryel could reply, the Sovran Agenor slapped at the air with a impatient hand. "An insolent rout of nomads, those Rismai. We think you intend to affront us with this fellow, Sovranel."

"I do not, father," the prince calmly replied. "Nor do I question your choices, whatever I think of them."

Agenor snorted. "Yours is a senseless whim."

Priamnor darted a scornful glance at the Ormalans. "Is it?"

The Sovran's cheeks purpled under their paint. "We warn you. Choose better, or not at all."

The Sovranel lifted his chin in a gesture that made Ryel start, so like to his own it was. "I will have this bannerman, or none."

Agenor shrugged with careless finality. "If you must. But I will put my faith in these Ormalan adepts. Guards, disperse this rabble."

Agenor again mounted his carrying-chair, and departed with the Ormalan wysards scurrying behind his entourage, closely followed by the Sovran's guards.

In the silence that ensued Priamnor addressed Ryel, that smile so like to Diara's playing about his lips. "My sister described you exactly. A young man, she said, with looks half Steppes, half Almancar. May I know your name?"

"Ryel," the wysard answered. "Ryel Mirai."

"You do not include your patronymic. Pray accept my condolences for your loss."

Ryel bent his head in thanks, much moved. "You are well versed in the customs of the Steppes, most exalted."

"My sister was fortunate enough to visit your homeland several times. I have never in my life left this city, but I have read much of your people." Again the prince scanned the wysard's features, with the same mild yet keen scrutiny. "What was your mother's surname?"

"Stradianis, most exalted," Ryel replied.

Priamnor considered a moment. "This city had a famous merchant by that name, a dealer in the rarest antiquities."

"He was my grandfather."

"And your father was a Rismai warrior." Priamnor seemed to muse. "An enviable heritage, yours. But come, I have taken you under my protection, and would have you be my guest during your time here. Mine is the Eastern Palace. Let us go there now that we may talk together a little, and that you may then rest until you are called."

The Eastern Palace was far different from the Sovran's. Its richness was that of simple elegance, its works of art excellently chosen, its opulence chiefly manifest in lush blooming foliage and flowing water. Priamnor led Ryel to his audience-room, a fair galleried chamber made cool and fragrant by a tree-shaded atrium further beautified by sculpture of marble and bronze shimmeringly doubled in a pool full of lilies, wherein tall cranes and herons stalked in silence.

"I have observed that your command of High Almancarian is perfect," Priamnor said. "I'm grateful for it, because I speak the vernacular badly." He gave an embarrassed little shrug. "My life's been rather a sheltered one... until recently. I confess that I am uneasy in my mind concerning those Ormalans."

"As am I," the wysard replied.

"I had expected my sister's illness to be quickly cured by able physicians," Priamnor continued. "It has greatly distressed me to find the Sovran's judgment swayed by mountebanks and magicians noteworthy only for garishness of dress. For that reason I today be-

gan to join my father in his selection of a physician, for I believe that
my views, uninstructed though they are, may be of aid in this unhappy time. My sister's derangement is caused by neither weakness
of mind nor taint of blood, though all the doctors who have treated
her so claim it to be. It is worse—far worse." The Sovranel's voice
faltered and he fell silent, his face deadly pale.

"Tell me what you have seen," Ryel said, remembering the voice
in his mother's yat and the rant of Michael.

The Sovranel spoke again, but only with visibly painful effort.
"It is difficult for me to speak of," he said. "It goes against all that I
have become. For the past several years I have sought to rid myself
of delusion. I worship no gods. I put no faith in charlatans or fakirs.
I scorn all belief in the supernatural. Thus it appalls me to think that
my sister's madness is the work of a daimon, but I can believe nothing else." His fine features were very calm, but his voice shook when
he replied. "I have seen it glaring behind her eyes. Have heard its
voice shrieking the foulest abuse, words my sweet sister would never
understand, much less utter … "

"But such is common with madness," Ryel said.

"Perhaps," the Sovranel said. "But I have also seen … horrors.
Unspeakable, inexplicable horrors …" His voice broke, and for a
moment he turned away to the garden, gazing on the sunlit flowers
until he was again calm. "Forgive me," he said, turning back again.
"But it is an appalling power, my sister's captor."

Ryel ventured a question. "If the Sovrena Diara is indeed held
captive by a daimon, would not a wysard be her best physician?"

At once Priamnor shook his head. "I have small liking for sorcerers, and no trust. I deeply regret that we can do nothing for my sister until those vile Ormalans have been tried. But at present she is in
the sleep-state that mercifully falls upon her from dawn to sunset,
and I would not disturb it even if I might."

"Nor would I," Ryel replied.

Priamnor fixed a troubled gaze on the uncertain future and
sighed. "This night may prove long. I would have us approach it
rested and forearmed. I always swim at this hour, when the sun is
high. Join me, and we will talk of any subject save the one that has
saddened us so far."

The prince's words were an unequivocal command, but so disarmingly couched that Ryel accepted with thanks. Together they passed through the palace's rooms and courtyards to the rooftop. Before them stretched a marble terrace extravagantly abloom, and a great oval pool roofed with a trellis of flower-laden vines that scattered and sweetened the relentless sunlight. At one end of the pool was a statue in life-size of a young man, his arms swung upward as if readying for a dive. The sculptor had fully understood and realized the strong curves and projections of the shoulders and biceps, the flexed tension of the legs, the lithe inbreathing upstretch of the waist. The polished bronze glowed like wet skin in the warm light.

"Finally." The Sovranel Priamnor threw off his fragrant robes with no more self-consciousness than he'd have shown if peeling an orange, and stood naked at the edge of the pool, stretching for pleasure of the sunlight. Ryel could not keep himself from first stealing a glance, then staring. For now the wysard saw the bronze image come to life, giving itself up to the sunlight. In the same moment he remembered another sculpture, one he had seen in the Sovranel's atrium—a statue of pure marble delicately tinted, wrought to the dimensions of life in the semblance of a water-nymph dreamily contemplating the smooth reflection of of her slender nakedness, lifting back her dark hair from either side of a face soft with revery. Ryel had at first looked away from it abashed, but its transcendent beauty had drawn him back to admire and wonder, until the only shame he felt was for his dullard prudery. Yet now as he remembered the pale quiescence of the marble nymph and looked upon the living bronze of Priamnor Dranthene, he saw that the two resembled each other in ways no variance of gender could disguise—the same graces of proportion, the same serene intimation of strength, the same classic beauty of feature.

Then with a start of shock Ryel realized that his wraithlike vision in the desert and the atrium's water-goddess were identically formed, and that the masterpiece of Priamnor's audience-chamber represented none other than the Sovrena Diara, all her beauty unveiled for her brother's private contemplation.

Ryel shuddered. Among the Rismai, incest was an outrageous crime, punishable by death. The words of the horse-tamer Belar came back to him, joking mention of how incest improved the Dranthene bloodline. *No*, he thought, appalled. *It can't be. They can't —*

"Is something wrong, Ryel Mirai?"

The wysard looked up to find the Sovranel regarding him with bewildered concern.

"Nothing," he answered, coloring at his lie.

"Why are you standing there? Don't you want to swim?"

"Yes, but … " Ryel bit his lip at this fresh reason for consternation. The Steppes peoples were noted not only for the modesty of their women, but of their men as well. Even when splashing together in the lakes, boys of the Inner Steppes invariably wore some form of covering however scant, and upon reaching manhood never showed themselves to any but their gods or their wives. Ryel and Edris in their years together at Markul had kept the customs of their land, even as they kept its language.

Priamnor understood at least partly, but he did not sympathize. "Your modesty shames you," he said. "Half your blood is of this city, Ryel Mirai, and not the strait-laced Steppes—and at any rate, you and I are alone here." He smiled. "Besides, it's terribly uncomfortable swimming with clothes on."

Ryel did not agree. But lest he seem too hopeless a barbarian, he stripped as far as his shirt.

Priam had walked round him, and now stood at his back. "I forgot to ask—*can* you swim? I've heard that few of your people ever learn."

Enthralled with the beauty of the gold-spangled water, the wysard abstractedly nodded in answer to the Sovranel's question. "When a boy, I used to splash about in the ponds around the summer encampment," he replied. "But that was a long—"

Suddenly he felt a shove, and water engulfed him. Taken utterly aback, Ryel at first scrabbled and thrashed in the airless realm, but in another moment he became used to the water and only too aware of his Steppes shirt, that trammeled his arms intolerably. He peeled off the hindering garment and threw it from him, then dove deep, feeling only pleasure as he gave himself up to this wondrous new element that absolutely enclosed him, lifting him free of earth. He had been the swiftest swimmer among his play-brothers, but never had he swum in water like to this—water not murky and weed-ridden, but clear as aquamarine crystal, shimmering with sunlit gold. And now he found to his delight that with the Art's help he could dart underwater from one length of the great pool to the other and back again and again without surfacing for a breath. It was like flying. Ryel looked down at the gold and many-colored mosaics that glistened like a fantastic far-off landscape, and at Priamnor's shadow moving swiftly past, and remembered the eagles he had envied as a boy.

When he at last resurfaced, he found Priamnor lifting himself onto the edge of the pool and shaking the water from his face. "I knew you'd enjoy the water if I could only get you into it," the Sovranel said. "But how could you hold your breath for so long without your lungs bursting?"

"I came up for air more than once," Ryel said, with all the matter-of-factness he could summon.

Priam accepted the lie, though with clear bewilderment. "Strange. I never saw you. But come out into the light with me, and we'll talk."

Amid the full heat of blinding afternoon they relaxed side by side on a cushioned vast divan, giving their bodies up to the unrelenting radiance. "Careful, or you'll burn," the Sovran said, glancing over at Ryel. "You look as if you've never been in the sun all your life."

"For much of it I haven't," the wysard replied.

"Ah. Because you were studying your art."

Ryel froze. Suddenly it was deep winter, teeth-clenchingly cold. "My what?"

"Your healing arts, I should say. Where did you learn them?"

"At Fershom Rikh," Ryel answered, inwardly flinching at having to tell yet another untruth. But the Sovranel seemed impressed by it.

"Studies there are most rigorous, I hear. You must have come very young to that place."

"Yes. I did."

Priam seemed to wait for elaboration, but Ryel offered none. After a silence the prince said, "Tell me, is the temple district of

Fershom Rikh as magnificent as I have heard it described? Many think it surpasses even Almancar's."

"It is nowhere near as fine, in my estimation." The momentary cold forgotten, Ryel wiped a skin of sweat from his forehead. "To me, Almancar is the only city in the World."

Priamnor smiled again, strangely now. "Is it?" He did not speak again for some time. "Do you not think we resemble each other, you and I?"

Ryel shook his head in perturbed denial at Priamnor's wholly unexpected question, and evaded the Sovranel's glance. "I would never dream of flattering myself so far, most exalted."

The Sovran fell silent a moment. "We have the same eye-color. The same shape of face, and many of the same features."

The wysard bit his lip. "I had not observed."

"But you have considerably more muscle. I wonder how you got it, pent up as you were studying medicine for so many years."

Ryel felt his nakedness clear to the core of his soul. "A doctor has as much need of his body's strength as his mind's, very often. I never forgot that."

"You'll need all your strength tonight, I fear," Priamnor replied. "But tell me more about Fershom Rikh. I have never been outside Almancar's walls, and would enjoy a description of another city than this."

The wysard cleared his throat. "Forgive me, but I'd rather discuss the trouble threatening Almancar."

"Trouble? Do you mean my sister's illness? We had agreed not to—"

"I mean the prophet named Michael. Surely you have heard of him."

"Worse. He and I have met." The Sovranel's face reflected faint disgust at the memory. "When he first came to this city several months ago, I learned of him, and was shocked hear of his poverty, a thing unknown and intolerable in Almancar. At once I had gold sent to him, but later learned that he had thrown it away and still lived in utter destitution, begging his food and sleeping in corners with only a single robe of black rags to cover him. His reputation for spiritual insight roused my admiration, and I summoned him to the palace for an audience in the hope that I might benefit from his wisdom. But all I found was a ragged and unwashed madman—a highly intelligent madman, yes, and an undeniably compelling one, but nonetheless hopelessly deranged. The Master he claims to serve is hardly a deity fit for this city, much less the realm." The prince's gentle features hardened. "Michael's insolence and his pride repelled me, yet I bore it out of pity. When at last he began to let fall insinuations regarding the Sovrena that no man mindful of his sister's honor could bear, I had him taken and whipped. My father was angry with me for that, since Michael is said to be nobly descended from one of the greatest families in Hryeland, and is near allied to the Domina Bradamaine—but I could hardly have cared less. Since then the prophet of the Master has devoted a large part of his public discourse to insulting the Dranthene dynasty."

"I've heard him," Ryel said. "He's dangerous. The Sovran should banish him at once."

Priamnor lifted a smooth bronze shoulder. "What harm can one poor fanatical halfwit do my family or this great city? But let's not speak further of that unwashed lunatic. You've been in the sun quite long enough—and we're both hungry, I'm sure." From among a number of fresh silken robes piled on a nearby chair he handed one to Ryel and chose another for himself. Then the prince called for the servant standing in readiness outside the door, who disappeared only to return moments later with other servants bearing laden trays. These they placed on a table set in a latticed bower near the water's edge, then departed. Music began, played by unseen citherns and flutes.

The Sovranel poured out two goblets full of gold-tinged wine. "I seldom drink anything stronger than water, but on occasions of importance I enjoy the vintage of Masir—and this is some of the best." He handed a glass to Ryel, and lifted his own. "To my sister's health."

Ryel raised his glass so quickly that some of the bright drink spilled out. "To the Sovrena Diara."

Never had Ryel tasted anything more delicious. Yet although he greatly savored the wine, so enjoyable was his converse with the Sovranel that the wysard hardly noticed what he ate, excellent though it was. But when the servants brought in the dessert, Ryel with a start recognized the sweets that he'd loved from childhood and shared with Nelora in the Rismai dawn.

Priamnor smiled at the wysard's surprise. "You're fond of *lakh* ? So am I. But try one of these, first." He reached for one of a dozen heavy fruits that filled a silver basket—fruits which Ryel had seen displayed as a great rarity in the market, and for which vendors had asked the price of a silk robe apiece.

"They're Eskalun pears," Priamnor said, his pleasure evident. "Fit for gods. Seldom do they reach Almancar in this state of perfection." Taking up a knife, the prince began to cut and core the fruit. Simple though the actions were, they made the wysard stare.

"You have equal skill in both your hands," Ryel said.

The Sovranel glanced from the knife in his left hand to the pear in his right, clearly chagrined. "So I do. You're observant."

Priamnor's answer had come reluctantly enough, but Ryel, who had made sure to seem exclusively right-handed since arriving at Almancar, pursued the subject. "Is ambidexterity a common trait of the Dranthene family?"

"No. Only I and my sister possess it." As he spoke, the Sovranel's bronze turned copper, and he set down the knife and the fruit. "In answer to your next question, I too have heard that such a skill denotes capacity for sorcery, and therefore have continually attempted to suppress it lest idle tongues noise it about. Doublehandedness is often as much a gift as an embarrassment."

"I'm sure it is."

They fell into silence that the prince broke hesitantly. "You say you have seen the temple district of Fershom Rikh. Are you also acquainted with Almancar's Temple of Atlan?"

Ryel remembered the first vision of Diara sent by the daimon, and nodded in bewilderment at the sudden shift of talk. "I am. But—"

"Then you doubtless know that from all over the world men make pilgrimage there to pray for lost virility, women for a change of lovers, rakes for fresh sport. I first entered that temple at sixteen, on my father's insistence. And that same night my first mistress came to my bed, likewise at my father's bidding—a beautiful Zinaphian slave, with wit as captivating as her looks. I became passionately infatuated with her, but the last thing my father wished was for me to become seriously enamoured. She vanished, and I later learned that she had been sent away from Almancar. It broke my heart, but unfortunately not for long. I consoled myself incessantly, emptily, with an endless array of lovers, until by rarest chance I found one whose beauty of mind fully equalled that of her outward form—a courtesan of the Diamond Heaven named Belphira Deva, the pleasure-quarter's queen at that time. She became faithful to me alone, refusing all her former lovers … but I was faithless. Until—"

"Until?" Ryel prompted, when the Sovranel did not speak again.

Priamnor stared into his wine as if some small loathesome thing swam there. "Until I became afflicted with a venereal malady that very nearly killed me. For many months I lay between life and death. Somehow I survived, but another of my companions did not: my dearest friend, my cousin Orestens, Prince of Dalnarma." He swallowed, and blinked rapidly for a moment. "I was vain, arrogant, riotous. Fond of flattery and homage. Now I see what a fool I was. The last four years I have devoted exclusively to study and meditation, shunning the world."

"I am sorry, Priamnor Dranthene," Ryel murmured.

The Sovranel was silent for a long time. "There has been one love I have kept innocent. Diara and I met for the first time seven years ago. It is Dranthene custom to keep fullblood siblings apart until they reach adulthood. She was thirteen, and I not yet twenty. I will never forget how beautiful I found her. But ours has since remained an entirely spiritual devotion."

Ryel let out a silent breath. "I'm glad to hear it."

"I'm sure you are, with those Steppes scruples of yours," Priamnor said, now with strange irony. "But my feelings for my sister are compelled as much by politics as by inclination." The prince's soft voice tightened. "By law, Dranthene siblings cannot wed together if the prospective husband is impotent or infertile. And my doctors have informed me that I may well be both since my sickness." With a gesture unwontedly fierce he waved away Ryel's attempt at sympathy. "It doesn't matter. When I consider that the Dranthene dynasty is on the edge of extinction, all I can think of is my little sister, tortured to the death by that evil thing within her." Keenly his jewel-blue eyes evaluated the wysard, with the profound appraisal of that first glance in the presence-chamber. His next words came almost sharply. "And you think to cure her? Do you not understand that you run the risk of death at my father's hands if you fail?"

Truth time, Ryel thought. *No more masks.* "Your sister Diara made me aware of the risks—even as she foretold that you and I would meet."

Priamnor started up. "But when was this? Where?"

"Last night, in the desert outside your city."

"But she was in my father's palace all last night," the Sovranel said, firm in his disbelief. "I was with her. I tell you she was there."

"Her body was," Ryel said. "But not her spirit."

The prince's sun-warmed color whitened. "Impossible. That cannot be."

"Did you not yourself have a vision of your sister?"

"It was no vision, but a dream."

"And you put faith in it," Ryel said. "You will have to believe a great deal more, I fear, before your sister is healed."

"What do you mean?" the Sovranel asked, his soft voice edged.

"That you will have to put your faith in fate if you wish the Sovrena to live." *More truth*, the wysard thought. *No masks, none.* "Many and many a one that calls himself a wysard is indeed a charlatan, I will admit. But I tell no lie when I assure you that I am far more than a mere Rismai tabib, Priamnor Dranthene, and it is your great good fortune that I am."

Ryel had expected at least a flicker of fear at those words, but the Sovran was all anger, coldly reproachful. "So. Another mountebanke, then. Yet I knew you for a liar when you spoke of Fershom Rikh. You could never have studied medicine there, for had you ever visited that city you would have known that it has no temple district of any kind, its people being strong skeptics. I was willing to overlook your falsehood, thinking you had some private reason for committing it. But now I find that all this time you have mocked me, and taken advantage of my trust. I had heard that your kind were cruel, but this—"

The prince's wrath, strong as it was, could not surpass the wysard's outrage. "Cruel? How dare you call me that, when I have given up my study of the Art and left my City to—"

"Your Art." Priamnor all but spat the word. "Did you use your dirty conjurings to make your looks mimick mine, the better to endear yourself to me? Show me your true face, fakir."

"I'm no shape-changer, Dranthene," Ryel retorted. "And even if I were, the last looks I'd choose to copy would be yours."

Priamnor only glared. "And which foul enclave is your City, warlock? Elecambron? Or perhaps Ormala?"

Ryel surged up from his chair, deadly furious. "I am a lord adept of Markul, noblest of the Four. My Art is for healing, not harm."

Priamnor's mouth twitched in its first ugliness. "Then heal this." The prince snatched up a knife, so violently that Ryel recoiled. But still greater was his shock to see Priamnor turn the blade on himself, gashing his arm deep on the underside beneath the elbow's crook. Instantly Ryel lurched forward, clamping his hand against the jet of vein-drawn blood as he blurted a word. When he let go, the wound was whole.

But Priamnor had turned pale. He stared at the red-smeared seam that even as he watched began to fade. "Incredible. I can't believe it."

Ryel finally caught his breath enough to speak. "Never do that again."

The Sovranel gave a short laugh. "I assure you I won't."

"Are you in pain?"

"None." The prince reached for water, washed the erstwhile wound, and looked again, more incredulous than ever. "Barely a mark. How is that possible? How—"

"The Art healed you," Ryel said, still fighting to breathe. "Be glad it did."

"You could have simply let me bleed. I deserved it."

Revolted nearly to sickness, Ryel made no reply. He leaned his head on the back of his chair, entirely exhausted, and closed his eyes. Then he felt Priamnor standing behind him, and one of the prince's hands resting lightly upon his shoulder.

"Forgive me, Ryel Mirai."

At that voice and that touch, both hesitant and remorseful, Ryel felt his strength return. "I blame you for nothing."

"Truly you are powerful in this Art of yours," Priamnor said. "But it seems that my healing caused you harm."

"I've dwelt in the World of men only a short time since leaving my City, and haven't yet grown accustomed to it," the wysard answered. "It's draining, this dealing with the body's hurts."

Priamnor's voice had doubt in it, and foreboding. "But tonight you will need all your powers—unless the Ormalans my father chose prove effectual."

"They are certain to fail. Only I can help the Sovrena."

"How can you know that?"

Ryel let out a long breath. "Because I alone am to blame for her torture." In the absolute silence that followed he continued. "The daimon has used your sister as a means to lure me here, seeking to embody itself in my form."

"But why?"

"For its greater pleasure. And you've seen what gives it joy."

When the Sovranel did not speak, the wysard understood. He pitied this young man born to immense power, indulged in all things. Stronger than his pity was an emotion born of that first look, and strengthened ever since—a devotion more than fraternal, explicable only by the Almancarian word *ilandrakia*. "I'll fight the daimon to my life's limit," he said aloud. "But I must ask that you trust me entirely, and believe that I would sooner die than do you harm."

A long hesitation. Then very quietly and utterly without fear the Sovranel spoke. "With all my heart I trust you, Ryel Mirai. A thousand questions I would ask, but it is time you rested, while time yet remains. Come, I'll take you to your rooms."

At the threshold of his chamber Ryel would have bowed in farewell, but Priamnor forestalled the gesture.

"I expect no deference from a lord adept of great Markul, Ryel Mirai."

"I only show my admiration," the wysard said.

The prince laughed quietly, as in all his ways. "By that logic I, too, should bow."

"As yet you have no reasons. But I hope to give you some, this night." And Ryel took Priamnor's hands in his own and held them for a moment against his brow, and bade farewell until evening.

Chapter Seven

The wysard lay in meditation as the blazing gold of afternoon surrendered to dusky purple sunset. One might have thought him dead, or dying. He barely breathed, nor did his eyes, open and focused far, so much as blink a lid. All he had learnt in his youth with Edris he passed in review, weighing and considering those things which might be of use against his enemy. Daimons of the Outer World he had met and quelled, rival wysards he had infallibly foiled, but the being now holding the Sovrena Diara was stronger than either.

You killed Edris, Ryel thought, his rage icily controlled. *Strangled him from within, and I helpless to prevent it. And now you torment another—not a strong man powerful in the Art, but a defenseless girl. I loathe you, Dagar. To my soul's core I loathe you. Come out of her helpless body, here to me. Face me in a man's form, and let me cut you to pieces.*

He felt his body heaten, his heartbeat quicken, his face sweat. And then suddenly night fell, bringing with it everything he'd hoped and feared to forget. Everything.

There were several Crossing spells, but none was easy. Ryel had chosen the quickest and most perilous. The philtres and the unguents to drug his body into absolute stillness had been long in compounding, and the incantations had taken day, but all the preparations ended in a single word. In the night's silence, in the midst of the lamps and narcotic incense, he had lain down and felt the drugs turning him to stone, and whispered the crucial single syllable through stiffened lips.

Then he died.

It had to be death. Nothing else could be so black and empty, or hurt so much. He could not tell if he was suspended motionless in the icy void or hurtling downward, but he knew he was lost, and might never find his way back. Just as his terror was resigning itself to despair, poisoned claws seized and gripped him, pulling him into shrieking pieces before crushing him to dust; and the dust dispersed on a blast of fire.

Yet something of him yet remained behind, in a place suddenly beautiful and strange. A little bubble of light he seemed, afloat in deathless peace, dissolved to a spark within a sphere.

I've reached it, he thought, and he glittered with ecstasy.

He was all thought now. He had survived the unbodying, and had been stripped to his essence, his *rai*. On the edge of the Outer World he hovered, divided from that place of shadow by a chasm he sensed rather than saw. Beyond the brink annihilation roiled and leapt, but on the other side the spirit-realm of power past all the World's strength vibrated and beckoned.

Everything I risked my life for is there, his rai sensed. *There and waiting. But it's too far. I won't survive.*

The nothingness compressed, enveloping his spirit-sphere in black lead, and a mocking croon oozed out of it.

"Spoken like a faint-hearted fool. I had expected better of you, Markulit."

The spirit-bubble enclosing the wysard's rai spun on its axis a full revolution, fighting the pull of the lead, seeking the source of the voice.

Who speaks? he demanded.

The voice replied instantly, with the same insinuating smoothness, but now it issued from the other side of the chasm.

"Why did you come here, if not to seek the life beyond death? And yet you hover on the edge in cringing terror, when you might float over it easily and without fear, unbodied as you are."

Poised and yearning Ryel's essence listened. *Who are you?* it asked.

"One who has been over and back. One who has watched over you with the most tender concern, ever since your birth. One who would teach you wonders, miracles."

The wysard's rai sparked sharply. *Tell me what you are.*

"You will learn when you join me, here where immortality awaits you," soothed the voice. "Come. Learn what I have learned, and return to the World a god."

Ryel's bright rai quivered, shimmering between fear and desire. *I can't. I'll die.*

"You will not die," the voice assured, softly and with infinite seduction. "Come."

The wysard's spark shot over the abyss, hovered above it.

I will be as a god, it thought, trembling iridescently. *I will be —*

But at that moment the rai's bright bubble started to dissolve, suspended over the endless chasm. The horror that imbued Ryel surpassed even the dissolution's agony, and he threw himself at the Outer World not caring if it claimed him forever, longing only for release from fear. But he could not move. Immobile, he disintegrated, his iridescence eaten away by the corrosive cruelty of the abyss. And then he dropped.

It was a long fall, long enough for him to yearn for complete death. But he kept falling. Falling and burning, shrunk to nothing but a single scream. All around rang laughter sharp as shattered flint.

Then the laughter stopped, silenced by imperative thunder. "Ry! Get out. Come back."

Hard hands plucked him out of the abyss like a pup out of water. Ryel's ethereal sphere solidified, and sprouted arms and legs. But death clung to him.

"Move, whelp. Wake up!"

He was being shaken very roughly, enough to rattle his life out. *Don't stop*, Ryel thought. *Please, please, don't —*

"You idiot brat." A brusque finger forced his lips apart, a hard heavy mouth clamped down and filled his lungs to bursting.

Too late, Ryel would have said. *Too late*. But he was dying at last, and very happy.

His joy proved momentary. With sick regret he awoke to his body's battered ache, his eyes' scorched throb. He could hear a woman singing, but could not tell if she was near or far. Cool fingers soothed his temples.

As he opened his eyes, he heard a gasp. He beheld Serah Dalkith. "Sister?"

Her face was drawn and ashen, but made a trembling attempt at a smile. "So, brother, you return to us at last. We had thought——"

Ryel ignored her. "I must see Edris. Bring him to me. Now."

"Shh. Wait, young brother. Listen." And Serah took Ryel's hands in hers, and softly told him what had passed.

She had found him in the great chair of his conjuring-room, lying across Edris' lap, caged in the frozen clutch of lifeless arms. Only her strongest spells had availed to free Ryel of that dead embrace. Instantly some of the brotherhood had said the needful mantras to preserve Edris' body, and bore it to the Silent Citadel while others carried Ryel to his bed, where Serah had kept constant vigil over his unmoving form for nearly a week.

"You attempted the Crossing."

Serah's words were not a question. Ryel stared at her. "How did you——" But even as he began the question he knew its answer. Seizing her wrist that was covered with a wide bracelet of smooth silver, he used the metal as a mirror, and gave a cry.

His eyes were gone. In Serah's struggling silver the empty orbs of a statue confronted him, black and vacant as the void he had hurtled through.

He fell back, all his body cold.

"An Overreacher," he whispered brokenly. "I am one now."

Serah reached out to him. "Ryel——"

He evaded her. "Tell Edris I am awake and must speak with him."

She gazed on him with deepest pity, her eyes welling with tears. "Ah, Ryel——"

"Tell him. I beg you, sister." He caught her hands. "Find him."

"Ryel, no. Don't do this." She pulled free of his grip—it was easy, he was so weak—and cradled him like a child, and like a child he fought her ineffectually until he, too, wept. Out of his vacant eyes no tears fell. The pain racked him like acid, and he sobbed and thrashed, ever shrieking Edris' name until Serah could hold him no longer and called for help.

"Ryel Mirai. Ryel, awake."

The wysard bolted up as if out of drowning water. "Ithradrakis. I remember. All of it, even to the last breath——"

"You speak to someone else, Ryel Mirai."

The wysard's eyes still ached, and he could not open them straightway. But he knew that voice, utterly unlike Edris'.

"I heard your cries—they were horrible," Priamnor's voice continued. "Was it the daimon?"

Ryel blinked and winced. "No daimon sent my dream." Even as he spoke, the wysard felt strength well outward to his extremities as if his heart were a sun—an invincible force. "I have it. All of it."

"All of what?" Priamnor asked, perturbed. "Can you stand?"

"Stand? I can probably fly."

Too relieved to smile, the Sovranel only nodded. "Excellent. But the hour advances. Here, I had clothes of my city found for you. Your Steppes garb, although admittedly picturesque, is somewhat too warm for this climate."

Ryel thought of Lord Nestris' elaborate robes in his journeybag, but willingly forgot them again as a servant entered bearing a number of fresh silken garments, muted in hue and plainly fashioned as the Sovranel himself was accustomed to wear. The garments' caressing rustle calmed and soothed like a sweet voice, but still more pleasing was the scent that seemed to be woven into the cloth, the fragrance Ryel remembered from the moment he and Priamnor Dranthene had first met. He breathed deeply, and strength surged in his blood as if he lived on air.

You can't be dead, ithradrakis, he thought. *Not when I feel your rai like light all around me—bright hot light. With that light I will destroy our enemy—burn it hollow, then crush it like the empty shell of some ugly insect. I will —*

"Ryel."

The wysard turned to Priamnor, wondering at the wet salt in those sea-colored eyes when there now seemed so little to fear or mourn for.

"Ryel." The Sovranel blinked hard, and continued with strained effort. "I have other sisters and brothers, but Diara is dearest to me. We have the same mother, she and I. If anything should—"

At that moment the door slammed open and a woman, from her rich dress and her manner one of Diara's ladies in waiting, rushed in.

She had been running hard, to judge from her flushed cheeks; running and weeping.

"Oh, sirs, you must come at once. She's dying. The sorcerers poisoned her."

Suddenly the short distance separating the two palaces seemed infinite miles. Ryel gathered up his trailing robes the better to follow Priamnor, who proved breathtakingly fleet, and together they left the lady to join them as best she could.

But thought's swiftness would not have sufficed. Bursting through the portals of Diara's apartments only a few steps behind Priamnor, the wysard halted appalled by the loathesome fetor in the room, a stench only worsened by censers burning strong perfumes. Amid the miasma he could discern a bed exquisitely wrought of silver, but its linen torn to shreds and soiled. On this rich and vile couch lay a still figure pitiably frail, and at its side knelt the Sovran Agenor distraught even to madness, while gathered around them stood lamenting courtiers, their jewels shimmering in the last of the dusk. But the two Ormalans Rickrasha and Smimir huddled together gibbering in a corner, their glassy eyes desperately bulging as they sought the chance to flee.

"Too late, my lord," another of Diara's ladies said to Priamnor between sobs. "Those foul sorcerers—guards! hold them!— envenomed her with some infernal bane, thinking to afterward instill her body with a feigning spirit that would make her appear healed."

Ryel knelt, and took the Sovrena's hand. It was cold and heavy as marble, with lead-gray nails. Next he lifted one of the princess' eyelids, observing the pinpoint contraction of the pupil, and as a last confirmation of his fear put his face close to hers, scenting her breath. He smelled wet wood and rusting iron.

"Xantal in its purest form," he whispered, feeling his blood run cold. "By every god ..."

The Sovran Agenor shoved him heavily away. "Don't touch her, Steppes fakir! Guards, cut him down!"

The guards wavered. At once Priamnor beckoned to two of them, commanding them to restrain the Sovran. He was instantly obeyed. As Agenor wasted his feeble energies in struggle, Ryel turned to the other sentinels.

"Clear this place. Drive out everyone except for the Sovran and his son, and then return at once. Go." He next addressed Diara's waiting-woman. "Have lights brought—as many as might be found. There must be no darkness here."

The soldiers and the lady in waiting obeyed without question, so sudden and strong was the authority that rang in the wysard's voice and darted from his eyes. Seeing their chance, the Ormalans would have bolted for the door, but Ryel shouted out a word and they froze entirely.

"By the god Divares," Priamnor murmured, stunned into involuntary faith.

The sun was setting, but branches of candles surrounded the bed against the gathering darkness. Each new flicker of light heightened both Diara's beauty and its outrage. It wrung the wysard's soul to find the girl so fair, despite the cruel vandalism of filth and self-inflicted blows and scratches, and fevered thinness mocked by heavy jewels and stained satin rags. Unable to look longer, Ryel rounded on the two Ormalan adepts, who helplessly whimpered as they met the empty-eyed stare only they could see.

"You gutter trash," the wysard hissed. "Yes, well you may flinch at the sight of me, for you view me clearly, and know what I am. I promise you'll burn for this."

The air tightened around him, dense and stifling, even as he spoke. And then the one named Smimir quivered violently, his face purpling, and flames spurted from his silently shrieking mouth and frantic eyes. Like a rotten tower set afire from within the Ormalan burnt, and a moment afterward the fear-maddened wysardess, both of them ablaze at their cores until they toppled at last. Out of a fold of Rickrasha's robes the fat chameleon dropped in a clump of staring dead cinders, and then the two Ormalans crashed to the paving-stones like fire-hollowed trees, their blackened ribs splitting open and spilling forth reeking embers and hissing clots.

"You murdered them," Priamnor whispered, his lips white and taut.

"It was the daimon," Ryel said, his voice fully as strained. "Get out, Priam. Go, at once."

"I can bear it," the Sovranel said, but he spoke through gritted teeth out of an ashen face. "I will not leave her when—but look! Look there!"

Diara sat upright, gazing around her. At the sight of the blasted corpses she began to howl and yelp with laughter. In her wasted face the eyes were entire black.

You, Ryel thought, electrically aware. *You the tempter, and the murderer. I know you, Dagar.*

"Stand clear of it," he said aloud, pulling the Sovranel away. "There's terrible danger here."

Priamnor fought Ryel's grip. "Let go of me! My sister is alive!"

"No," the wysard panted, his lungs crushed by the air's weight. "She is worse than dead. Have the guards take your father from the room, at once."

He spoke too late. Somehow Agenor broke free of his soldiers and rushed toward the bed, seizing Diara's usurped body in eager arms. The thing flung back its head and howled with laughter, and then clutched a handful of the Sovran's amulets and necklaces, yanking them taut and driving the jewelled chains deep into the double chins. And even as Dagar throttled the old man, he leered sideways at Ryel, his vacant eyes asquint with mockery.

Clearly Dagar expected the wysard to counter with some spell, but in answer Ryel seized Diara's hair, wrenching hard. The daimon screeched in pain and loosed his hold, but with malicious spite he gave Agenor a parting blow that hurled the old man to the other side of the room.

"See to the Sovran," Ryel commanded the guards, never taking his eyes from the daimon. "He's still alive? Good. Carry him out, and don't return. "

Glad of their escape, the guards hastily bore their ruler away. Ryel next addressed Priamnor, lifting his voice over the daimon's obscenity and babble.

"You can't stay here. He'll seek your harm next."

Fiercely the Sovran shook his head. "I will not leave her or you."

Ryel motioned Priamnor back. "He's rising. Get out!"

Dagar leapt from the bed, still shrieking laughter and blasphemy, and greedily fixed his empty eyes on the scorched remains of the Ormalan sorcerers. With an apelike bound he squatted beside what was left of the one named Rickrasha, thrusting his claws into the steaming entrails. Then he scooped out a dripping clutchful of charred guts and devoured it gruntingly, casting a sly sidewise glance at Priamnor as he smeared Diara's beautiful ravaged face with reeking filth.

At that appalling sight the Sovranel gave a choked cry, then swayed and fainted. Ryel caught him as he fell, and faced the daimon with a rage that left no room for fear or even speech.

Giggling and cursing the daimon staggered toward them and darted his defiled fingers at Priamnor's face.

Ryel struck his arm away. "Damn you—let him alone!"

The daimon recoiled, baring its slime-caked teeth in a grin. "He's pretty. "I wouldn't mind playing with him next."

The wysard lowered Priamnor to the ground and stood in front of him. "You'll never touch him while I live, Dagar."

The daimon tittered. "Don't you love me anymore, young blood? Perhaps you prefer black women? Or yellow? Or green?" As he spoke, he shifted from color to color. "No? It's taking all my wiles to win your heart, sweet eyes. But resist these charms and graces if you can."

Rising up in the air as he tore open the stained bodice of the gown and lifted its bedrabbled skirts, Dagar threw Diara's battered and neglected body into a series of weightless contortions so inhumanly grotesque in their obscenity that Ryel's only care was to make sure Priamnor was still unconscious and unseeing. The wysard watched the daimon with all attention, lest goaded by his indifference it attempt still worse enormities. Weary at last of his posturings, Dagar sank to earth and stood unsteadily, wheezing and gasping.

"Did you enjoy that, young blood?"

Ryel gave a scant nod. "Enthralling—and so original."

Dagar gave a malignant squint, then a scum-toothed grin. "This weak girl bores me. Perhaps you could suggest a clever way to kill her."

Such overmastering hatred that blazed within him Ryel had never felt before. Unused he had ever been to that evil emotion, and the intensity of what he now felt for this nameless thing all but overpowered him, fused as it was with fear. Seizing Diara's body by the shoulders, he stared unflinchingly into the void of Dagar's eyes and closed his hands around the girl's slender neck, leaning both thumbs into the fragile cartilage barely guarding the throat.

Dagar squealed in delight. "Ah! So you enjoy my kind of sport. That's good. That's very good indeed, young blood."

Ryel applied more pressure. "This is a work of mercy, spider. This will be no more to me than putting a sick animal out of pain— save that in this case I will rejoice in a *rai's* deliverance. Rejoice knowing there is one part of Diara Dranthene that you can never again reach to hurt or humiliate or destroy."

The daimon gagged and twisted. "Fool. Death of the body is death entirely—did you not learn that lesson well in Markul?"

"I've since found out the truth, Dagar."

The dead black eyes narrowed at the name. "Thank me for it, then. Give me a kiss, young blood."

Ryel tightened his grip. "You lured me to destruction, hell-born. You laughed as I fell."

"Because I had you, beauty," the daimon panted. "Your body would have been mine—had your fool of a father not interrupted."

Ryel forgot Markul and his mother's blood in a drench of Steppes vengeance. "You killed him!"

"He shouldn't have gotten in my way," the daimon sneered. "His heroics did him no good, after all; they only slowed down the inevitable. You've seen that the Void can't hold me. I'll have you, sweet eyes." His empty black stare locked with Ryel's. "Yes. I marked you for my own, as I marked Michael, and my Ormalan friend Theofanu. We'll have fun, we four." He grinned as his voice dropped to a vibrant bass, eerie in the girl's mouth. "Soon all will know the name of the Master. But enough for now—I've seen what I wanted to see, and I'm sick of this game. Here, take the tiresome little bitch."

The empty eyes shut, and the bruised body toppled into Ryel's arms even as the stifling air thinned. Drawing a starved breath, the wysard put his ear to the Sovrena's heart, and found to his unbelieving joy that a pulse beat there, although with exceeding faintness. Too spent to lift her up, he dragged her to the bed and dropped her onto it, then called to her in the language of the Highest. The girl made no response but lay motionless, all but unbreathing. Ryel again called to her, using every reviving word he knew from his study of the Art, but to no avail. He tried various stimulants he had brought, and others he recognized among the many bottles and phials left by previous unsuccessful healers, but to no effect.

"Has it left her?" Priamnor Dranthene stood at Ryel's side, so pale that the wysard forgot the Sovrena momentarily, all attention fixed on his friend.

"Priam. Sit here, next to me. Are you hurt?"

The Sovranel struggled for breath, and found it. "Never mind that. How is my sister?"

"Her tormenter's gone," Ryel answered. "She survived."

The prince clasped the wysard's hand, his own fingers strengthless but warm. "My eternal thanks." He smiled wanly. "I wanted to face the thing. Call it out and kill it. But I couldn't even look at it."

"I almost could not either, Priam," Ryel said.

With his silken sleeve the Destimarian prince blotted the Diara's face clean of its filth, infinitely gentle. "But now my sister is free. Will she remain so?"

Ryel nodded. "I believe she will. Her captor has played its play, and obtained what it came for. Now it remains for me to heal the hurts she has received both in mind and body while you see to your father." The wysard as he spoke inwardly winced as he recalled the way the Sovran Agenor had struck the wall, the thud of flesh and snap of bone.

Priamnor read the wysard's face, and wearily stood up. "I must go to him. But I will return, ilandrakis."

At that last word the wysard felt his eyes burn. "My thanks, Priam," he replied.

"Tell me what else you require before I go."

"I ask that you send away the courtiers waiting in the hall," Ryel said. "And I would have you summon a few of the bravest of the imperial guard, and command them to stand outside this door and guard it with their lives."

The prince nodded. "I will. Good fortune be yours, Ryel."

"And yours, Priam."

Before he left, Priamnor summoned several of his escort and had the two dead Ormalans removed, to Ryel's entire relief. After all had departed, leaving Ryel alone with the Sovrena, the wysard drew a long breath and abruptly gagged on it. The room was foul with the stench of steaming dead guts, unwashed incontinent living flesh, and heavy perfumes gone sour. Uncurtaining the windows, he threw the casements wide. A blossom-laden breeze from the Eastern Palace wafted in, and he drank it eagerly. The air had lightened deliciously, as if from a sudden sweet hard shower of rain.

Ryel returned to Diara and took her hand, then slid from her wrist to her arm. All her body was cold, and if she were not warmed she might yet die, he knew. Exploring the other rooms, he soon found the one he sought—a large chamber with a great alabaster bath. Two curious taps of wrought gold emerged from the vessel. Ryel pushed them, found hot water emerge from one and cold from the other, and smiled at Almancarian luxury even as he blessed it. He let the hot water run and poured invigorating essences into the flow, then returned to the Sovrena.

As it had been in his vision, her hair was dressed in many braids, woven with ropes of pearl. But now the plaits were greasy and tangled, and the ropes broken and straggling. Ryel unknit the braids one by one, and cast the jewels to the floor. All the gems at her neck and on her wrists and fingers and ankles Ryel likewise removed and dashed to the ground, kicking them out of his way. Her tattered and stained garments too were fastened with many rich ribbons and brooches; Ryel drew his dagger and cut the intricate knots, and with impatient fingers loosened the clasps. Next he slit the wide sleeves and the front of the gown from neck to hem, and then did the same with the shift, until Diara lay naked.

Ryel had longed for this in some of his dreams, the waking ones he'd steeled himself against time and again. But what he now beheld inspired not lust, but rather desperate pity. Here was no ethereal vision: all the girl's body was mottled with bruises and seamed with red scratches, smeared and crusted with the vilest dirt. The skin was rough and taut with starvation, the flesh wasted. Ryel's eyes blinked and burned at the sight. Drawing upon his Mastery, he did what he could to heal the marks of Dagar's cruelty. Expending the absolute

last of his forces, Ryel carried the Sovrena to the bath and lowered her into the water. After a few minutes that seemed infinities her cheeks colored deep, and her eyes opened drowsily, meeting his.

"*Keirai*," Ryel whispered.

"*Keirai d'yash*," the princess replied sleepily as she smiled with recognition. "It's you."

From a source hitherto unknown Ryel gathered strength enough to speak. "Yes, my lady. We meet a second time."

"But still not face to face. I feel removed. Here, and yet not here."

"Because you are not fully awake, but in the dream-realm," Ryel replied as calmly as he could.

Her lovely eyes became puzzled. "Why?"

"You were for some time not in your right mind," the wysard said. "I have put you in the dream-realm to soothe and heal your wits before you return to the World."

"You're kind." She swallowed. "I'm very thirsty."

"I'm sure you are." He brought her cool water, and she drank deeply, then lay back in the bath looking down at herself with bewilderment.

"This can't be me. Why don't I hurt, when I'm so bruised and torn?"

"One feels no pain in the dream-realm," Ryel replied.

"Apparently one can feel very sticky, however." She scratched her head, then lifted up her hand, regarding it with mild despair. "My fingernails look like talons. And my teeth feel fuzzy."

"We'll start on those," the wysard said.

When her nails were trimmed and her teeth clean, Diara thanked the wysard with a bright sweet smile. "That first meeting of ours in the desert, under the moon—do you recall it?"

"I never will forget, my lady."

She looked up at the glass lacework of the ceiling. "But now it's day." Again she gazed at him, and her lovely eyes lit brighter than the dawn, although as softly. "Day, and I here—with you." She laughed like the chime of breeze-stirred little bells. "Let's drink to our meeting again. Is there any wine?"

By chance there was, a crystal ewer full of the Masir vintage Ryel had drunk with Priamnor. The wysard filled a glassful and held it to the princess' lips as she drank until she waved him away.

"Your turn now." She wriggled deeper into the water, revelling in the warmth. "I want to get drunk, but you have to join me."

The wysard decided he deserved it. Putting his lips to the glass, he took a long swallow, then another, until the glass was empty. He refilled it and offered it to Diara, who drank it down and then leaned her head back, eyes closed.

"I'm afraid you're going to have to bathe me," she murmured. "I don't have the strength."

The sudden realization of her eyes, the soft sleepy music of her voice, both directed at him alone, had been hard enough to bear, and he had drawn upon all the asceticism of his Markulit Art to look upon her nakedness with dispassion. But now he was asked to lay hands upon it. *This is too much*, he thought, bitterly resentful. *I realize that there are tests and tests, but this—*

"I should never have asked," Diara said. She looked away. "It was a disgusting request."

"What?" Of all things he hadn't expected to hear that. "Oh, no. Never that, my lady. Never." With the care of a mother, the calm of a physician and the thoroughness of a nurse Ryel made her clean, but first he poured milky blue balm into the water to render it opaque.

She watched him bemusedly while she lifted and shifted as required. "What a marvelous place, this dream-realm. Awake, I would never allow my women to do this much for me. How amusing to feel no shame."

Ryel for a terrible moment remembered another woman, shameless in another bath. He replied brusquely, "Sit up and I'll get to your back."

Diara did so, lifting her long black hair clear of her neck. The wysard remembered the gesture of the marble nymph, but immediately afterward recalled where he had seen it, and to whom it belonged.

"Your brother will be glad to see you well again," he said.

The Sovrena nodded. "I've missed him. He is my dearest friend."

"I'm sure he is."

"And he has taught me so much. Things no one else ever could."

Ryel felt his heart catch on something sharp. "Has he? Such as?"

"All the things my tutors leave out. Stars, which we observe together, up on the roof of the palace. The epics of Destimar, which I love because Priam reminds me of one of the heroes—of Diomenor, the brave prince who had the sorcerer Redestens as his friend. Have you read of them?"

Ryel drew a deep breath of relief, despite Diara's last remark. "Yes. Many times. What else have you been taught by your brother?"

The girl reflected a moment. "The ways of ruling justly and choosing good advisors, in case Priam should fall ill again."

"I didn't know a girl could assume the sceptre of Destimar."

She turned to stare at him. "I am a woman, Ryel Mirai—and not an ignorant one. I was educated as Priam's equal from my earliest years, and I've seen more of the world than he has. As for womanrule in Destimar, legend has it that this city was founded by the Sovrana Parysina thousands of years ago. And don't forget that warrior-maidens appear often in the epics, especially the twins Mevanda and Nelora."

"I'm aware of it. My sister was named for one of them."

Diara's heaven-eyes widened. "Nelora? But I know her! I met her when I last visited the Inner Steppes with my uncle. She was a sweet little girl of ten, very pretty, with the loveliest golden hair I ever saw."

"She's turned into a self-willed brat since then."

"I hope that means she hasn't been brought up in utter ignorance and submission like most women of the Steppes."

Ryel had to laugh. "Not a chance of that."

"Good. I hope to meet her again someday."

The wysard reflected that there was small chance of that ever occuring. "We were discussing your education. What else have you been taught?"

"Too much, according to my father. History. Languages. I can even bore you with mathematics and natural philosophy."

Ryel smiled. "I doubt you'd ever bore me."

"And regarding more practical matters, I wager I could swim rings around you. Priam made sure I learned that."

Ryel started. "You and the Sovranel swim together?"

Her eyebrows lifted, in astonished innocence. "Why, certainly. He taught me how, after all."

"Naked?"

The wysard had blurted the word, and made her laugh. "Of course we're naked," she said amid soft silvery peals. "Only barbarians wear clothes in the water. But I've bathed long enough. Now you have to help me up, rinse me off, and dry me."

Ryel felt his face burning from a hundred abashed infuriate emotions. Still, he did as he was commanded, with stoic matter-of-factness. Then, having at the Sovrena's direction massaged sweet essence into her hair—the same fragrance that had imbued Priamnor's garments—he took up a comb and steeled all of his concentration on coaxing the ivory teeth through the night-black tresses. He would not meet her eyes, her sea-colored eyes, the loveliest in the world.

But she had other ways to torture him. "I remember you in the desert," she murmured, very softly. "Your body. Your arms." And in another instant she had insinuated herself between them, wreathing herself about him. He could feel her hands behind his neck, softly urging him down to her lips.

It was far more than he could bear. Untwining himself carefully but firmly, he stood clear. "Let's get you dressed."

"My hair's almost dry," Diara observed. "Will you braid it for me?"

"No. Where do you keep your gowns?"

Very reluctantly she showed him, and he selected a dress at random. When at last she was clothed, they faced each other again at a distance Ryel deemed safe.

Her voice had become hesitant, unteasing. "Did you destroy my captor?"

For some reason the question eased his pain. "Beyond all things I wish I could have," he replied. "But I merely routed it."

"Then it may return."

Soft as her voice was, Ryel heard terror in it, resigned and desperate. He took both her hands in his, warming them against his chest. "I will prevent its ever returning, Diara."

"You cannot. I know you cannot, and you know it too."

Tears jewelled her dark lashes. They looked long on each other, hands clasped and trembling. Unable to bear any more Ryel murmured a word that made Diara close her eyes and lose her balance. Her clean dark hair tumbled over his arm as he caught her, and he gasped at the feel of it. As her head fell back against his shoulder he could no more keep his mouth from hers than he could his heart from beating. Her breath was fragrant with wine, and as if drinking drunk he kissed her again and yet again until he ached from her weight, slight as it was.

He half-carried, half-dragged her out of the room. Priamnor awaited him, flanked by mail-clad soldiers. Eagerly but half in fear he took his sister into his embrace.

"Ryel. Is she—"

The wysard nodded, brusque with fatigue. "Yes." The air before him seemed to darken, and all his limbs began to melt. He fought to speak. "Listen. This is important: she must never return to that room. The best place for her now is in the Eastern Palace, among flowers and water."

"I'll have her taken there at once," Priamnor said. "But you're not well. Let me give order for—"

"No. I'll live. Listen." Ryel continued, fighting hard for what remained of his strength. "When she wakens tomorrow morning, she'll remember nothing of this night or the days of her torment. Let no one speak to her of them. Have music played for her, soft music with singing. She'll be hungry, but give her only fruit and milk and bread to eat for three days. At evening let her have wine to drink—enough to get her drunk if she wants it." He paused to catch his breath, and continued, "For too long she's been in darkness. She needs sunlight from dawn to noon. And exercise, too—swimming would be best." He realized what he'd said, and winced. "Or walking. She must wear no jewels until three days have passed, and her maidens must not bind up her hair in any way until then, or paint her face. And don't let a doctor near her. Promise me you'll see to these things."

"I will, ILANDRAKIS."

"Go, then. I'll follow."

But Ryel did not follow at once. Unsteadily he walked out to the columned gallery, eager for the fresh night air. His body ached entirely, flesh and bone and nerve, and his head was afire, his eyes burning like live coals. Embracing one of the marble pillars, he pressed his cheek against its polished surface. No sooner had he touched the sweet cool stone than the air blackened before him and he felt himself sliding, and he never knew when he hit the ground.

Chapter Eight

 λ wonderful scent like all the flowers of the earth woke him. The wysard opened his eyes to bright day, and breathed eagerly of the warm air that wafted through the open windows.

"Priam."

The Sovranel of Destimar smiled, but faintly. "Ilandrakis—I thought you might never wake. A good thing I thought of Transcendence. It did the work no doctor could."

Ryel struggled to sit up, and drank gratefully of the water Priam offered him. "Transcendence?"

"Attar of a Thousand it's also called. Its use is forbidden to all save the Dranthene—although every perfumer in this city has tried to imitate it, with no success. Here." As he spoke, Priam took a small cylindrical vial from his robe's sleeve and handed it to Ryel.

For a moment the wysard admired the lovely carnelian stone and its exquisite carvings, then breathed deep of the fragrance he knew and loved so well. "It has life in it."

"Meaning you feel better?"

"Very much so," the wysard said, marveling as he spoke. "Completely well, in fact."

The Sovranel lifted a dark brow. "Strange. But not on second thought."

"What do you mean?" Ryel asked. He had from their first meeting sensed an answer. "You seem as much in need of it as I." He would have returned the scent-cylinder, but Priamnor waved it away.

"Keep it, as a remembrance." He rubbed his unshaven cheek. "Perhaps I've lost some rest from spending the nights of your illness here."

"Nights?"

"Three nights."

The wysard stared. "Three?" Unspeakable fear, then. "Your sister—is she—"

Priamnor nodded swift reassurance. "She enjoys excellent health and spirits—and is more lovely than ever before, which is much. And yet ..." When he spoke again, it was with much hesitation. "You saved her life. And yet she does not want to see you. When I asked her why, she had no answer. Perhaps you could provide me with one."

The wysard understood only too well. Were he and Diara to meet again, it would make them fall more deeply in love, and put the Sovrena more deeply into danger. "Your sister knows that the sight of me would make her re-live the torments she was forced to endure," he said at last. "I understand her feelings, and will comply with her wishes."

"Very well." Priamnor looked away toward the great windows that let in all the freshness of early afternoon, all the beauty of sculpted towers. "You have observed the color I wear, have you not?"

"Yes," Ryel said, surprised by the quesion. "Complete white. But why—"

"It is the mourning color of the royal house. The Sovran my father is dead."

Ryel had expected as much. "I'm sorry, Priam."

With visible effort the new Sovran of Almancar at last turned back to Ryel, his face more weary than grieving. "For your sympathy, my thanks," he said, with a touch of irony. "He died after the daimon struck him, the next night." Priamnor stood and went to the window, leaning against the embrasure as he looked out over his city. So drawn and pale had he become, with such silent despair trapped in his unblinking eyes, that the wysard's heart went out to him.

"Priam, you're exhausted."

Priamnor's gentle voice held a sharp edge of strain. "I might be. These many days I have not known water, save to drink, nor touched food save with loathing in my disquiet for you."

"For all your care I am grateful," Ryel replied, immeasurably moved. "You haven't slept either, it seems."

Priamnor's fingers ceased drumming, and clenched about the stone. "Sleep has been impossible. Scarcely do I close my eyes than I dream of terrible things—of wars and battles, inhuman cruelties of man against man."

"Let me help you, Priam."

"I doubt any wysard arts can aid me, ilandrakis. But I would have you rise and join me, if you would. I most require sunlight now."

Strengthened by Transcendence, Ryel rose and went with the Sovran to the vine-shaded pool. The wysard dove at once into the silent gold and crystalline world he loved, hovering in breathless bliss. But he was troubled by Priamnor's restless shadow hurtling past as if fleeing some sea-born horror, wearing itself out against the water. Later at table, Ryel noted that the Sovran ate little or nothing, but drank much of the wine of Masir—far too much, until at last he shoved his glass aside and stood up, abruptly and unsteadily.

"Am I drunk?"

"To my certain knowledge, yes," Ryel carefully replied.

"I hate it."

"Then why did you?"

Priamnor gulped and shuddered. "To poison the daimon."

Ryel felt his blood icing up. "The what?"

"Daimon. It's been within me for days," Priam said. "Three days. But I'd mastered it, I swear. Kept it captive—until now. I felt it steal over me as I swam. Tried to outdistance it in vain. It has me."

No, Ryel thought, his breath coming fast. *No.* "Priam—is it the same daimon that possessed the Sovrena?"

Priamnor shook his head in numb negation. "I think not. It isn't cruel. I don't think it wishes my harm, but I want free of it. I can feel it in my blood, like wine." He turned to Ryel, his eyes dazed and desperate. "It's killing me."

"I won't let it," the wysard said. "Here, sit down again. Lean against me." And Ryel gently pushed the Sovran into his chair again and stood behind him, cradling and soothing the short-haired skull, murmuring comfort. "No, don't move. It's all right, I'll deal with it. Be still."

Icily Priamnor's fingers gripped Ryel's. "I can't. I'm freezing cold. I don't know this place."

Something indeed holds you, the wysard thought wonderingly, *but not the daimon that tortured Diara. I would know by the heaviness of the air, by the breathless oppression, were you in its power.*

"Tell me where you are," he said aloud.

Priam's voice came ever more dazed and hesitant. "On the wall of a city."

"Almancar?"

Priamnor frowned slightly. "No. No. A place shrouded by mist. I can see dark towers. Beautiful, but cold, so cold—" He shivered, then suddenly tensed. "I hear someone riding up to the gates."

"Turn and look, and tell me who it is."

For a moment Priamnor was silent. "A man. No, a boy. Slender and tall, with long hair. Black hair. He has dismounted, and looks up at me."

"What color are his eyes?" Ryel asked, his heart racing.

"Blue." The Sovran paused. "Blue like my sister's and my own, but slanted in the Steppes way."

"Do you know him?"

"Yes. Perfectly." A long silence. Then Priam's voice deepened and stilled. "I love him beyond my life. I would throw myself in fire for him."

Ryel felt every flame of that fire behind his eyes. The voice was that of Edris, resonant and profound, speaking in Steppes dialect. The wysard's thoughts came in jolts, as if drugged with quiabintha. "Tell me who you are."

"*You* tell me, whelp."

"Ithradrakis. By every god—" Ryel brushed his lips against Priamnor's temple, and tasted sweat. Joy made him whisper. "I knew you weren't dead. I felt it. I always knew it."

A sardonic rumble of laugh in reply. "You're happier about it than I am, lad."

Ryel winced at his eyes' burning. "I'll bring you back," he said.

Edris snorted. "You don't have the Art, brat."

"I promise I will," Ryel said, desperate. "But don't go."

"I have to. I'm taking a chance being here—and I'll suffer for it. But I had to find you. You're in danger."

Ryel held Priamnor closer. "From Dagar? But I fought him, ithradrakis. Fought him and won."

Edris could never have been less awed. "Don't think yourself so great, brat. Tonight was nothing."

"But I'm strong. You know that ... father."

At Ryel's last word, more breathed than uttered, Priam's smooth wet brow furrowed. "You won't overcome Dagar alone," Edris said. "You'll need help."

"Who is there to help me? Another like yourself?"

Priamnor shook his head. His eyes were still shut hard, his voice still Edris'. "No Art can save you, lad, but one of the World might."

"Who?"

"One of two from the North. Soldiers. Captains of the wars to come."

Ryel felt himself frowning. "Wars? I don't understand. Tell me more."

"Don't plague me, whelp. There isn't time."

"Tell me their names at least," Ryel implored.

"Starklander," came the deep-toned answer. "Redbane. Beware of one of them."

"Which one?"

"You'll learn. Once you go North"

Ryel's heart plummeted. "North? But—"

"I said don't plague me, brat." Edris hesitated, stiffening as if in sudden wariness. "I can't stay."

"Is it Dagar?" Ryel asked. "Has he done you harm?"

"He does all he can. Don't worry about me—look out for yourself."

Desperate with impatience Ryel shook the unconscious cold body with Edris' voice. "But will we be together again? Can I bring you back?"

"Find Srin Yan Tai, on the slope of Kalima," Edris replied. "She'll tell you."

"But father—"

Priamnor tensed and moaned, clutching Ryel's wrists. When he next spoke, it was in his own voice, now tight with pain. "It's so cold. I'll freeze to death."

"No, Priam. You're going to sleep."

Panic, dazed and thrashing. "I don't want to dream. Don't let me dream."

"You won't." Ryel bent and breathed a word in Priamnor's ear. The prince slid downward and would have fallen from his chair had not Ryel held him.

You were here, the wysard thought numbly, grazing his cheek against the Sovran's cropped black hair. *You were here, father. Truly Priam must have the Art within him, asleep but strong, to have embodied the emanations of your rai, however briefly. If your rai is within the Void, and there exists a way to rejoin your body with your spirit, I will find it. But what dangers must I pass through first? And who are these Northern captains, and what is this talk of war?*

No answers came. A while the wysard reflected on what had passed, and arrived at the painful conclusion that he was choiceless. He would have to find Lady Srin Yan Tai as soon as might be, which meant the next day at first light.

The wysard looked down at Priamnor. "You won't want me to leave," he murmured. "So I won't tell you. But I'll return as soon as I can."

This said, Ryel took the carnelian scent-vial and opened it close to Priam's face. Ineffable sweetness overwhelmed the air. The Sovran murmured incoherently, then with a sudden start looked about him, wide awake.

"What happened to me? Where was I?"

Ryel drew his first deep breath for a long time, filling his lungs with fragrance, feeling it give him strength. "I wish I knew, Priam."

"Did I say anything?"

"Talk of strange cities and wars. Don't you remember?"

Priamnor again shook his head. "Nothing." The Sovran appeared to consider a moment, then gave a tentative stretch. "Everything that gave me pain is gone. I was sick with wine, but now I'm well. And I was weary unto death, too, but now I'm as alive as if I'd slept a dozen hours. What magic did you work on me?"

"None, I swear," Ryel replied. "It was Transcendence that restored you."

Priamnor smiled from sheer deliverance. "That's exactly how I feel—restored. Returned to what I was. I'm still cold, but some of that sun will warm me again. Come, join me."

In the delicious radiance they again lay side by side, basking in the cloudless heat. His chin resting on his folded arms, Priamnor gazed out at the rooftops and the towers of Almancar the Bright, now burning gold in the fullness of the late afternoon. "I have heard that Markul greatly differs from this city."

You should know, Ryel thought. *You have seen both.* But aloud he said, "The richness of Markul rivals that of Almancar, but as night does day."

Priamnor mused. "Do you think I'd make a wysard?"

It had occured to Ryel that Priam would make a very capable Tesbai, given the right instruction. "You could, if you wished. You're as double-handed as I am."

"But never as self-controlled." Priamnor watched a butterfly float past in a shimmer of emerald and orange. He held out his hand, where the bright-winged insect settled like a quivering jewel. The delicate iridescences of the butterfly's wings seemed to color his thoughts. "Now that we speak of pleasures, there's someplace I would take you—someplace I haven't been for a long time, and which I doubt has an analogue even in great Markul. But the clothes we've been wearing won't pass there. We'll need robes of the true Almancarian style—gorgeous and garish. I'll find some for you."

Ryel remembered Lord Nestris' parting gift of rich garb, now carefully packed in Jinn's saddlebags. "I have them."

"You might have worn them before this," Priam said. "They would have helped you in my father's presence-chamber." The young Sovran gently waved his finger, and the butterfly floated away. "We'll go and dress, and meet again as soon as I'm done conferring with the imperial archivist."

"Some matter of state?" Ryel asked.

Priamnor regarded the wysard steadily. "A matter that might interest you, as it happens. I may discuss it with you tonight when we've reached our destination."

"But where will you take me?"

The Dranthene emperor smiled for the second time that day. "To worship," he replied.

They scarcely recognized each other when they met again.

Ryel found his voice first. "And I thought *I* was gaudy."

The new Sovran of Almancar had swept in like another sunset, arrayed magnificently in trailing raiment of deep rose satin brocaded in emerald-blue. A light mantle fell in a rustling torrent of gold-silk mosaic. Jewelled bracelets enclasped his sun-darkened arms, and a rare pearl hung from his right ear, but he wore no rings save one, a fair cabochon spinel the color of his eyes. The wysard noted with astonishment that the Sovran's face was now lightly painted in the manner of Almancar, with kohl-rimmed eyes and reddened lips, increasing his resemblance to Diara so forcefully that Ryel could do nothing else but stare.

Priamnor adjusted a robe-fold, suddenly mindful of Ryel's wonderment, although wholly unaware of its depth. "I hope you weren't kept waiting long for me."

"Not at all," Ryel finally replied. "How was your conference with the archivist?"

"Enlightening." Distractedly the Sovran plucked at an encumbering sleeve. "These will take some getting used to." He rubbed his pearl-powdered cheek. "As will this paint. I would suggest that you use some yourself, did I not know you a thoroughgoing Rismai." He in his turn studied the wysard's dress, critically approving. "So. Excellent, those robes of yours, and almost as garish as mine. But where could you have found them? That antique cut is the highest fashion at present. I'm half envious."

"These are probably a century old," Ryel replied with a smile. "They belonged to one of my City."

Chin in hand—a smooth-shaven chin, now—the Sovran surveyed Ryel. "He must have been notable in *my* city both for excess of riches and dearth of subtlety. But flame-orange is a color that suits you, fortunately."

"My thanks—I think." Ryel did not mention that instead of the requisite under-robes he wore his Steppes gear, shirt and breeches and boots, beneath the light voluminous silk. He also thought it best not to divulge that he had visited the stables while Priam was with the archivist, and that now Jinn's saddlebags were ready packed for the secret departure he intended to take at first light, with his horseman's coat and Edris' cloak tightly rolled up and fitted easily and unobtrusively into the deep leather casings along with his journeybag. His sword, however, he kept, to which Priam made no objection since he too was armed. But the Sovran's light rapier was quite clearly more for show than use.

"We should be on our way at once," Priamnor said. "We have barely an hour."

"But where are we going?" Ryel asked.

"I told you—to worship. To one of the city's greatest temples."

"When did you become religious?"

"I didn't. Come, we're wasting time." A little while later, Ryel was holding a torch and leading Jinn down an underground corridor, following Priamnor who likewise held a burning brand against the dark as he guided a priceless Fang'an gelding.

"This passage was built many hundreds of years ago," Priamnor said, his soft voice echoing against the walls. "As the cobwebs indicate, I haven't used it recently."

"Where does it emerge?"

"You'll see."

Uneasily Ryel studied his friend. "You appear very agitated within."

At those words Priamnor suddenly halted and turned about, holding up his torch to Ryel's face, examining it with that piercing scrutiny he had used at their first meeting. "Do I not have reason? Say you had by merest chance found a treasure beyond price, one upon which your life depended, only to learn that it had been yours for many years though all unknown to you—would you not greet that knowledge with emotion?" His beauty flickered in the torchlight, grave and searching. Without staying for reply he turned again, and continued down the corridor. Baffled as to what Priam might mean, Ryel followed.

They came at last to a great portal of solid iron, where two strong servants awaited them and opened the door with much effort.

The men only with greatest reluctance accepted Priamnor's gift of gold, and wished to accompany their ruler for his greater safety, but were refused.

"You've devoted slaves," Ryel remarked as they mounted and began to ride.

Priamnor shook his head. "I keep no slaves. All my servants are free men and women, a custom I hope will someday be the rule in this city." He glanced at Ryel. "Would that change please you?"

"Very much."

"Good."

He said nothing more. After a time Ryel spoke. "We're among gardens."

"The city's loveliest," Priamnor said as he drew a fold of his cloak around his face. "They adjoin the temple grounds."

Many others were out enjoying the evening air. Under flowering trees hung with lanterns, richly-garbed groups of revellers sang and played musical instruments and heralded the rising moon with lifted wine-cups. The canal along which Priamnor and Ryel rode was crowded with slim lamp-lit boats carrying passengers likewise rejoicing in the warm night.

"This is beautiful," Ryel murmured.

The Sovran laughed, though not with overmuch mirth. "It gets better. Look, and tell me where we are."

Ryel followed Priamnor's indicating gesture, and found a vision made real. "But this is the Temple of Atlan!"

Priamnor reined in. "The very same. Moreover, it is the entrance to the Diamond Heaven, Almancar's pleasure quarter."

"But what if you're recognized?"

"The Diamond Heaven has not known me for five years, and in those days my hair was longer than yours, and my face bearded," Priam replied. "If anything, you will be mistaken for me—we resemble one another remarkably, as I observed earlier. But it hardly signifies, since we'll both be disguised with these." As the Sovran spoke, he took two silken half-masks from his saddlebag and handed Ryel one. They were exquisite and fantastic, hooded and owl-horned, glittering with jewels and precious embroidery. Priamnor donned his and turned to Ryel. "Tell me now if you know me."

I will always know you, Ryel thought. "Won't you be recognized by your smooth face?"

"I think not. The moment I shaved clean, it became all the fashion among the young bloods. But come, we're just in time for the night's first ceremony."

Many others had left the park and the canal to ascend the temple steps. But there were some who did not climb the great marble stairs—not aristocrats or rich merchants, but laboring folk of the Fourth District come to marvel and envy. In their midst a compelling voice thundered forth.

"Yes, gape upon them! There they go, the pampered sycophants of the Whore-Goddess, to wallow like gilded swine in debauchery paid for with your brows' sweat and your life-blood!"

Priamnor and Ryel had been tying up their horses, but now they turned to that voice which both of them knew well. The prophet Michael stood on a mounting-block nearby, glaring into the torchlit dark with burning black eyes. Already followers clustered about him, and some of the maskers halted on the stairs to listen and jeer.

"An hour of my instruction would teach you Atlan's mysteries, Michael!"

The wysard monk's wolfish eyes darted to the masked woman who'd spoken, and blazed with devouring fire as they swept across the carnal snares revealed by her clinging satin. His deep voice snarled disdain.

"There speaks some drug-sotted slut, or some drunken adulteress, come to pant at the lewd gyrations of the Golden Whore's slave priesthood, then tumble and roll in a brothel's bed! This is your aristocracy, O Almancar! This, your fabled greatness! This, the filth that the Master will wash clean, and soon!" With consummate scorn his glare swept the glittering maskers on the temple steps, from top to bottom, then fell upon Ryel and Priamnor. His cruel lips parted over his dazzling teeth, and he grinned like a daimon before turning his gaze upward to the pale towers and tall buildings.

He lifted his bare hard arms, shut his eyes, raised his voice. "Yes, unhappy Almancar, this is your royalty, this your wisdom, fallen at the feet of strumpets and minions! Even your new Sovran, the chaste Priamnor, comes here to revive his brute lust, his father not yet cold in the grave!" His cruel eyes opened again, raking the crowd like knives, fixing on Priam. "What brings you here, last of the Dranthene? Was it not enough, the clap that nearly killed you? What would you do with whores, impotent as you are? Or would you now play the woman, being unfit for anything else?"

The listening crowd gasped as one and Ryel would have spoken in fury had Priamnor not caught his wrist, gripping hard.

"No words. Let him rave." But he was pale beneath his mask.

One of the soldiers of the city guard turned furiously on Michael, half-drawing his sword. "Watch that gutter tongue of yours, ranting fool! The Sovran Priamnor forsook the Diamond Heaven years ago!"

Michael eyes flashed like edged steel. "How can you be so certain, when Atlan's lechers go masked? How would you know if he were at this moment in your midst?" As the crowd murmured among themselves, high and low alike, the mad prophet spoke again, his voice an echoing shout as his eyes darted from one mask to the next. "You are of Atlan's crew tonight, Priamnor Dranthene, you and your wysard favorite! May these good subjects that you scorn bear witness to your love for a teller of truth!" He tore the ragged robe from his shoulders, and with damnable pride bared his scarred back to the crowd. A woman nearby shrieked and fainted, and guards at once came forward and broke up the throng, driving Michael from the temple steps with blows and shoves that Ryel knew Elecambron's greatest adept would not bear for much longer. Priamnor would have to be warned of the prophet's real powers, and the terrible danger they threatened.

However, now was not the time. "Much as I pity the poor fanatic, I'm glad that's over," the Sovran murmured, regret mingling with revulsion in his voice. "Come, we're late for the service."

Ryel followed Priamnor, forgetting the dirty black-ragged preacher in the feel of the gently jostling crowd, of the soft stray impacts of rich fabric and the mingling of a hundred rare perfumes liberally applied to skin consummately well-washed, of bright laughter and the caressing accents of the city's sweet language. Without exception everyone was gorgeously and fantastically masked and robed, and Ryel wondered at it.

"The laws require, for the better reputation of the city, that Atlan's adherents go richly disguised—a means of encouraging both expense and anonymity," Priam replied. "The worship of Atlan is more than a little costly, but I've come well provided for us both," the prince continued, smiling at the wysard's astonishment as he threw a double handful of gold into the vessel held out by a forbiddingly huge door-guard. "Here's something for you, too, ilandrakis." He thrust a silken pouch heavy with coin into one of Ryel's hanging sleeves. "Now you'll be irresistible. Let's go in."

Ryel hesitated. "But what if your identity is suspected and your mask removed by force?"

Under the mask's edge, Priamnor's mouth smiled again, this time somewhat tightly. "I doubt that will occur. The penalty for such transgression is death." As he spoke the last word, he and Ryel entered the temple.

Often in time to come the wysard would remember the Temple of Atlan, and with each remembrance find his Rismaian upbringing and his Markulit training severely tested. He had grown up in a hard land among a stern people distrustful of luxury. The many whims of the flesh he had studied dutifully and with as much detachment as he could summon during his study of the Art, and had wondered at their power over mankind. Atlan's worship made him fully understand the essential sanctity of pleasure, and he was awed and humbled by the depth of that comprehension. Every sense that might bring delight to the spirit was exalted, from the silken scented cushions whereon the worshippers reclined at their ease, to the music of ravishing sweetness, and wine so heady that a single taste brought euphoria, passed hand to lingering hand in cups of gold. In dancers of the rarest beauty, whose bodies slid and twined and enlaced in ardent exaltation of the flesh, seconding the ever-accelerating music with rhythmic clicks of gems. Ryel felt his eyes dazzle, his mouth dry. He glanced over at Priamnor and wondered how the Sovran's masked gaze could be so clear and searching, studying the dance with complete dispassion.

The music died, the dancers dispersed, the rites ended. Ryel released the breath he'd been holding and sank back on his cushions, his wits unsteady, his blood in riot.

"Most edifying. Most awe-inspiring," came the Sovran's voice, controlled and amused, at his side. "Can you walk?"

"Not very well, probably," Ryel muttered.

Priamnor laughed. "Religion has its uses. The sacraments of Atlan are wisely designed to put the worshipper in the correct frame of mind to worthily enter the Diamond Heaven." He stood up, and helped Ryel to his feet. "You seemed suitably impressed. But come, Heaven awaits us."

Heaven it was indeed to the wysard's already dazzled eyes. Amid the rich throng of revellers come from every corner of the World, silk-curtained chairs borne by liveried slaves conveyed indolent glittering favorites to assignations, while in the meandering canal that divided the Jewel Path lovers reclined at amorous ease in gilded shallops, or pleasure-parties sang and played in lighted barges, scattering flowers in the clear water. Ladies leaned from the roof-galleries of splendid houses, trading wit with the passersby below, and often tossing down flowers with artfully folded notes tied to their stems.

A thrown rose softly struck Ryel's cheek. He bent and gathered it, and as he did, female laughter pealed from on high. Looking up, Ryel and the Sovran saw that several masked ladies clustered at a railing on the rooftop garden of one of the quarter's most opulent mansions.

"Come taste our wine!" the boldest of the bevy called. "It will cost you nothing but a sweet look from your fair eyes, my lords."

"That I rather doubt," Priamnor wryly murmured.

The mansion was ornamented all over with mosaics and sculptures of a nature that made the wysard first stare, then look away. "There's a paper tied to the stem," he said, dissemblingly indicating the flower.

"Of course there is." Opening and glancing at the note, the Sovran gave a short laugh. "Just what I expected." He handed it to Ryel.

The wysard read aloud the message that was scribbled with negligent grace across spangled fragrant paper. "'The silver moon/ Though cold and high/ Falls melting-ripe/ Into a jeweled hand.' What does it mean?"

"You'll learn," the Sovran said, his smile ironic now. "Symbolism here is never too occult."

The ladies had not silenced. "Come up to us, young heroes! We have awaited you all this night."

The Sovran bowed and kissed the rose with a flourish as the ladies applauded. "My friend and I have errands elsewhere, my beauties," he said. "But we'll return."

"Promise!" one of the ladies called.

"You have my word," he said.

Another beauty gave an unbelieving laugh. "Ah, but is it good?"

"As good as if the Sovran himself gave it," Priamnor said.

Louder laughter at that. "The young Dranthene is an anchorite worse than that dirty ranting Michael!" cried the one who'd thrown the flower. "But were he here, I'd try his famous chastity."

After some other badinage—exceedingly polished and witty for an avowed recluse—the Sovran bade courteous farewell to the ladies of the Joy Realm and took Ryel's arm, leading the wysard further along the street.

"I've amazed you."

Ryel bit his lip at the Sovran's amused tone. "To hear the ascetic Priamnor Dranthene bandy words with bawds and harlots is something of a surprise, I must admit."

Priam endured the reproach calmly. "You see me as I was, ilandrakis. But now ... " he looked around him, his mouth beneath the mask unsmiling, his eyes joyless. "I'll thank you to call me by my Heaven-name, if you would. It used to be Atlantion, but tonight it shall be Diomenor, in honor of the stern young god-hero of the epics. And what will yours be?"

"Redestens," Ryel answered, not so much to Priamnor's question as in remembrance of some words Diara had let fall.

At that answer, uttered without a moment's hesitation, Priamnor's jewel-blue eyes shone behind the mask. "Ah. Redestens the Desert-hawk, Prince Diomenor's comrade in arms with the magical powers. Excellent. You're well and aptly read, ilandrakis. If we're to be epic heroes, high time we found some adventure. Follow me—but first I must caution you that the ladies of the Garden of Dreams are the most beautiful and accomplished of all the Heaven. Unless times have greatly changed, they'll require an inordinate amount of gallant wooing. Can you bear it?"

"I can if you can."

They entered the Street of Sighs, and halted before a lovely house of pink marble, its columns amorously wrought. Ryel followed Priamnor up the stairs to the rooftop, into a dazzling world of lush flowers and voluptuous statuary, wild vines tendrilling over silver trellises, and lamps glimmering like stars. Ravishing music added further sweetness to the perfumed air. But richest of these sights was the bevy of courtesans that made a fragrant sparkling cloud of butterfly-winged masks and gossamer robes and flickering downy fans. As the wysard and the Sovran looked about them, another lady bustled up, a lady no longer young but gaudily defiant of the fact, clearly the mistress of the house. Her overpainted eyes peered closely at Ryel and Priamnor through the slits of her virginal visor, assessing first their faces, then their garb. Although she seemed not sure of the former, the latter decided her to the utmost courtesy. "My honored lords, all the beauties of the Garden of Dreams are at your beck, impatient to entertain you. Shall I select your company, or have you some particular nymphs in mind?"

"We wish to speak only with Belphira Deva," Priamnor replied. "That is, if she is not engaged to another."

The bawd—for so Ryel privately named her—gave a forced smile. "Lady Belphira has not been engaged for many years, my lord, in any way save as a singer. A deplorable loss. Yet although the lady has long forsworn the delights of Atlan, she is nonetheless the glory of my house, and accustomed to the greatest courtesy—and generosity."

Priamnor inclined his head. "We will disappoint her in neither, madame. I give you my hand on it." Which he straightway did, after first filling his palm with gold coins.

Pocketing the money with a deep curtsey, the lady led Priam and Ryel to a private bower, and gave orders to her servants waiting in readiness. At her word a low table was instantly spread with candles, and wine, and spiced confections. With many compliments to Ryel and Priam she departed to receive another party of masked adventurers.

Priamnor leaned toward the wysard's ear. "So. Are we in Heaven yet?"

Even as he spoke, the fairest of all the courtesans of the Garden of Dreams approached them, formed like a goddess and clad in purest white adorned with pearls and diamonds, her half-mask's snowy plumes trembling as she rested her eyes on Priam. Clearly her blood was Northern, to judge from the dark green of her eyes, the deep heavy gold of her hair. But the painting that colored her eyelids, cheeks and lips made Ryel think of the statue of Diara in Priamnor's atrium, of borrowed hues conferring feigned life on dead white marble.

Both men at once rose to their feet. Priamnor looked long upon the lady before bowing deeply. "I am fortunate indeed to address Belphira Deva, the celebrated queen of the Diamond Heaven."

The lady gazed on him as if stunned, and her reply came slowly. "I am honored by your compliment, most gentle lord. And what am I permitted to call you?"

"Diomenor, by your leave."

She tilted her head at that name. "Diomenor. I might have erred and called you Atlantion, my lord. I thank you for the correction. And what of your friend?"

Ryel bowed. "Redestens, my lady."

Belphira's delicate brows arched behind the mask. "Your name is most ill-omened," she said to Ryel. "Redestens was a sorcerer, my lord, as cold and reasoning as his friend Diomenor was unruly and insatiable. He would never have willingly entered this Heaven's gates."

Priamnor laughed. "I forced him to. Have we permission for more converse with you, my lady?"

"As much as you wish," the courtesan named Belphira replied, but it seemed her voice trembled.

They seated themselves, or rather reclined among a cloud of cushions. Priam poured out wine first for Belphira, then for Ryel and himself, then raised his glass toward the lady.

"To all of your beauties, Belphira Silestra."

The lady bowed her head amid a quivering of plumes. "You do me too much honor, my lord." Lifting her face again, Belphira gazed long on Priamnor. Clearly she knew well with whom she spoke, and sought only the pleasure of his eyes on hers. "This is a glad meeting, my lord Diomenor."

Priam met her regard with equal tenderness. "I have traveled far to see you, my lady."

"You have indeed," she replied. "But that distance is not measured in miles."

Priam turned to Ryel. "Lady Belphira has the gift of divination," he said. "She can tell you all that you are. Do you wish to hear?"

Ryel had known from the first that Belphira was no ordinary woman. Looking upon her, he was keenly aware that the Art slept within her, very strong. "Tell me who I am, my lady," the wysard said, half fearing the answer.

Lady Belphira turned her emerald gaze to the wysard, and it seemed she looked into his very soul. "Like your friend Diomenor you have journeyed far, Redestens," she said at last. "Yours are the Inner Lands of the Steppes. I know it by your accent, despite the absolute fluency of your speech. As I have read, there are young men of the Inner Steppes, the Rismai principally, who vow to forswear all soft dealings and to devote their lives to war—I feel that you are one of those."

Priamnor shook his head. "My friend has never fought in battle, fair one."

"Ah, but there is combat far more bitter than that of sword against sword," Belphira said. Ryel looked into the lady's eyes, and saw great understanding there, and wonderful gentleness. "The struggle of heart against mind, of self against world, is unending war to some; and there are greater struggles still, in which men render up their lives for reasons beyond love and hate. Such a warrior I sense in you, my lord Redestens."

Greatly moved, Ryel took Belphira's hand, and would have touched his brow to it. But he remembered where he was, and carried it to his lips instead. "I am no lord, madame."

She smiled. "In some city, surely, you are a great one."

"In that City you would be a lady fully as great," the wysard replied.

Priamnor looked from Belphira to Ryel, a glint of something very close to jealousy in his jewel-colored eyes. "I well recall our first meeting, my lady," he said. "At the palace of the Sovran Agenor during his *sindretin*, the great celebration of his fiftieth birthday. My recollection of that night has never faded."

Belphira only half smiled. "Nor has mine ... even though the rest of me has been less fortunate."

"You have not changed a day, my lady," Priamnor said. "But I still recall the night with some anger, because of the insult offered you by that unmannerly brute, Guyon Desrenaud."

The lady flushed suddenly and with vehemence. "Lord Guyon never meant insult."

"He became your lover," Priam said, now with an edge of rancor.

Belphira inclined her head in slow assent. "He did. But that was long ago. And Lord Guyon was the last lover I ever took—until you came into my life. These past five years we have not met, you and I, but in that time I have taken no other admirers, choosing instead to entertain the guests of this house with my singing alone."

Priamnor, although very evidently pleased with Belphira's words, still seemed not entirely satisfied by them. "Tell me about that night in the Sovran's palace, my lady. Tell me what made you favor that ill-bred Northern lout."

"Why would you wish to know, my lord?" she asked.

"To learn if he still has a hold on your heart."

The lady looked down. "He did once, and strongly. But that was before he traveled to the Northern Barrier, and became the lover of that land's ruler, the Domina Bradamaine. Before he became the famous Starklander."

At that name Ryel caught his breath. "Starklander?"

Belphira stared at him. "The name seems to excite you, Redestens."

"Because it's ... because it sounds so strange," Ryel replied hastily.

Belphira lifted a silken bare shoulder. "Did you dwell in the North, you would not think so," she replied. "Among the Northern nations Starkland has ever been another name for the Ralnahrian highlands, in recognition of the dour toughness of the men who dwell there, amid crags and cold. In recent years Lord Guyon gained fame in the neighboring realm of Hryeland, where he became leg-

endary for his bravery and generalship in the army of the Domina
Bradamaine. His young manhood was spent at Ralnahr's royal court,
as the chosen friend of Prince Hylas, son of King Niall. He came to
Almancar as Hylas' interpreter at the Sovran's sindretin, where he
and I met."

"I need to hear the story of that meeting," Ryel said to Belphira.

She stared at him, astonished by his tone. "You would? But
why?"

"I have very important reasons, my lady," the wysard replied,
struggling for calm. "I implore you to tell me all that you remember."

Belphira hesitated, glancing at Priam. "My lord Diomenor will
not wish to hear my tale, I fear."

"I can bear it," Priam said. "In fact, I'd be glad to learn the entire story from your own lips, my lady. By all means recount all you
can." He smiled. "I remember how fair you were that night under
the stars. I lost my heart to you the moment you appeared, and no
wonder. For you were chosen as the fairest lady of Almancar, to
grace the assembly with your beauty and your singing."

"Your praise honors me overmuch, my lord," Belphira replied,
coloring under her mask's edge. "In truth, I believe I was invited to
the sindretin because my mother, in her day the loveliest courtesan
of the Diamond Heaven, always maintained that my father was a
Northern prince of the blood. According to her, I had every right to
call the Sovrana Lys, Agenor's Ralnahrian wife, my aunt."

"I am aware of those rumors concerning your birth," Priamnor
replied. "But your singing went beyond all mortal nobility. It was
celestial. All of the guests—and there were hundreds, come from every part of the world to honor the Sovran—fell absolutely silent as
you sang. All save that Northern ruffian."

Ryel spoke, then, to Belphira. "Describe Lord Guyon to me, my
lady, as carefully as you can."

Her face reflected equivocal memories, and she replied slowly,
her green eyes gazing far. "I see him even now."

Chapter Nine

Lord Guyon had drawn Belphira's eye at once, for amid the magnificent attire of all the other guests his made a strange and striking contrast. Indeed, Belphira had never in her life seen anyone more oddly dressed, or more carelessly—nor, she had to admit after the fact, with more fascination. A black and white Shrivrani headcloth concealed everything of his face save for the eyes, and a worn brown desert cloak half-hid his travel-beaten black Northern riding-gear. But the eyes were most arrestingly piercing, and the rusty garments sat close to a form remarkable for its height and perfection of shape. Nevertheless, it was a singular costume for a sindretin guest, almost insolently negligent, and the Sovran glared it up and down, and demanded who had allowed into the palace a ragged *aliante*. At this insult Lord Guyon's eyes blazed behind the Shrivrani cowl, for in the tongue of Destimar an aliante was a soldier of fortune of the lowest kind—one that would kill for a crust of bread, sell himself to any master and then as lightly betray him.

"'Aliante I may someday be, but never yours, Agenor Dranthene,' the tall Northerner had replied, angrily prideful as he stood at his full height, straight-backed with his hand on his sword-hilt. He spoke in perfect High Almancarian only a little slurred by drink, the subtle intonations so much at variance with his rough aspect that everyone began to whisper. But the murmured surprise turned to silent amazement when with abrupt defiance the seeming mercenary tore away the concealing headcloth, letting it fall about his shoulders.

"'You speak to Guyon de Grisainte Desrenaud, Earl of Anbren,'" he said to the Sovran. Belphira had listened as if to proud music, unable to take her eyes from his face.

"As you may be aware, my lords," she said to Priamnor and Ryel, "in Almancar physical beauty is considered a visible sign of the gods' continuing presence among men. As I looked on Guyon I could not help but feel holy awe and wonder. He was just turned of twenty-four years old, very tall, and wonderfully well made. His tawny hair was cropped close to his head, drawing all attention to his face, and never before, even in my city so famed for the loveliness of its denizens, had I seen features more striking. Pure highland Ralnahrian they were, of the finest cast. They had not known a razor for several days, but the beard-stubble in no way obscured their noble harmony and forceful beauty. The eyes were full of intelligence wary and stern—dark celadon as a winter sea were they colored, acute and steady as a hawk's, turbulent and cold as they braved the Sovran's rage. I marveled. I did not know then that he was in mourning for the woman he had loved with all his heart, and in his grief had turned to bad courses, seeking to kill the pain within him by wearing out his body in riot and disorder.

"The Sovran Agenor liked his looks even less. 'Throw this dirty ruffian out,' he commanded his guards. Even as Lord Guyon flung off his cloak and clutched the hilt of his sword, the Sovrana interposed, swiftly and decisively.

"'Peace, Agenor, for once at least.' Like the Sovran she looked Desrenaud up and down, but not with disfavor—not at all. 'Yours is high blood indeed, to judge from your looks,' she said. "What part of the North claims you?'"

"'Along the frontier of Ralnahr on the edge of Hryeland was I born, most exalted,' Desrenaud replied proudly, amid the silence that had fallen with his desert cowl. 'In the western borderlands, where the mountains meet the sea. It is my honor to serve in this company as interpreter to Ralnahr's heir apparent, Prince Hylas.'

Belphira paused, rapt in memory. "I will never forget how strange it was to hear the palace language of Almancar in the mouth of this man—to listen to its difficult elegances perfectly uttered, with only the faintest traces of Northern tang and Sindrite brandy, by one so apparently a stranger to any civilization. The kingdom of Ralnahr is distant and small, and fluency even in common Almancarian is not expected of its court, whose wonted tongues are Ralnahren and the trade-language of the Northland, Hryelesh. Therefore Lord Guyon's mastery was doubly surprising, and I wondered how and why he came by his knowledge.

"Then by chance our eyes met, and in that moment he threw me a glance that froze my blood with its scorn. Suddenly I saw myself through his storm-colored eyes—saw an empty-headed bedizened doll smiling blankly as she was borne in like a master-cook's fluffy dessert, cloying and insipid. A garish bauble to be chaffered for and used at pleasure, maybe pulled to pieces, by anyone willing to meet the price required. A mindless child I saw, devoid of volition, ignorant of all hardship, empty of any passion. I further realized that Desrenaud was a man made up of self-will and strong desires, hardened by rough upbringing and aged beyond his years, rankling with old sorrows and recent grief—a man whose entire existence had run entirely counter to mine, whose contempt dismayed me and whose strength I envied ... and whose desolation of spirit I pitied with all my heart.

"At that moment the Sovran requested me to sing for the guests. I chose a love-ballad of ancient times, and sang as I had never sung in my life, all of my heart poured into every word. As I sang, I felt Desrenaud's gaze like an inexorable hand under my chin, and I looked up amid my first tears ever shed in shame or pain only to find his winter-eyes as wet as mine.

"How long we remained thus electrically enmeshed I have no idea. But then all at once he pushed through the listening throng and dropped to the ground before me, wrapping his arms around my skirt, pressing his forehead against my knees as a supplicant does a ruler or a god in the old tales. An act of madness—and yet I did not find it so, any more than I heard the outrage of the guests. The world had fallen away from Desrenaud and I, isolating us in a sphere of flame. For the first time in my life I comprehended the inexorability of male strength, the depth of male longing—and all I could feel in return was terror and hunger. I had drunk wine, and my wits swam; I would have given all my other lovers' gifts and fortunes for a kiss of Lord Guyon's mouth. I had only enough time to caress his hair, whispering that I knew, I knew—yet I could never have explained what I knew, or how ... "

Belphira halted, fetching her breath with trembling lips. In that interval of silence Priamnor spoke, his voice unwontedly hard.

"I remember the fellow's insolence. Had I been armed, I would have cut the ruffian down."

At those words Belphira smiled as her inward eyes beheld the past. "The Rei of Zalla very nearly did."

The Sovran of Destimar nodded with the same memory, but with a smile very different from Belphira's. "He would only too gladly have run Desrenaud through with that evil-looking diamond-hilted dagger of his. But you would not allow it—would you, my lady? No, you needs must fling yourself in front of that Northern churl and dare the Rei to strike."

Belphira saw herself in that remembrance, and laughed. "I admired the Rei's courage, although I deplored his action."

"It wasn't courage Akht Mgbata showed—it was devotion," Priam said. "I don't doubt the Rei would still murder Lord Guyon for your sake—and that you would still prevent him."

"I very well might." Belphira gave Priamnor a near-teasing smile as she turned to Ryel and continued her narration. "Only the pleadings of Prince Hylas kept Lord Guyon from prison, and perhaps worse. He was bodily thrown out of the sindretin, and forbidden ever again to enter the palace."

"But he found his way to the Diamond Heaven," Priamnor said, grudging now.

Belphira met Priam's rancor levelly, with no discomfiture whatever. "Yes, my lord. He found his way to this place ... and to me. But before you condemn either me or him, you should know that I was no easy conquest. He did not want me to be. *I* did not want to be. After so many heartless beds and empty nights, we both required tenderness. He wooed me in a hundred different ways, but always with worship. And I, who unlike him had never before known love, accepted his homage with delight—and terror. For love is a tremendous thing, if real. There is no emotion more strong or lasting. The deepest hatred can waver in the light of reason, or fade with time, but the deepest love knows no reason, and is deathless."

Ryel listened awed, and even Priam seemed moved instead of angered. Belphira continued.

"It was strange to be surrounded by the Diamond Heaven's pleasures, yet remain chaste. To play at courtship as if it were an elaborate endless game. Strange, yet inexpressibly sweet." Her beauty clouded, then. "But ours was not always an unendangered paradise, for there was one constantly watching us, who could never comprehend any feelings save the most vile."

In a few words she explained. Among Prince Hylas' entourage there had been a rude puritanical lordling named Derain Meschante, notorious as a stern hater of all things fleshly. He would steal into the Diamond Heaven to berate the courtesans and their clients for what he considered their sins, using language and actions both rough and foul. Again and again he was expelled, only to return again and again.

"He always wore rented finery," Belphira said, not disguising her contempt. "There are many shops outside the Heaven's gate that provide such. It disguised him well enough for him to constantly evade detection. Were not my dislike so strong, I would have pitied him, for he could never comprehend pleasure or know joy, but always loathe and mistrust all that was beautiful. His hatred of Lord Guyon was strongest of all his hates. Thus it fell out that when one night Meschante again sneaked into the Heaven to quarrel and condemn, he and Lord Guyon came to blows, here in this very place."

Priamnor's mouth tightened. "Brawling in the pleasure-district is a capital offense," he said.

Belphira nodded. "True, but the punishment is very seldom carried out, especially if wealth and rank intercede. Prince Hylas pleaded for the lives of both Guyon and Meschante, and his request was granted—on the condition that the two enemies instantly leave Destimar, and never return. Before Lord Guyon departed, he bought my freedom at ruinous cost, and I joined him as part of Prince Hylas' entourage when it returned to Ralnahr."

"I remember," Priamnor said, his umbrage undisguised. "You were gone for years."

"Two years only," Belphira replied, unhesitatingly. "I was glad to return to my native land. It was sweet to breathe the sharp air of the highlands, and feel the caress of snow on my face."

In Ralnahr she had become one of Queen Amaranthe's ladies-in waiting, and had been given the title of countess. Soon afterward she and Lord Guyon betrothed themselves to one another, and passed from courtship to love in all its fullness even as a leaf-sheathed bud becomes a bright blossom heavy with perfume. Folk soon began to whisper that a great change had come over Guyon Desrenaud: that he had given up his rakehell ways and wild companions and turned his mind to serious matters. He particularly studied statesmanship and diplomacy, and with his skill rendered great service to King Niall. Belphira was esteemed by all for bringing about so wondrous and admirable a change—by all save Lord Derain Meschante, who contrived his utmost to come between the lovers and their happiness.

"I loathed Meschante," Belphira said, her soft lips trembling as they formed the despised name. "Loathed his coarseness, his bigotry, the dirty smallness of his mind. And ever as Guyon's reputation for greatness increased, Meschante's hatred grew with it. Fortunately, all unlike Guy, Meschante had few if any friends—only Prince Hylas, whose kindness to him was little more than pity and forbearance. But the prince had never been strong in health, and soon sickened of a disease the doctors had neither name for nor cure, and so died. Instantly Meschante accused Guyon of murder by sorcery, a ridiculous accusation that none believed."

"Sorcery?" Ryel asked. "What do you mean?"

"Double-handed people seem to draw their kind to them," Belphira said, looking from Ryel to Priam as she spoke. "Guyon never strove to disguise his ambidexterity, any more than I do my own. But it is a trait strongly associated with enchantments and witchcraft, and Meschante was loud in his insistence that Guyon's black arts had proved Hylas' death. King Niall and Queen Amaranthe, disgusted by such outrageous slanders, had Meschante exiled from the court. Guyon's heart was broken by the death of the prince, who had been to him dearer than a brother. Grief made him desolate and restless, until in the end he could no longer bear it, nor could I help him. For I know well that in the matter of one man's grief for another, a woman's sympathy is useless. He left Ralnahr to soldier in the pay of the Domina Bradamaine, fighting in her war against the White Barbarians. Without him I could no longer bear the Northern cold, and returned to this place. He and I have not met again since. That was seven years ago."

She fell silent. After a time Priamnor spoke.

"Continue your story, my lady."

"That is all of my tale, dear my lord," Belphira said gently. "To end it, I can only say that to have known the love of Guy Desrenaud was the first joy I had ever felt in my life. Until this moment, I had resigned myself to believing it the last."

So I've found one of the two, the wysard thought, his pulse again a-rush. *Surely the mysterious Redbane cannot be far behind.* Aloud he said, as calmly as he could, "And does Lord Guyon still soldier in the North?"

With a sigh Belphira shook her head. "No. He had not been but two years in Hryeland when he committed an impardonable act of treason against the Domina and then deserted the army of which he was lieutenant-general, fleeing the Barrier in secret."

Damn the luck, Ryel thought, bitterly checked.

Belphira looked toward the mirror of the moon. As she gazed, bright silver welled up in her eyes and spilled down, hidden by her mask. But then she remembered the place she was, and the men she spoke to. Instantly she dried her eyes, and brightly smiled once more.

"I entertain you very badly, my lords Diomenor and Redestens. Let us turn the talk to some other matter. All the news in this city is of the prophet Michael, who in his loathing of the flesh sounds even worse than Meschante. What are your thoughts concerning him?"

"Tell us yours, first," Ryel said.

Belphira smiled wryly. "I think Michael knows full well how much black rags, close shaving, and bare feet become him, and I think every rip in his raiment and every smear of dirt on his face are arranged with care and forethought." Her smile faded, then. "And I think he is very, very dangerous. The folk of the Fourth District hang upon his every word, and with reason."

Ryel observed how Priamnor's lips tightened to a line. "Tell me of that, my lady," the Sovran said.

With a jeweled hand Belphira indicated the brilliant revels going on about them. "Here we are, my lord, amid all that the world can offer in the way of delight," she said. "But at this very moment, little children of both sexes are being unspeakably used in a place scornfully called the Dog's Ward by the rich of this city. Many others are undergoing every kind of perverse torment and humiliation for a few small coins." She gazed upon Priam's face, searchingly. "That alarms you? You did not know?"

"I did not know," Priamnor murmured. Ryel caught all of the pain in those four whispered words, as did Belphira.

"Few among the elite of this city know of the Fourth District's ills," the beautiful courtesan said. "Few, save for those who take base advantage of them. The new Sovran of Destimar would do well to learn the truth."

"I will make certain that he does," Priamnor replied.

"I believe you will," Belphira said. At that moment a servant approached and whispered something in her ear, at which she nodded and rose to her feet. "I have talked far too long, and forgotten an appointment," she said as the servant departed. "I am expected in one of this house's banqueting-rooms to sing for the guests."

"Then we will not detain you," Priam said, standing with her. "But accept this, with my deepest thanks." As he spoke, he took from his finger his only ring. "For a lady of your riches, this token is as nothing, but it may serve as a charm to open a door."

Accepting the jewel, Belphira contemplated it silently. She seemed to think now of joy, now of sorrow. "One unlocking demands another, lest you later think your generosity ill-advised." With those words she removed her mask, disclosing a face of empyrean beauty. "Such am I now, still unaided by the surgeon's art. But five years ago some thought me fair."

"They were very wise who did," Priamnor said, dwelling on the dark green eyes, the rich hair of heavy gold, the noble yet sensuous sweetness of every feature. "And they have yet more reasons now." Taking both her hands in his, he touched his lips to them, but his eyes as they again met hers mingled misgiving with desire. "Five years ago I thought myself a man. But now ... "

His voice faltered. She gazed up at him, seeing far past the mask. "This moment was enough," she whispered. "And it will always be, whatever comes after." She freed her hands from his, but only to strip off every one of her many rings and cast them down like litter. She slipped the Sovran's jewel onto her finger, and held out her hand to him. "It fits as if made for me."

"Because it was." Taking her hand, Priam drew her to him, and bent to her lips. Their kiss lasted no more than a moment, but promised infinities.

"Come to me. Soon."

Priam had spoken in a whisper, and Belphira replied as softly, "I will."

Taking their leave of that house, the wysard and the Sovran once more regained the Jewel Path, which had grown more tumultuous now than ever.

"We'll never last the night unless we have some chal," Priamnor said, blinking wine-weary eyes in recognition of a shop-sign. "And here's just the place to find some."

Soon they were sipping from vaporing bowls at a pavilion over-hanging the canal, somewhat retired from their fellow revellers like-wise seeking a respite from excess.

Priamnor swirled his chal-cup, studying the jade-colored liquid. "In my years of seclusion I never forgot the beauty of Belphira Deva's singing. I used to hear it in dreams." He looked up. "I loved her, Ryel. Tonight I realized I still do. But I was once able to show my feelings ... entirely."

Ryel hardly knew how to reply. "From what I sense in Belphira, the spirit is of far greater significance to her than is the flesh."

Priam gave a close-mouthed ironic laugh. "She is a woman, ilandrakis, a woman of great beauty and strong passions. He that would win her heart—and all the rest—must be a man in every sense." Before Ryel could speak, Priamnor continued, seemingly off the subject. "I had forgotten my father's sindretin. But now I recall that Guyon Desrenaud was remarkably well-made, with an animal vi-rility I remember being jealous of, boy that I was." He swirled the chal meditatively. "Belphira has never forgotten him, but I must. My present concern is for the people of the Fourth District, and the ter-rible degradations they suffer. It shames me that I never knew until now of their troubles. No wonder they are discontented, and readily give ear to the fanatic Michael."

"He will only become more powerful," Ryel replied. "You have never visited the Fourth District?"

"Never," Priamnor said. "But I will, and soon."

"To see it truthfully, you should go in disguise."

"Wise advice. I'd be glad of more of your counsel—and I'm sure you think I need it."

Ryel shrugged."Well, you have, after all, lived an unusually privileged life—"

Priam faintly grimaced. "Sheltered, you would say."

"In some respects, yes," the wysard agreed. "You'll need to be careful in your choice of advisers. What you most require is an able chief minister. Someone you can trust entirely."

Priamnor nodded gravely, but then he smiled. "I've already found one. But I warn you, you'll have your hands full."

Ryel knocked over his chal-cup. Patiently the Sovran of Destimar poured the wysard's cup full again, set the chaltak aside, and continued in all seriousness. "I had planned to ask you after tonight, but why not now? Stay here in my city, Ryel Mirai. Stay, and take your place as my closest adviser. We will rule Destimar together, even as Diomenor and Redestens ruled the imperial realm of Kasrinagal."

The wysard looked away, glad of his mask. "You honor me far too greatly, most exalted."

"Don't call me that," Priam said, impatiently. "You are more exalted still, in a City far greater than mine. But answer."

Deeply embarrassed, Ryel cast about for a fit reply. "The honors you would confer upon me are befitting only to one of your family, most ex—"

"Never call me that again. You *are* of my family."

Ryel froze all over; froze and burnt. "Not possible."

"Try to believe that after you hear these facts," Priamnor said. "Shortly after we met, you let fall that your mother's maiden name was Stradianis. As it happens, her name figures in the Dranthene archives."

The wysard could only blink. "But why?"

"You may have heard that your grandmother the Countess Ysandra was a great beauty in her youth. My father's youngest brother Mycenas was her most ardent admirer, and continued to be so even after her marriage to Ulrixos Stradianis ... who was an old man at the time, and rumored incapable of siring children."

The wysard colored hot. "What proof have you of our kinship other than the archives?"

"Evidence of a highly specific and physical nature," Priam replied. "Certain characteristics of the Dranthene bloodline breed true in every generation. In the archives it is further recorded that when your mother was one year old, she was presented at the Temple of Demetropa, as are all children of Almancar. The priestess who examined her observed that the little girl had several traits peculiar to the Dranthene."

Ryel swallowed. "And what were they?"

"The eye color, first of all," Priam replied. "They had a hint of violet not common anywhere in Destimar save with my family. You have those eyes, Ryel."

The wysard glanced away. "That isn't enough."

"You might not have noticed the shape of your mother's ears, but this configuration is pure Dranthene." And reaching out, Priamnor gently flicked one of the wysard's lobes. "Mine are exactly similar. More significant still, there's your response to Transcendence, which cured you after that terrible night with the daimon. None but the Dranthene are physically affected by the scent. A final conclusive test is severe intolerance for cats—all the Dranthene are deathly allergic to those animals, which are strictly banned from the Diamond Heaven. But I half wish there were a cat nearby now, so that I might test you and be sure—"

"I'm glad there's not," Ryel said. "I'd sneeze myself silly."

Priam stared open-mouthed and Ryel laughed, and then they were both laughing. The young Sovran reached out, and the wysard met him halfway.

"I knew it from the start," Priamnor said as they embraced. "Knew it from that first look."

"I felt it, too," Ryel replied, his heart full.

"Then you'll stay."

"I must," the wysard said. "You need me now more than you could ever imagine."

Priam drew away to study Ryel's face, startled by the sudden gravity of his tone. "What do you mean?"

"The prophet Michael is no mere demagogue, Priam. He serves the daimon that took your sister captive."

The young Sovran's smile vanished, and he grayed under his pearl-dust. "But then he is ... "

Ryel nodded. "A wysard, even as I am—a lord adept of Elecambron, with strength to equal my own. His Master has sent him here to incite first discontent in Almancar, then insurrection throughout the realm."

The young Sovran of Destimar grew pale. "Then this land is in great danger."

"Not just Destimar, Priam. The World."

"Then what help is there?"

At that despairing question Ryel put his hand on his kinsman's wrist. "There's me," he said. "Me, and my Art."

Priamnor's eyes held Ryel's, ineffably gentle and grave. "Ah, cousin. What a hollow fiction the demigod Redestens seems compared to you. But come, let us return at once to the palace that you may tell me more."

"What of your promise to the ladies at the Garden of Dreams?"

The Sovran's mouth quirked half-exasperated beneath the mask's edge. "I had forgotten them. But I gave my word, after all. Well, we'll visit them a moment—but only that I may drink your health, and celebrate your decision to remain in Almancar."

They were welcomed eagerly at the Realm of Joy, where the rooftop was crowded with revellers far less decorous than those of the Dream Garden. The Sovran and the wysard were soon drawn into a tumultuous dance, with laughing courtesans on either hand. Sometime during the dance Ryel was wooed away by yet another beauty to join in a glass of frangin. As he sipped the liquid green fire he watched Priamnor, who had called for a somewhat slower tune and now led the others in an Almancarian zarvana, partnered by the fairest lady of the house.

"Ah, but he is beautiful," breathed the lady at Ryel's side. "Is he not?"

Ryel could only nod, but it was not of Priam he thought. He set his glass aside that suddenly weighed his hand like lead. Dagar lurked in the night, preventing all remembrance of Diara, but feelings took the place of memory a thousandfold. Ryel felt the same torment he had known that night in the desert outside the walls of Almancar, after the vision of the Sovrena had left him, the same helpless, aching need.

The lady at his side took his hand. "Come with me," she whispered. "There is someone who most deeply desires to speak with you."

The courtesan led him from the rooftop down the stairs and into a wide columned corridor dimly lit, lined with doors. Behind many of the doors came sighs and murmurs that made the wysard shudder and burn.

"Here," the lady said. She opened a portal, motioning Lagan inside.

Ryel wavered on the threshold. "What awaits me?"

Soft plumes brushed his face as the lady murmured in his ear. "The fulfillment of your desire, my lord. Stay and make ready, and it will soon come to you."

With those mysterious tantalizing words she departed. Ryel found himself in an apartment furnished with every magnificence, where great mirrors reflected a wide bed. On a table were a ewer and a basin, and Ryel filled the silver vessel, then pulled off his mask to dash water on his face with both hands, seeking to quench his heat. But the water was scented with a fragrance that crassly counterfeited the transcendent essence he had combed into Diara's hair, and he wiped it from his skin in loathing.

A tickling hand touched his shoulder, light as a spider. He whirled around and gave a cry. Diara stood before him—Diara the Sovrena of Destimar, masked and robed in the light livery of the Diamond Heaven.

"No," Ryel whispered hoarsely, recoiling from her. "Get away from me."

She smiled and tossed aside her mask, and let her robes fall. Under a film of lawn her white body glowed like moonlight. Lifting her hands to her head she removed and cast aside the jewelled pins, freeing her dark tresses. "Perhaps this guise is more to your liking," she said.

Ryel's heart beat hard as a memory-flash brought back that night in the desert, outside the walls of Almancar. But still he shrank from her.

"You're not her," the wysard whispered. "You can't be."

She smiled at him half in scorn, half in pride. "Come closer and find out." She held out her hand as if dropping alms. "Many a one would kill for a single touch of this."

She had an imperious self-assurance, an insolent vanity, utterly unlike the artless charm of the girl she so unsettlingly resembled. Her voice, too, was chill and thin, devoid of Diara's soft music, and no violet lights added heavenly graces to the ice-tinged transparency of her eyes. Nevertheless she was beautiful, fair beyond bearing.

Ryel took her hand. For a time he stood motionless, feeling her smooth fingers warm his own. Then suddenly he pulled her into his arms, so hard that she gave a little surprised cry of pain. Her cry instantly altered to a laugh, and she clutched the back of his head, crushing her lips against his, thrusting her tongue into his mouth. Locked and reeling they fell onto the bed, and Ryel reached down to clutch the hem of her shift, yanking it upwards as her legs opened under his to clasp his sides, spur the small of his back, grind damp heat into his groin.

Her hands were in his hair, pulling and tearing. "Fuck me. Fuck my life out."

As the wysard struggled with his robes and cursed them, somewhere on another world came a great crash and a shouting, and then something even stronger than his lust pulled him away from the girl. Blaspheming daimonically he jerked about, and faced Priamnor, and lost his voice.

But Priamnor had all of his and more. "A house full of women and you needs must shame my sister? Is that your kinship, dog?

He struck Ryel across the face, sudden and blinding as lightning "How did you corrupt her? How? Or what sorcerer's drugs did you use?"

Ryel licked the blood from his mouth-corner. It shocked like raw spirit, and he grimaced and spat. "Are you blind? This isn't the Sovrena, but a whore that by chance resembles—"

Another blow, harder and angrier yet. Ryel put his hand to his face. *I'm drunk*, he thought, tenderly feeling the pain throbbing beneath his fingers. *Drunk, and drugged, and ready to kill, and so is he. It's strange.*

He stood up and flung off his Almancarian robe, revealing the Steppes garb hidden by the garish satin. He turned to the giggling trollop on the bed. "Reach me my sword."

She tossed it to him, shrieking with harsh laughter that rivalled the ring of steel as Ryel tore the weapon from its sheath. For a moment Priamnor seemed to freeze at the sight of the naked blade, but then he, too, stripped off his mask and drew.

As they circled, watching their chance, Ryel spoke. "You're all wrong about this, cousin."

"Never call me that again." Priamnor struck aside Ryel's blade and lunged, but the wysard evaded the thrust with no trouble whatever, and could have taken instant and fatal advantage of the Sovran's loss of balance caused by treacherous trailing silk. But something held him back.

I don't want this to end, he thought. *Not just yet.*

Something had to take the place of lust, while he was still hot— something just as urgent and insane. This would do beautifully. Priam was the perfect adversary, good but not quite good enough, easy to hold at bay, push aside, beat back. It made the wysard laugh, this risky sarabande fought to the shrill music of a slut's laughter.

"Cut him!" the harlot screamed to Priamnor. "Say this!" She yelled out a word that clanged like clashed metal. With a raw shout Priamnor repeated the word as his sword shot forward. Razored steel drove deep into the wysard's side in a thrust of amazing pain, and Ryel cried out, his echoing howl throbbing in red waves against his eardrums. Somehow his hand found its own way to the wound, and struggled to wrestle back the blood that broke from around its palm in a flood of slow fire. Instinctively the wysard grunted a staunching-word as he dropped to his knees, head bowed, blind with agony. All at once the air shut in around him, driving the breath from his body.

"Finish him! " the whore screamed. "Gash his throat!"

With sickening effort Ryel turned toward the bed. In the harlot's shrieking laughing face the eyes were entire black, hard as onyx. Ryel stared and trembled.

"Priam," he panted, choking on the blood in his throat. "Priam, look at her. Only look. Can't you see it's the daimon? Can't you—"

Priamnor Dranthene swung his red-drenched blade aloft in both hands. "Let this shut your mouth, warlock!"

"You bastard," Ryel whispered, but he was not speaking to the Sovran. Flinging himself forward, he drove his shoulder into Priamnor's knees. The Sovran staggered back, hitting the wall and falling hard.

"Murder!" the false Diara screamed. "The Sovran of Destimar has been killed! Help, someone!"

"Bitch," Ryel hissed. But the bitch's eyes were blue now, and the air had lightened. Momentarily regenerated by a few famished lungfuls, the wysard threw on his flame-colored robe, then yanked the cloak and mask from Priamnor's unresisting body and donned them headlong, and made his escape even as the hallway's many doors began to open and half-clad courtesans and their gallants emerged in every state of confusion and undress.

Once on the Jewel Path the wysard hesitated, catching his breath through gritted teeth. Some noticed him but only smiled, believing him merely drunk. He edged and excused his way through the crush, ever smiling lest he arouse suspicion, but the burning throb in his side froze his face into a rictus. In the courtyard of the Temple of Atlan yet another rout of maskers was assembling for the midnight service, and Ryel struggled past them. Stumbling down the steps of the temple into the courtyard, he found Jinn waiting where he'd tied her. Such was the stringency of Almancar's laws that his saddlebags were untouched, but revellers had twined roses in the mare's mane. Unable to mount, the wysard clung to Jinn's neck, guiding her toward the gardens and a deserted grove with its lanterns still burning. With the help of the gay little lights Ryel found that Priamnor had stabbed him just under the ribs of his right side, deep enough to reach any number of crucial veins and vitals.

"Good work," he muttered. "You'll make a warrior yet, ilandrakis."

He flung aside his mask and lay down in the grass to breathe in the fresh air of the night, staring up at the dainty lamps, unsure if a stray breeze or disorienting agony was making them sway. For the first time since leaving the Aqqar, he missed his City.

I can't heal this, he thought, more than a little amazed at his detachment. *All I can do for myself is either ease the pain and bleed to death, or stop the blood and lie here trying not to scream. Not a World of choice. Not a World of hope.*

He would have liked to sleep. The night air was warm, the grass soft and fragrant as Diara's hair, sweet against his cheek, but it hurt too much to sleep.

"I was going to stay with you, ilandrakis," he whispered, his eyes afire. "We were going to rule Destimar together. We—"

The air crushed in around him, squeezing like a great snake, and he gasped and strangled as the hated voice crooned in the middle of his brain.

You've made this city too hot to hold you, sweet eyes. Time to escape, while you yet can.

"No," Ryel panted. "I'll talk to Priam. Tell him the truth."

He won't listen, beauty. I can assure you he won't—not with the ideas I've put in his pretty head.

"You bastard."

The voice only laughed. *At any rate, you haven't time to find him. You're dying, but your healer awaits you at the western gates.*

Ryel spat yet more blood. "I'll never get there."

Oh, but you will.

Ryel groaned. "How?"

You know how. Go.

Before Ryel could say or think another word, the air lifted and cooled. Drawing a starved breath, the wysard lay and gathered his will.

I know what to do, he thought, gritting his teeth. *I only hope my healer does.*

Tightening the wide sash of his Almancarian robe hard over the

wound, he whispered the pain-allaying spell. Instantly his blood
burst forth, but he felt only its spreading heat as he pushed himself
up from the ground. Moving as quickly as he might, he swung into
the saddle and muttered the staunching-word. The pain came back
like a fresh thrust from a sharper blade, and he groaned. Alternating
spells in favor of bleeding when torment made him sway too much,
he rode half-senseless through a pale blur of streets and walls, a wel-
ter of crowds and voices. The streets began to close in upon him,
and the voices called out, offering horrible pleasures. Now and again
a painted child with drugged eyes was thrust in his way.

Suddenly a wild shouting, deep and strange, wakened him from
his pain-dream.

"Blight is on this city! The corruption of courts, the whoredoms
of false Atlan! Blight and doom!"

The ragged black fanatic Michael now stood in the courtyard before the western gates haranguing the crowd, which was large
though the hour was late because of the caravans making ready to
leave or enter the city. Drivers and muleteers, drudgers and toilers
stood in a rapt throng, thralled with every loud mad word.

"Death!" Michael exulted. "Death is upon this city of whores
and wastrels! Death upon those gilded degenerates, and their vain
idols of the guts and groin! Even as you stand here, torn from a
weary bed to sweat and haul, your high nobility swaggers and riots
in the whore's quarter—but the Master has compassion on your suf-
ferings, and has taken his first step toward vengeance! Your stripling
Sovran Priamnor lies at this moment in some house of lust, senseless
from debauchery and worse, far worse!"

Risking the blood-loss, Ryel stunned his pain with the right
words, halted Jinn, and glared at the grim preacher. Michael suddenly ceased his diatribe and his empty eyes again met Ryel's. His
hard lips parted in a daimon-grin, and his nostrils flared as if he
scented blood and liked what he smelled. Dismissing his listeners
with a peremptory gesture he approached Ryel who scarce could
keep the saddle, and grinned up at him with teeth white as stars,
eyes black as empty space. "Well met, my lord brother."

Michael spoke now in his native tongue, harsh gutteral

Hryelesh. "Get away from me," Ryel muttered in Risma dialect, incapable of any other language.

Amazingly, Michael understood. "All in good time, Steppes gypsy." The Elecambronian said a single Art-word stronger than any of Ryel's, undoing both spells. Torture and blood alike overwhelmed the wysard, and he reeled as the deep music of Michael's voice engulfed him in velvet hell.

"Take it like a man, Markulit. A mere man, this time."

Drained past all speech, Ryel impotently struck at the grimy hand on Jinn's bridle. With a laughed curse Michael pulled him down and slammed him against Jinn's side, ignoring his gurgles of agony. They were alone now in the shadow of a wall, with no help nearby even if Ryel had had the strength to shout for it.

Hot breath and cruel mockery burnt Ryel's ear while hands irresistibly strong tore open his robes. "So what became of you, gypsy? Wounded at the brothel district were you, brawling for a slut? You shouldn't be where you don't belong, sweet brother of chaste Markul. Where's the pain—here?"

Dirty fingers thrust into Ryel's side, deep into the gash, while the other hand clamped over his mouth and stifled both shrieks and retchings. With inhuman cruelty Michael clutched the wound, wringing the lacerated flesh as he growled spell-words in his throat. Never had Ryel known that kind of pain. It was like burning coals being driven into his body. Dirty wool blackness overcame him and he collapsed, but arms hard and hot as white-forged steel hauled him upright again.

"Thank me, Markulit. You'll yet live, and work the Master's will."

Ryel shuddered and gasped, but suddenly the pain vanished like a rat down a hole. Stunned by his deliverance, the wysard felt himself going limp in that loathed yet imperative embrace, too weak to move or think. His mind emptied dry, and the only things that came to fill its void were Jinn's anxious whickering, the acid scorch of vomit in his throat, rank dominance conferring the merciless essential encirclement of cruel white arms, and low-toned music soft with rage, borne on breath wonderfully and bewilderingly sweet.

"Your strength is nothing to mine, Markulit—I could break you like a reed. I begged the Master to take me and use me as He would, but He wants only you—a weakling boy who can't even survive a scratch, much less cure it. Do you still hurt?"

"No."

The arms unlocked, leaving Ryel dizzy and cold. "Get out, then, Markulit, while you still have time. But first take this, that the Master bade me send you."

Michael seized Ryel's head in both his hands, kissing his mouth with savage ferocity. At that kiss the wysard again blanked into blackness, but in another moment came to and wildly looked about him. His grim tormenter and savior had disappeared. Ryel leaned against the wall dazed and spent, still breathing the reek of Michael's sweat, tasting the baffling sweetness of that breath, licking the bruises on his lips left by those white teeth. He put his hand to his side, dreading the pain that would surely erupt from the touch, but none came. With increasing boldness and disbelief he explored the place where Priamnor had stabbed him, that now betrayed no hurt whatever. Jerking his robes away, he found only a dried red smear where the wound had been. He felt no weakness, despite all the blood he'd lost, and none of that blood had left any stain on his Steppes garments, although his torn flame-colored silken robe was drenched with it.

"By every god." He stroked his side and found all his flesh smooth and whole. But he had little time to marvel at Lord Michael's cure, for the shouts of the city guard reminded him of that he was still in danger. With all haste he flung off his stained Almancarian finery, then re-mounted as a Steppes horseman spurring toward the gates of the city.

Although only false dawn had broken, the western portal of Almancar was open and teeming with traffic of departing and arriving caravans. Behind him Ryel heard soldiers shouting for the gate-wardens to stop anyone who sought to get through, but Jinn's wild gallop forced all who stood near to leap aside.

A commanding shout rang loud, deep as a death-knell. "Stop that rider! He has killed the Sovran!"

The voice was Michael's. Before anyone could mount and follow, Jinn was scouring the desert road toward the mountains, the night-wind her only rival.

Chapter Ten

Ryel raced toward the foothills of Kalima, plunging for cover into one of the clumped groves of stunted trees. Once hidden he dismounted, throwing himself on the ground and burying his head in his arms, his eyes throbbing.

He rolled over, dry leaves crackling under him. Numbly he contemplated the sky, now brightening as the dawn came up. For some time he lay distraught, his ideas confused and desperate. He had never felt more tired. Perhaps if he just rested a little while ...

When he awoke, he had no idea how long he'd slept. Less than a couple of hours from the look of the sun in the heavens, but much longer than that from the way his body felt. His eyes were all but gummed together, his mouth felt like a cave full of bat droppings, and he was ravenously hungry. He'd neither time nor water to make the chal he longed for, but while searching Jinn's saddlebags he found a packet of lakh and a blessed little flask of frangin, surely tucked there in secret by Nelora. They made a delicious breakfast, and Ryel soon felt a surge of energy from the tart liquor and the sugary sweets. Inwardly thanking his little sister as he remounted, he began the ascent of Kalima and the seach for Srin Yan Tai.

Taking care to make his way unobserved, Ryel cut across the winding roads until he had left the jewel-mines behind him. The road upward stretched forth deserted, and he might make as much use of it as he wished. Instead he steered Jinn into the trees, giving himself up to the woods. He had no desire to make use of his enchanted mare's swiftness. Instead he needed the solitude, the fresh unhindered growth, and the shaded coolness after Almancar's cloudless heat and endless stir of buy and sell. He needed silence and meditation after the violence of the night before. Most of all he needed fresh green hope after gray despair, for his soul's healing.

This was his first forest. All his life, both in the Steppes and in Markul, he had dwelt on empty land. Now he entered the woods with reverence, as if crossing the threshold of a temple. The trees of the desert surrounding Almancar had been dwarfed and ill-formed, but those of the mountains loomed free of any curse. The great-girthed trunks towered upward, mingling together their high boughs, while at their roots long needles covered the ground and cushioned Jinn's gait to muffled thuds. Fully a hundred yards high were those great trees, and between their first branches and the ground was room enough for a horse and rider to pass with many feet of space to spare. The early sunlight pierced the heavy foliage in glowing shafts, making dappled gold patches on the ground, and the still air breathed a clean wild fragrance of pitch. A stream tumbled past, its live water shimmering in the light, and Ryel leapt down for a much-needed drink. When he had finally quenched his thirst, he threw water on his face, wishing that he might as easily wash away the excesses and evils of the night before.

All that day and the next Ryel spent among the trees. He began to climb more than he rode, testing his legs against the unaccustomed steepness of the slope. At night he sat in meditation, wrapped in Edris' cloak and clutching a hot bowlful of chal against the keen air of the mountains. Water was plentiful owing to the many snow-fed streams, and food he had enough, thanks to his mother's insistence—horseman's rations of peppery dried slices of antelope and thin wedges of grain-dense bread, only a little crumbled from being wedged into a corner of his saddlebags. Quietly he tended his fire, listening to the furtive scurryings of the night-feeders, the cries of owls, waiting for Dagar's loathed voice to invade his mind like some corrupt ooze, but it did not. Too relieved at the deliverance to wonder at it, the wysard turned his thoughts to Srin Yan Tai.

Ryel had never met Lady Srin, who had left Markul some time before his arrival. Of her skill, however, he had heard and read much. Hers was deep thaumaturgy, dealings with the Outer World that went beyond mere summonings and commands. Like him she had seen the edge of the Abyss and been marred by it, and like his, her eyes were empty black. She was of the Steppes, even as Ryel, but farther to the east and north, in the Elqhiri Kugglaitan. Hers was warrior's blood, high and stark, and she had been in her youth, now long past, a redoubtable fighter. Equally accustomed to grimmest hardship as well as most flagrant luxury had she been, in those days: strong of will as of body, yet beautiful beyond telling, and fond of the delights of the flesh—of wine and mandragora, lovers and gold, dainty food and fine havings. None of these had been able to satisfy her at any depth, and therefore out of sheer restlessness she had come to Markul in her fiftieth year, riding up in armor of gold and steel to demand entrance.

Many had watched her from the walls, and one of them had been Edris, who had described the sight in his Book: "A voice like the booming of a bell she had, and black hair down to her waist, fantastically knotted. And when she stripped to enter the City we were all of us amazed, for hers was the body of a girl of twenty, but muscled and strong. Too strong for my taste—too much shoulder and not enough hip and buttock, and breasts like the wrist-shields her people use to ward away arrows, hard as bronze."

I'll certainly know her when I see her, Ryel thought. *Now if only I can find her.*

On the second day the slope steepened even more, and when Ryel again came to the road, he found it shrunk to a mere path. Clearly few if any travellers had made use of the Kalima route for some time, but Ryel noted that a horse and rider had journeyed westward to only a day or so before, riding at a hard gallop whenever the ground allowed. The imprint of the horseshoes bore a cipher, and Ryel knelt to examine it.

"A messenger of the imperial house of Destimar," the wysard murmured, feeling his voice catch.

He went back into the trees, fleeing the sight of those tracks and the memories they evoked, centering his thoughts on Srin Yan Tai.

"You know someone's looking for you," he said, his eyes shut hard in concentration. "That much I can sense. Now let yourself be found. I have to know—"

Jinn halted so hard she nearly threw him. Lurching out of his trance the wysard scrambled for balance, cursing energetically. Then he saw what Jinn had stopped for, and swore again, now breath-lessly.

He had wandered into a hollow set in Kalima's side, and found a wondrous place. A fair large green field stretched between two em-bracing arms of rock, and in the midst of this field was set a lake little more than a pond. In the midst of the lake lay a grassy flowery island perhaps fifty feet across, and in the midst of the island rose a single tree that seemed to Ryel a great slim-wristed hand holding aloft a bubble of cinnabar silk. The deliberate fantasy of the place made Ryel smile, and he urged Jinn into the glassy water that he might cross to the island. Scarcely had Jinn ventured a hoof than the stream erupted as if a thousand snakes were fighting to the death therein, boiling hot as molten iron. The horse reared back, shrilling terror, and Ryel hurtled through a vivid swirl of blue and green and cinnabar before crashing into red darkness.

Steel, sharp and cold against his throat, choked him into con-sciousness. Squinting upward, the wysard found himself straddled by a tall broad-shouldered figure obscure against the sun, clad in the way of the Kugglaitana Steppes. One of its hands held his sword, the other his horse.

"Talk, you prying whoreson," boomed his captor's voice. "And say it in three words, or die squealing."

Ryel groaned. "Srin Yan Tai."

The sword was tossed aside, the horse set free. Yanked to his feet by an inexorable arm, Ryel looked into empty black eyes set in a wonderful face.

The voice boomed again. "So—you finally showed up. What took you, whelp?"

Ryel stared. No one but Edris had ever called him that. "You know me?"

Lady Srin laughed at him. "I've seen you naked as my hand, lad. I know all about that mole on the right side of your groin. But come on—it's time for food and fire. I speared a young boar this morning, and it's been seething ever since."

"But—"

"Later, later. In good time. Follow me."

Stepping-stones led to the island's shore—chunks of rock crystal, invisible in the transparent white-sanded water. Jinn hung back and would not be persuaded to cross.

"Just as well," Lady Srin said. "I dislike the notion of my flowers being trampled—although at least with this horse there'd be no horseapples."

Ryel stared. "How did you know—"

"I know everything, whelp. Let her be, and come on."

The boar stew simmered in an earth oven. Once unburied and uncovered, it sent up a delicious vapor. "Good," said Lady Srin, stirring it with her dagger. "Bring it and we'll eat."

Fortunately, climbing the tree was easier than Ryel had forseen, even with the encumbrance of a heavy and bubbling-hot cauldron. Steps invisible to the casual eye accomodated him wherever he chanced to set his foot, and in a moment he had joined Lady Srin on the platform supporting the tent.

"It's a fine day. We'll eat here."Lady Srin ducked inside the tent, emerging with plates and cups and wine. The plates were silver, the cups gold, and the wine red and strong. The two wysards filled their vessels and ate side by side, crosslegged at the platform's edge. Too hungry for talk, Ryel fell to with grateful good will.

"An unusual mode of living for one bred on the Steppes, this of yours," he said after a time. "A tent in a tree, with mountains all about."

Lady Srin shrugged. "A yat's a yat."

"How do you know I'm the son of Edris?" Ryel asked.

"I helped him bring you into the world. I've seen you in my Glass on every one of your birthdays," Lady Srin answered, filling their goblets again with dark red wine, lifting hers to the wysard, and giving a wide flash of grin. "I'm your magic godmother, lad."

A shock of memory struck Ryel like a bolt. "Was it you that—"

"That saved you during a lightning-storm when you were twelve? The very same, lad. You'll hear the whole story in good time. For now, we eat."

Lady Srin must have been seventy years of age by now, but her face had barely a wrinkle. Folk in her part of the World kept their youth longer than did those of other places, and she had the advantages of Art to preserve her looks. Her smooth bronze visage was slant and heavy of eyelid, jutting of cheekbone, wide across the brow—a beautiful barbaric mask plundered for its jewel-inlaid eyes. Those eyes had been pale gray, like moonstones, according to what Ryel had read in the chronicles of Markul. As for the hair, it still hung in long narrow braids and loops, but now the lustrous darkness was streaked with silver. Her clothing was manlike and splendid. An outlandish and gorgeous figure she made as she sat in her tented tree, spearing chunks of meat with her dagger-point and quaffing down her wine.

But picturesque as the wysardess and her home were, Ryel felt disquiet. "You don't seem too well protected in this place," he observed, looking from her to the land beyond, where Almancar lay glowing.

Lady Srin shook her head. "Few eyes indeed think of prying here—although now that I recall it, in the past a few over-curious interlopers were boiled alive in my moat. Since then I've made use of a strong spell-fence to keep undesirables out."

"I felt it, but I got through."

She only snorted. "You were meant to, whelp." She ran a many-ringed finger around her empty plate, licking it with relish. "Time for talk. Let's go inside—evenings get cold this high up."

Lady Srin's tent was much larger within than it seemed without. Furniture there was none, nor any decoration save an array of painted and gilded chests and strongboxes—and a brightly tiled Almancarian stove, which gave Ryel a brief but acute pang of homesickness.

"Yes," said Lady Srin, observing the wysard's interest as she filled a kettle with water and set it on the tiles. "Handy inventions, these."

"You might have heated your tent with the Art."

The wysardess' lips—still full despite almost a century of sneers—curled in disdain. "As if I'd waste my powers on piffling silly trifles. Have you perhaps noticed that the World is not Markul?"

Ryel leaned forward. "Tell me about the storm when I was twelve."

"In time, in time. Impatient youth." Srin Yan opened the door of the stove and extracted some glowing coals which she placed on brazen dish. "Fasten the tent-flap tight."

Ryel did so, and turned back to see Lady Srin throw a gray-green handful of crumbled herbs on the coals. Instantly a thick smoke arose and filled the tent with a provocative redolence somewhere between stench and perfume. Lady Srin knelt over the smoke, breathing deeply with her hands on her knees.

"Ah. Now we can talk as friends, easy and unforced," she said. "I trust my herb is to your liking."

"Seldom have I made use of mandragora," Ryel replied, a little misgivingly. "It is a mystic's drug, productive only of dreams and visions."

"It's good for you." Lady Srin Yan opened a chest, extracting from it porcelain bowls and a silver box. Taking some jade-dark powder from the box, she dropped it into the water on the stove. A subtle fragrant vapor mingled with the mandragora haze. Soon they were sipping chal, and Ryel again asked his question, or began to.

"Tell me about the storm. Was it foretold?"

Lady Srin nodded almost matter-of-factly. "Where you're concerned, nothing happens by accident, lad."

"How did you know to come to my help?"

"I'd had premonitions. Dreams. And I just happened to be in the neighborhood." She poured herself more chal, and her next words were a question, a strange one. "How many elements are there, whelp?"

"According to the ancients, four," Ryel said, mystified. "Earth, fire, air and water. But why—"

"Just so. And elemental forces have worked on you, Ry. When the lightning struck you in your twelfth year, you took to yourself the powers of water and air. Your rival Michael likewise had an elemental epiphany, but his came later in life, during one of those endless Northern wars. He was captured by some of the barbarian enemy, bound hand and foot and thrown into a deep-dug grave brimful of fire. Needless to say, those tender attentions were meant to confer an excruciating death, but Michael rose up from the flames not only quite alive, but utterly unhurt. Thus began his affinities for fire and earth."

Ryel recalled his own effortless submerged swimming in the Eastern Palace with never a need to take breath. "Is Michael impervious to fire, then?"

"Yes, even as you are to water. And your Mastery, if well-wrought, can compell the weather as you wish. But Michael's capabilities are much more dangerous—as you'd expect. Earthquakes come to mind, and holocausts, and whatever other disaster you please."

"By every god," Ryel murmured.

Lady Srin gave a wry grunt of laugh. "No amount of gods are going to help you, lad."

"Who—or what—conferred these powers upon us?"

"I hope, whelp, that eventually *you'll* enlighten *me*. Well, enough of that—now tell me about the death of the old Sovran, how you healed Diara, and your fight with Priamnor."

Ryel stared at her. "How could you have known about my going to Almancar? By what Art—"

"It didn't take Art." Lady Srin leaned back, benign with mandragora, and smiled on the wysard as if about to reveal a most amusing secret. "By the way, did you know you're dead?"

The wysard received this news very blankly. "What?"

The wysardess grinned with much self-satisfaction. "At least as far as young Priamnor Dranthene is concerned, you've been a corpse since yesterday, when the imperial guard took your body back to Almancar. Your very dead, horribly mutilated body." In her maddening way Lady Srin poured herself some more chal, sat comfortably with her back against a rug-covered chest, and spoke at complete leisure. "Actually, it was the body of an Almancarian messenger—one of Priamnor's elite soldiery. Some robbers caught and killed this particular courier, but I doubt they enriched themselves much. Imperial envoys ride light. I found the poor lad's corpse quite by accident, with the letter still upon him. You'll have to excuse the bloodstains—he was carrying it under his shirt, next to his skin."

Ryel remembered the hoof-marks with the Dranthene cypher that he'd seen during his climb up Kalima, and felt his heart constrict with regret for that young officer, galloping headlong to his death. "Who was the letter meant for?"

"No one but you, lad."

Ryel felt very confused. "But Lady Srin, only yesterday I was in Almancar. It isn't possible that—"

"No, no, lad. A couple of days ago you were there, very true."

"But how ... in the name of All, did I really sleep two entire days?"

"You did, much to the good of your health. Almancar had worn you out. Too much stimulation, specifically in the area of daimon-dealings and debauchery. I decided you needed a bit of rest, and did the necessary things to make sure you got it."

"I wish you hadn't," the wysard replied, not caring if his resentment showed. "You made me waste time."

"Nothing was wasted, whelp." Lady Srin regarded the wysard's stunned face with serene complacency. "Thanks to your little nap, matters turned out very well. From Priamnor's missive I was able to deduce your activities in Almancar, and thus had your remains ready to hand over to the soldiers when they came searching for you yesterday. Fortunately the courier was tall and slim enough to resemble you exactly once stripped of his uniform, cut under his right ribs, modified here and there with a touch of Mastery, and left under a hot sun for awhile."

"It'd better be a convincing fraud," the wysard said, looking away. "Priamnor and I have swum together."

"As I've said, I know your every hair," the wysardess serenely—and disconcertingly—reminded him. "At any rate, your advanced state of decomposition will do much to keep the fastidious young Sovran at a safely unsuspecting distance. As far as he's considered, you're an extremely dead man. And I've little doubt he's taking it hard, if this letter's any indication." Lady Srin held out the blood-grimed paper. "Here—it's all yours."

Reluctantly the wysard did so. The first lines made him knit his brows in perplexity.

"It's in code," Lady Srin said, noting his expression. "Not only that, the code translates into the loftiest of High Almancarian. If you need help—"

Ryel did not look up. "I don't."

The wysardess, warned by his tone, fell silent. But ever as he read, Ryel was chagrined to feel Lady Srin's eyes on him, intently assessing every twitch of his face, every change of color.

"To Lord Ryel Mirai, greeting:

"The doublehandedness which embarrassed me at our first meeting has proven of great service now, for my right arm is broken and will take long to heal, and I cannot entrust these words to any scribe. I here employ the most difficult and secret of the imperial ciphers, well aware that no code devised by man is proof against your Markulit skill of wysardry.

"I write this not sure if you are alive or dead. Every moment I relive the excesses of the Diamond Heaven, my drunken madness, your blood drawn by my blade. The daimon's false illusion deceived me, to my everlasting shame. No sooner did I emerge from unconsciousness, my arm broken and my wits clear, than I saw how grossly the courtesan of the Dream Garden counterfeited my sister. For my injury I hold you blameless, only too well aware that I deserved a far worse punishment. I can only hope your Art has saved you, and that my torment of mind will soon be ended by news that you are alive and in health.

"Although greatness such as yours transcends any earthly title, in recognition of our blood-bond I have conferred upon you the rank of Prince of Dalnarma, together with all its privileges and appurtenances. This I will make known to all the rulers of the lands with which Destimar is allied, in hopes of hearing some word of you.

"Since your leaving, my sister has learned of Agenor's daimon-wrought death, and is in deepest mourning. Nevertheless her sorrow is nothing to that of your desolate kinsman,

Priam."

Ryel felt his own eyes scorching. "I broke his arm."

"He hurt you rather worse, from the sounds of it," Lady Srin said. "Although he puts the blame on Dagar. Still, he's made handsome amends by declaring you a Dranthene prince of the blood. Which gives you triple nobility—of the Steppes, of Markul and of Destimar. Not bad."

Ryel wasn't listening. *Priam*, he thought. *Ah, ilandrakis. When you see that body you'll never forgive yourself.*

Lady Serah seemed to have acquired telepathy of a sudden. "Priamnor Dranthene must keep on believing in your death, at least for a while. You have much to accomplish in the World. Very much, lad."

"Too much, maybe." Ryel drew a tired breath. "Edris is Dagar's captive in the Void. I spoke with him. He sent me to you."

Lady Srin nodded, in no way surprised. "That was the plan. I'm the magic godmother with all the answers—or at least some—to help you in your fight. You're going to have to win, young brother, for your sake, and the World's." Lady Srin's empty eyes held the wysard's, unblinking. "Dagar called me as well, long ago. Wanted me for his use, as he wants you—until he apparently decided I was too old, and the wrong sex. He marked me, as he has marked you— his way of putting his seal on those he intends to make use of. That's a surprise to you, I see. Nevertheless, it's fact that no Over-reacher was ever marred in the eyes until Dagar's death."

A long moment she allowed this information to make its impression, then continued. "Dagar kept vigilant watch over the Crossing. The old and unable he maimed or destroyed, and the strong he singled out as his own. Young manhood such as yours surpassed even Dagar's desire. Don't flatter yourself by thinking it's your purity Dagar seeks, your unsullied soul—he craves your flesh. He has burned for you, believe me, ever since he saw you before the walls of our City."

The thought of that covert scrutiny upon his nakedness made Ryel's skin crawl. "Why would Dagar not choose Michael of Elecambron?"

Lady Srin considered. "I'm sure Michael would more than willingly give over his body for Dagar's misuse, and damn his own rai to the Void forever. But the bane of the Red Esserns runs in his blood, and makes him of more use to Dagar as a vassal."

"Bane of the Red Esserns? What do you mean?" Ryel asked.

Lady Srin's brows, straight and heavy, bent hard. "You've never heard of the curse? Never read in the Books about Markul's wicked Lord Aubrel? Had you been a better student of our City's records, you would have learned much concerning the greatest of the First, Aubrel Essern."

The wysard started at Lady Srin's last two syllables. "By every god. But surely Michael cannot be ... "

Lady Srin nodded, relishing Ryel's emotion. "Just so. A lineal descendant of a Builder of Markul. Lord Aubrel's family ruled Hryeland many centuries gone, and his family is to this day powerful in the North. Aubrel was the eldest son, and marked for kingship, but the Art called him. For a long time he and the other First Ones dwelt harmoniously and profitably together, learning the Mastery. But then Aubrel sought to explore the boundaries between life and death, and made the first Crossing. It didn't kill him outright, but he returned infected with the malignant energy of the Outer World. It drove him mad, and among his many acts of insanity he attacked and raped one of the wysardesses, Fleurie of Ralnahr. She conceived by him, and of course should have aborted the child. Instead she left Markul and made her way North, where Aubrel's family took her in. The birth killed her, but Aubrel's son grew to manhood, carrying his father's infection in his veins, with his outward form likewise tainted—colored strangely, blood-red of hair and unnaturally pale of skin, peculiarities that continue to the present day. He too died mad, but not before marrying and begetting. Since that time the daimonic sickness has established itself among the male Esserns of the direct line. The unfortunates who carry the curse invariably die raving witless after lives of unremitting and indescribable pain— short lives, mercifully, but not too short to preclude procreation, more's the pity. In a twisted sense, the curse has proven Michael's blessing, for even as the Art helped him to control the pain, the pain goaded him to ever greater Mastery. Unfortunately, it also predisposed him to listen to Dagar's persuasions."

"What Overreachers are there alive besides you and me, and Michael?" asked Ryel.

"One only. Theofanu, an Ormalan wysardess who now masques as a priestess up in the Barrier lands—high priestess of the cult of the Master."

"So that religion began in the North."

"Yes, and has flourished so well that Dagar has seen fit to send his apostle Michael to propagate the faith in Destimar. That's not good, trust me."

"I remember Dagar mentioning Theofanu," the wysard said. "Is she one of the Foretold?"

Srin Yan heavily sighed. "Very probably, I'm sorry to say."

"And just how do you know who's Foretold and who isn't?"

At Ryel's tone Lady Srin frowned. "I've written proof, whelp." In another moment she'd flung open another chest, one full of papers and scroll-sheaths and books. "I know it's in here someplace."

Ryel leaned over the open chest with her, sniffing the musty faint reek of crumbling parchment and clinging mildew. Reading what he could, he caught his breath. "But these are all Markulit writings. They look incredibly old."

The wysardess smacked his fingers as he reached for a paper. "No groping amongst my treasures. The lightest touch crumbles them. I've been collecting them for years—bit by bit they come to me, by chance and accident. Ah, here's what I was looking for. Listen carefully, now." With extreme care she took out a ragged scrap of vellum and began to read aloud, slowly and chantingly like the tolling of a great low-toned bell:

'Out of the emptiness, One wishing All,
Old in its evil. Into the World, one well-created:
Born to the Art, bred in wide lands,
Storm-blooded, bonded with water and air.
Brought young to the walls of the Greatest and Best,
Grown manward 'mid wonders, grown strong in all strengths.
Two against the One, father and son.
Two of the Bad to serve the Worst,
One of those two fire-tried, earth-compelling;
Four of the Good to fight them.
Two brothers, Art-bad, World-bad;
Two Art-sisters, evil and good.
From the father's death, the son's life;
With the son's life'."

Ryel leaned forward, his impatience desperate. "Don't stop! Go on."

Lady Srin only shrugged. "That's all there is. The parchment's torn away after that."

"But we know what comes next," Ryel said, his heart quickening. 'With the son's life, the father's.' It has to be."

Srin Yan Tai shook her head warningly. "That's more than we know, whelp, but I can make a few guesses as to the text we have. You yourself are very clearly described, and Edris is more than hinted at. Fire-tried and earth-compelling can be none other than our friend Michael Essern. As for the two brothers—I'm not sure. It might be that Michael has a male sibling—I hope it's not worse than that. The two Art-sisters are Theofanu and, I hope, me. As for the last words, I strongly advise that you don't read too much into them."

Ryel remembered Edris' deep voice, so strange in Priamnor's body. He recalled the mention of Starklander, revealed to him as Lord Guyon Desrenaud, and the yet mysterious Redbane—two men who would have to be found for the World's sake. But Ryel had begun to weary under the weight of so much destiny. "When I left Rismai, I told my mother I'd be back in two weeks," he said. Even in Markul he had never felt farther from home.

The wysardess dryly tsked. "Foolish boy." But then her eyes took Ryel's and held them hard. "I know it seems a great deal of work, but consider what happens if Dagar gets his way. The World will simply become too tiresome to live in. Tyrannous regimes never last in the World, because people eventually tire of being always afraid and bored. They grow ashamed of having to be always mean and vile. Eventually they respond to the call of their higher faculties, and fight to the death for beauty and nobility and peace. But if Dagar achieves incarnation, the tyranny will last forever. That's a rough thing to ponder, whelp."

The wysard shuddered at the crawling of his skin, but then warmed again with the memory of wine-tinged lips, night-black hair falling across his arm, bright water and bronzed nakedness, endless sun glittering on all the treasures of the earth. "Almancar is too rich to be swayed by Michael's rantings."

Srin Yan Tai laughed, short and dry. "You're not seeing enough moves ahead, lad. Once Michael incites the Fourth District to revolt, young Priam will be too distracted to notice his half-siblings' grab for the throne."

Vaguely Ryel recalled Priam's mentioning that he had other brothers and sisters besides Diara. "Which half-siblings are those?"

"The twins Catulk and Coamshi, by Agenor's first wife, a Zegry princess. Black-skinned twins with pale yellow eyes, a striking combination that unfortunately had far more physical affinity with a certain Falissian captain of the guard than with the Sovran, who divorced the wife and executed the lover. Together with their mother the twins rule the poisonous jungles of the Azm Chak, which boast a numerous and belligerent population very fond of jewels. They're vicious, those Zegrys. This won't be their first attempt on Priam's life."

Ryel stiffened. "What do you mean?"

"The Azm Chak is famed as a hotbed of repulsive and incurable diseases," replied Lady Srin. "One of them is *jirankri*, an especially troublesome venereal complaint. The twins envenomed a beautiful woman with this disorder, and sent their pretty fireship to Almancar's pleasure quarter to infect Priamnor and his favorites. Among jirankri's more annoying manifestations is its necrotic effect on the male organs of generation, which after much noisome suppuration and untold agony eventually drop off—a nasty surprise for its victims. I happened to be in Almancar at the time, and managed to persuade Agenor to let me cure his son before the worst could occur. Only the utmost powers of my Art could save him—although Priamnor's mother the Sovrana, a good but unreasoning woman, gave all the credit to the goddess Demetropa."

Ryel winced as he remembered the counterfeit Diara of the Diamond Heaven, her false flesh surely laced with danger worse than anything from the Azm Chak. "I must return to Almancar and help Priam."

"Priam will have to help himself," said Lady Srin. "You've more important business." Turning about, she opened one of her wooden chests and brought out something thin and flat wrapped in a piece of gold-shot silk. "Here—this might prove useful to you from time to time."

She unfolded the cloth, disclosing several pieces of broken mirror. Taking a fragment up, Ryel looked into it but found no reflection.

"This is a Glass," he said.

"All that remains of mine," Lady Srin answered, dryly rueful. "It burst into bits when I looked eye to eye with Dagar during the Crossing. I'm lucky it didn't blind me." Carefully selecting one of the larger shards, she tore off a bit of the golden cloth and wrapped it up, then handed it to Ryel. "Take this with you on your way. You might have need of it."

With no eagerness Ryel took the gift. "My way where?"

Lady Srin fixed him with her blank eyes. "You know as well as I, lad. Tomorrow morning you're heading North."

End of Part One

*In Part Two, the concluding volume of **The Wysard**, Ryel Mirai encounters yet more challenges to his Art. He finds the mysterious Redbane in the Northern city of Hallagh and becomes a member of the Sword Brotherhood, but by terrible mischance is infected with daimon-bane that for a time warps his Mastery to evil uses. At the sea's edge Ryel discovers the long-sought spell that will bring Edris back from the Void, but Dagar steals it from him with the help of Michael Essern, who battles Ryel in hand-to-hand combat that pits air and water against fire and earth. Ryel seeks and discovers Starklander in the vile wysard-City Ormala, and afterward is lured to the ethereal realm of beautiful wanton Riana, the One Immortal, where he learns the great secrets of the Art. But will his heightened Mastery thwart Dagar's plans for the downfall of Almancar and the North, and then the World? Can it avert the war that threatens the destruction of great Destimar, and the lives of Priamnor and Diara? Will it bring Edris back to life? As the One Immortal warns, Ryel might get everything he wishes—but not as he wished it.*